JULIANNA KEYES

OMNIFIC PUBLISHING
LOS ANGELES

Omnific Publishing
1901 Avenue of the Stars, 2nd floor
Los Angeles, CA 90067
www.omnificpublishing.com

First Omnific eBook edition, October 2013
First Omnific trade paperback edition, October 2013

Library of Congress Cataloguing-in-Publication Data

Keyes, Julianna.
    Just Once / Julianna Keyes – 1st ed.
    ISBN: 978-1-623420-66-6
    1. Contemporary Romance — Fiction. 2. Dude Ranch — Fiction.
    3. Colorado — Fiction. 4. Summer Love — Fiction. I. Title

10 9 8 7 6 5 4 3 2 1

Cover Design by Micha Stone and Amy Brokaw
Interior Book Design by Coreen Montagna

Printed in the United States of America

For my parents,
who support my dreams, no matter how far-fetched.
I love you too

Chapter One

I stare out the passenger side window at the pretty mountain scenery bumping by, smiling at the realization that nothing has changed since I was last here. I remember my first time riding down this well-worn dirt road: heart in my throat, fingers gripping the door as I peered out at a world that had nothing in common with my Manhattan home.

I can still feel faint tremors of that excitement, the thrill of entering an unfamiliar world just waiting to be explored. The only difference is that now I'm old and weary. Old and *wise*, I correct myself, directing a frown inward. And unlike what some people might say, I'm not jaded, just discerning. No more foolish decisions, no more living on a whim like there are no consequences. There are consequences — this I know.

"Nothing's changed, huh?" Hank Endersley asks. His kind eyes crinkle as he smiles from beneath a battered brown cowboy hat.

"Nothing," I half-lie, returning the smile. The ranch hasn't changed, but I have. I'm exhausted. I feel like I'm thirty going on sixty. What have I been doing to age myself so prematurely? I'm a travel writer, not a warrior. I don't save lives or defuse bombs, I don't teach in the inner city or solve crimes. I don't even donate blood. I'm just tired. And I'm old. And, in my weakest, darkest moments, I admit that I'm lonely.

In ten years of travel writing, I've been almost everywhere, done and tried most everything. I've met thousands of people, shared drinks, kisses, touches, beds, but they've all been fleeting. Some fun, some sincere, but all finite. All ending with me getting on an airplane, promising to keep in touch, then inevitably forgetting. Distance will do that. It's why I haven't been back to the San Juan mountains of southern Colorado since I was nineteen, why I haven't seen Hank Endersley's kind face in ten years.

The old blue pickup rattles down the road, its ancient inner workings jostling against the rusted frame. I peer ahead through the dusk at the familiar arch that spans the dirt road, announcing *Ponderosa Pines Ranch* when you arrive and *Via Con Dios* when you leave. A hundred yards beyond the arch, the main ranch house comes into view: a low, sprawling wood cabin nearly a hundred years old and made to last a hundred more. Colorful flowerbeds line the pathway, and hanging baskets decorate the porch that runs the length of the front. It's warm and beautiful, and while my career has taken me to extravagant, luxurious, tropical locales, this is the one place that has always made me feel like I'm on vacation—which is ironic, since I'm here to work.

Hank steers us past the ranch and down the road a little way to the equally old and rustic home he shares with his wife, Mary. Evidently she hears us coming—who on earth couldn't, really—as the front door opens and she steps out, wiping her hands on a tea towel and grinning from ear to ear.

I'm exhausted, but her smile is contagious, and as soon as Hank stops the truck I'm out and covering the distance to the house.

"Kate!" she murmurs in my ear. Her softly accented voice envelops me almost as tangibly as her arms.

"Hi, Mary."

"It's been too long."

"I know."

"Too, too long."

"I'm sorry."

"We have all your stories. I read your book three times."

I smile into the thick curls of her gray hair. "You did not."

"I did."

I hear Hank's plodding footsteps as he approaches. "Let her go, Mare," he orders. "What's for dinner? We've got to feed her. I could hear her bones rattling."

"That was the truck," I protest, resisting the urge to sob as Mary releases me. I follow them inside the house, into its familiar smells of roast chicken and lemon. Instantly my traitorous stomach rumbles.

"Told you," Hank says from somewhere down the dim hall.

Mary leads the way to the kitchen and dinner, which for me is two plates too many of chicken and mashed potatoes and apple pie. It's delicious, and I can't remember the last time I had a home-cooked meal. I'm comfortable in restaurants. I'm comfortable dining alone and making notes on the notepad I keep in my purse. As much as I love Hank and Mary, as much as the years between us fall away with each passing second, their scrutiny, their caring, makes me squirm. Finally I can't suppress a yawn, and Hank clears the plates as Mary fusses over me.

"Tea?" she asks. "Milk?"

"I couldn't." I shake my head. "I'm stuffed."

She looks satisfied. "Good, then. Good. We're so glad you were able to come back."

"Me too. The timing was perfect." I smile at them, grateful that two of my favorite people in the world haven't forgotten me after a ten-year absence. Then I yawn again.

"Let's get you to bed," Hank says. "I had one of the girls set up your room in the bunkhouse, but you can sleep here tonight. Who knows what time they'll settle down."

Ah, the bunkhouse. The thought of it makes me smile. And I know just what time those girls will settle down: never. Not until the last day of summer has passed and they're all heading home and the rules of real life return. I worked here for three summers as a teenager, and I'm pretty sure I never slept more than four hours a night.

Now, however, is a different story. A twenty-hour trip from Thailand and a stomach full of mashed potatoes and gravy makes me think I could sleep forever. I let Mary lead me up to the second floor, into the small bedroom with dormer windows and a single bed with a patchwork quilt. The room is cool and quiet, and while I know I should go downstairs to collect my luggage, I don't. Once the door is closed I climb under the covers in my jeans and sweater and fall fast asleep.

As many times as I've woken up in strange places, you think I'd be used to it, but I never am. A rooster crows and I open my eyes, confused and squinting against the lemony sunlight spilling through the thin curtains. I take in the slatted wood on the ceiling, the soft green paint on the walls, and eventually it comes to me. *I'm here*, I think. *I'm back*.

I shower quickly and pull my blond hair into a ponytail while it's still wet. I smile as I think of my mother, a professional socialite if there ever was, and her constant warning that my thick hair — my "best feature" — will fall out if I don't style it.

I'm downstairs by seven, but Hank and Mary are already there, the breakfast dishes cleared. Mary offers to make me something, but I decline. I rarely eat in the mornings, but I do need coffee.

"They have the good stuff in the kitchen," Hank says, referring to the lodge kitchen. "Guests'll be in now, so just help yourself."

"Go around back," Mary suggests. "You remember the way?"

I nod. "Is Saturday still exit day?"

"It is."

Hank and Mary own and operate an exclusive dude ranch — a four-star resort that invites the wealthy and weary to escape their stressful everyday lives and spend a week in the mountains. They put on blue jeans and cowboy hats, ride horses, eat gourmet meals, and go to bed early, exhausted by the fresh air and exercise. Guests arrive Sunday evening and stay until Saturday afternoon, and because today is Saturday, the guests will be leaving after lunch. My plan is to stay out of the way while the staff finishes up — there'll be time for introductions later.

"You're sure the chef won't mind a stranger in his kitchen?" I shudder at the thought of Chef Jacques, whose delicious food barely managed to rival his vicious temper. The last time I was here he ran the lodge kitchen like a drill sergeant, cursing furiously. If I look on the bright side, he prepared me for dealing with every intimidating person I met from that point on, but still, the memory of his angry face strikes fear in my heart.

"Alec is tame compared to Jacques," Hank laughs. He laughs *now*. He was just as afraid as the rest of us back then.

"Okay. I'll take my stuff upstairs while the staff is out, then venture into the kitchen. If anyone gets mad…"

"Tell 'em Mary sent you," Hank finishes.

I laugh and collect my two suitcases from beside the door, then wave goodbye and step outside into a wall of chilly fog. The sun breaks through in intermittent patches, warm when I manage to feel it. It's a five-minute walk to the lodge, and while I hear the faint sounds of ranch life, I see no one.

My assumption that nothing much has changed since my last stay appears to be correct: the girls' bunk is still tucked on top of the main lodge, and there's a steep wooden staircase on the end of the building that leads to a permanently unlocked bunkhouse door. Despite the fact that there are probably about sixty people eating downstairs, it's quiet up here.

The girls' bunk consists of a narrow hallway running the length of the building, along which are several private rooms for the senior staff. A short hall runs off to the left, leading to the two shared bathrooms and larger rooms filled with bunk beds for the rest of the girls.

I call out "Hello?" and get no answer, then tug my bags down the hall until I find a door labeled with my name. I smile as I step inside the small, sparse room: I was kitchen/cabin manager during my third year at the ranch, and this is where I slept then too. It's unfortunately positioned directly over the kitchen and faces east, so it traps all the heat of the morning and becomes an unbearable sweatbox by the afternoon.

Even now with the fog outside, the room is hot enough that I strip down to the tank top beneath my sweater and flick the switch for the ceiling fan. When I'm not immediately rewarded with a cool breeze, I look up and gasp in horror: the ceiling fan is gone. All that remains is a mocking piece of metal from which a fan might hang.

"Oh, hell no," I mutter. Hank and Mary said the girls had set up the room, but "set up" meant tossing a pillow and a stack of sheets on the bed, along with a quilt no one else wanted because an entire corner appears to have been chewed off by mice. They didn't open the lone window that faces the front of the ranch, and the musty smell suggests this room hasn't enjoyed any fresh air since its last occupant left.

The window is old and tight, but after a brief but determined battle, I step back, victorious as cool, foggy air washes over me. It helps a little, but this ceiling fan business must be addressed right away. I slept well in Hank and Mary's house, but I prefer to unpack and settle in to a new place as soon as possible, and there's no way I'll be able to sleep here without the fan.

I change out of my airplane-and-sleep-wrinkled clothes and into a new pair of jeans and long-sleeved top, then head downstairs in search of coffee, and after that, a fan.

Once outside, I wind my way around the back of the lodge, which looks quite a bit like the front, minus the porch. There are flowerbeds here too, and a variety of doors lead to different parts of the lodge: the lounge, the hallway past the main offices to the dining room, access to the laundry room and supply closet, and a small phone booth—the only phone on the ranch, apart from the two in the office.

When I reach the end of the lodge, I turn the corner and find the fenced-in area that encloses the second kitchen entrance. I push open the gate and secure the latch behind me. This is where the Dumpsters are, and where people come to smoke or eat when they don't want to be seen. It's small but tidy, and a short staircase leads up to the back kitchen entrance.

I hear the familiar rattling of the sanitizer, the machine that sterilizes all rinsed dishes, and the murmur of voices. And then, as I climb the steps, I smell the coffee my system so desperately craves.

I peek my head in at the back of the kitchen, a square space with a pantry to my right and a long counter that runs to the front of the kitchen on my left. There are staff coffee pots on the end closest to me, and seconds later I'm sipping the hot brew like my life depends on it.

"Ahem."

I open my eyes—I hadn't realized I'd closed them—to find a man I assume to be Chef Alec staring at me. He's got a spatula in one hand and spatters of food on his white apron.

"Morning," I say, swallowing too quickly and burning my tongue. "I'm Kate."

"Uh-huh."

"The new kitchen/cabin manager," I clarify.

His face registers some recognition, like he knew someone was coming to fill the position, but he looks me up and down sternly before meeting my eyes. "You've worked here before?"

"Yes. Years ago."

Suddenly there's a thud, followed by a surprised cry and the sound of breaking glass. I already know what's happened: there are two doors from the kitchen to the dining room, and for obvious reasons, they're labeled the in door and the out door. This is supposed to prevent collisions, but the system doesn't always work. Obviously.

"They've been here two weeks," Alec informs me. "You've got your work cut out."

A pretty blond teenager in the standard uniform of jeans and ranch-issued polo shirt peers briefly over Alec's shoulder, then disappears, most likely to report on the stranger stealing coffee.

"I start tomorrow," I say, when it's obvious Alec expects me to do something immediately.

I prepare myself for an angry tirade, but he merely sighs. "Not a minute too soon."

As I turn to go back outside with my coffee I bump into a second man in a white uniform, this one closer to my age, with close-cropped brown hair and a kind face. "Hey," he says, surprised.

"Hey. I'm Kate."

He shakes my proffered hand. "Mark. I'm the sous chef."

"I guessed."

"Mark!" Alec bellows.

"I'd better — "

"Do you know who I'd talk to about getting a ceiling fan?" I blurt out before he can escape.

"A ceiling fan?"

"Yeah."

"Ah, Shane probably?"

"Shane. Okay. Where might he be?"

"Try the barn."

I smile politely as Mark rushes past me, then continue outside. Compared to Chef Jacques, Alec is more than tame. He's decent. I still remember dropping a sizzling hot plate one time and bursting into tears when Jacques screamed at me so long and so loud that the entire dining room gazed at me with sympathy when I returned.

The barn hadn't been built when I was last here, but is easy enough to find: it's large and red and located opposite the lodge, next to the horse paddock. I cautiously approach and look inside. It's dim and cool beyond the open doors, and instead of the expected stalls, I find myself looking into a massive, somewhat unkempt office, with a quadrant of desks on the far side next to a few dented filing cabinets.

Just inside the doors is a padded bench with a stack of weights I couldn't lift if my life depended on it and a long row of toolboxes and various ranch implements. Eventually my eyes adjust and I can make out a man sitting at one of the desks, his back to me. "Hello?" I call.

He turns at the sound. Holy hell. The man is beautiful. He's wearing a baseball cap pulled low on his head, but even from here I can see he's got the cheekbones of a model and the broad shoulders of a professional athlete. Clad in jeans and a plaid shirt, he looks like something out of a Sexy Southerners calendar.

"Shane?" I ask, taking a few steps inside.

The man unfolds himself from the chair and comes forward to meet me, long legs covering the distance quickly. He touches the brim of his hat, and when he's close enough, I can see the short edges of his blond hair and striking blue eyes. Why does this guy work in a barn office?

"No," he says finally, shaking my hand. "I'm Brandon. Who're you?" He looks me up and down much the way Alec did—blatant but at the same time disarmingly non-sexual.

"I'm Kate Burke, the new kitchen/cabin manager. I was told Shane might help me find a ceiling fan."

"Kate Burke," Brandon repeats. "You do not look like Jolene."

I frown, not knowing what that might mean. "Who?"

He laughs. "The manager before you. She stuck it out for the first week, then packed her bags. Couldn't cut it."

"Why not?"

He shrugs. "Not everyone's made for ranch life." Again, he looks at me from head to toe.

I arch a brow. It's not like I'm wearing a ball gown. And I'm sure he's used to being checked out, looking the way he does, but that doesn't mean I'm up for being inspected—and being found lacking, if his expression is any indication. "Duly noted. Is Shane around?"

"Around, yes. Do I know where? No."

"What's his job, exactly? Handyman?"

Brandon shrugs. "Foreman. General manager. Boss. You name it."

"Okay, well, if you don't mind, please tell him I'm in dire need of a ceiling fan."

"Dire?"

"Yes. Use that word. *Dire*."

"Got it." He's trying not to smile.

"What?"

He shakes his handsome head, and it takes me a second to realize I feel nothing...sexual. A year ago he'd have been exactly my type. Swap out the plaid and denim for a suit and tie, and he could've been my date to any number of yacht parties, gallery openings, or exclusive five-star restaurants. But now, despite the fact that I still have an apartment full of designer clothes and an entire closet dedicated to shoes, I get none of the thrill I used to feel when faced with something so pretty. I grew up wealthy and worked hard—and partied harder—to make a name for myself as a travel writer, and I've always been drawn to fancy, frivolous things. But six months ago I decided—not without some outside influence—it was time to grow up and leave behind my foolish impulsiveness. I would be older and wiser, no matter what, and I'm irrationally pleased to find I'm not fantasizing about a fling with Brandon. I came here to focus and behave myself, and the last thing I need is a silly summer romance to throw me off course.

With nothing better to do, I go back to my room. One step into the upstairs hall, however, I come to a standstill.

"Fuuuuuck!" comes a groaning voice from somewhere in the bunkhouse.

"Hello?" I call out.

"Fuuu—Wait. What?"

"Is someone up here?"

"Come help me!"

"Where are you?"

I'm answered with indiscernible mumbles and grunts, but I follow the sounds past the bedroom for female wranglers to the kitchen/cabin girls' bedroom, home to half a dozen bunk beds, one of which has an ass sticking out from beneath it.

"Is that you?" a female voice asks.

I crouch down on the floor next to jean-clad legs and cowboy-booted feet. "What's going on under there?" I press my head to the wooden floor and try to see into the darkness beneath the bed. There's a faint sliver of a face pointed toward me, both arms extended over her head, obscuring one eye.

"I dropped something under here and when I reached in to get it, my hair got caught on a nail," she explains. "I've been here forever."

"You can't pull it loose?"

"Not without ripping my scalp off. I tried."

I pull back and survey the beds, which are as I remember: hand-made wooden structures designed to stand the test of time. Not even our drunken antics broke them, even when we tried.

"Okay..." I say slowly. "Are you stuck to the wall or the bed?"

"The wall. I think." She straightens her legs so she's lying prone on the floor. "That's better," she sighs.

"What's your name?"

The word is muffled. "Hailey."

"Okay, Hailey, I'm going slide the mattress off to see if I can spot the nail you're stuck on, okay?"

"Sure."

I toss the pillows aside and slowly wiggle the mattress off the bed. It flops onto Hailey, who grunts but doesn't complain, and when it's mostly off I climb onto the wooden slats that form the base of the bed, eventually spotting the snagged hair and working it free.

Hailey groans in relief and shimmies her way out. I start to speak, but now, with her hair out of the way, I'm able to see the item she was reaching for: a bottle of vodka.

"Um..." I turn on the bed to stare at her.

Now that she's standing in the light, I see Hailey is a little older than I expected, probably in her mid-twenties. Her mass of red hair is shampoo-commercial gorgeous, and she's got surprisingly tan skin with a faint smattering of freckles across her nose.

She looks at me. "What?"

"Why are you searching for vodka at..." I glance at one of the alarm clocks scattered around the room. "Nine thirty in the morning?"

Hailey crosses her arms. "Remind me who you are and why that's any of your business?"

For the second time that morning, I find myself arching my eyebrow. What is it with the people around here? "I'm Kate Burke," I inform her. "The kitchen/cabin manager. Who are you?"

She freezes. "Let's start again," she suggests.

I try not to laugh.

"I'm Hailey, one of the kitchen/cabin girls," she says. "Who might you be?"

"Kate Burke. The new kitchen/cabin manager."

"Pleasure to meet you."

"Uh-huh. Why are you drinking in the morning, Hailey?"

She sighs and sinks to her knees, gripping her hair in one hand before sliding back under the bed to retrieve the bottle. "I wasn't drinking—and I wasn't going to," she says before I can suggest it. "I was just checking that the other girls hadn't taken it."

"Which girls?"

"Janie and her minions, Lisa and Becca. You'll meet them."

"They're drunk?"

"Oh, who knows. Everybody here is either drunk or hung-over half the time. But they're eighteen, so when I see them snickering and running off together, my first thought is: vodka."

"Naturally."

Hailey shrugs. "Anyway. I have to get back. I only meant to come up here and check. I've been gone nearly half an hour."

I watch as she tucks the bottle into the back of a drawer, arranging bras and panties in front of it.

"Nice meeting you," she says before ducking out.

After shoving the mattress back on the bed I return to searching for the elusive Shane. I couldn't help but notice that the girls' bedroom had a fan, so I feel further validated in my quest for one of my own. I've done my share of staying in cramped, hot hostels, but I'm not twenty-two anymore and the appeal of stifling, crappy sleeping quarters has worn off. Not that they were appealing before.

I introduce myself to everyone I meet, most of whom are perfectly nice, but none of whom know where to find Shane. I pass the kitchen at one point, and Alec asks if I've seen "my" girls. The guests have gone, but the kitchen and dining room are in disarray, and with the exception of Hailey, there's no one cleaning up. I promise to keep an eye out and soon find the three missing girls crammed into the phone booth, sharing a cigarette. Taking a deep breath, I rap on the door, wondering whose bright idea it was to hide in a clear glass booth.

After a second the door cracks open and a plume of smoke wafts out. I inhale—just a cigarette.

"Can I help you?" the blonde from earlier in the kitchen asks. She's pretty in a mean-girl way, and because she appears to be the leader, I assume she's Janie and the other two are the "minions" Hailey mentioned.

"Are you the kitchen/cabin girls?"

"So?"

"I'm Kate," I tell them. "Your boss. Alec is looking for you."

"Tell him we're busy."

I push the door open the rest of the way, and they topple out. "Tell him yourselves."

The other two look cowed and afraid, but Janie just glares. "In a minute."

I fix the other two with a stern look. "Now."

They look like frozen deer: they don't want to displease Janie, but they don't want to get in trouble either. I don't know what I could do to punish them — firing people is a last resort when your business is as remote as this one — but I try to give the impression of being ready to act on my unspoken threat.

"Let's go, Janie," another blond one mumbles, shuffling her feet.

"Yeah," the third girl echoes, a brunette with bad skin. They all look to be eighteen or nineteen, and Janie and the blonde could be sisters, but right now I don't care. I'm already starting to understand why Jolene left. I found one girl upstairs stuck under a bed looking for vodka, and three geniuses hiding in a clear box — all while they're supposed to be working.

Janie takes one last drag and stomps out the cigarette, grinding it into the ground with the heel of her cowboy boot. "Fine."

They walk off, Janie slightly in the lead, as though it were their decision. I take a deep breath and remind myself that I'm in the right here. I try to avoid conflict, but sometimes I can't, even if it makes my hands shake so bad I have to stuff them in my pockets. *You're right,* I tell myself again. I'm an adult and I'm behaving like one, which is probably why it feels so strange.

Chapter Two

A short time later I linger just out of sight as the staff waves goodbye to the departing guests and the ranch vans drive off. I feel as though I've met everybody but the one person I'm looking for, and I've badgered them all with my need for a fan. With the exception of the kitchen/cabin girls, everybody here seems competent and comfortable, and I hope I'm making the same impression.

I run upstairs to dig my credit card out of my bag, then hurry back to the smoky-smelling phone booth and dial the only phone number I know by heart. After three rings, a familiar voice picks up. "Hello?"

"It's me."

"Where are you?"

"At the ranch."

He sighs. "Seriously?"

I squat down on the overturned milk crate that serves as a seat and lean against the dingy wall. "Seriously."

Stanley Goldblatt, my agent, best friend, and tormentor, launches into his now-standard plea for me to return to Boston where he'll kick out my tenants so we can be apartment neighbors again.

I can't help but laugh. "I promised I'd stay," I remind him. "I'm here for the summer. And I want to be."

This is true. I promised Hank and Mary I'd spend the summer, June to September. Despite not having worked in hospitality since my last summer here, I should be able to manage. Over the course of my career I've stayed in hundreds of hotels and eaten in thousands of restaurants—I know what guests like, even if I'm not normally the one to give it to them. In return I'll get a season free of the stress of city life, three blissful months where I can wake up in the same bed every morning to the sweet comfort of a dull routine. It's the perfect opportunity to put myself back together. I'll walk away confident and composed in September, finally ready to return to the life I know and love.

"You'll go crazy," Stanley chides me. "I know you. You'll lose it. You barely survived six months at home."

"Those six months were wonderful," I assure him. "But I'm ready to work again."

"You're having a nervous breakdown."

"Am not."

"You'll get bored. You won't have any friends."

"Why wouldn't I make friends?"

"You won't have anything in common with a bunch of cowboys," he says. "Or cowgirls. You'll be lonely."

"I'm surrounded by people."

"And horses."

"And peace and quiet."

"Kate, if all you needed was peace and quiet, you had that at your beachfront cottage in Thailand."

He's got me there, so I try another tack. "I know Thailand didn't exactly go as planned, but this will work out. Trust me. I need a break. Something different. You know that better than anyone."

"You had a break! You said you were better!"

This is true too. Before Thailand I spent six months "not working" at my apartment in Boston, until I started feeling antsy. You know something's wrong when you're in your own home, next door to your best friend on the planet, and you still feel like you're in the wrong place.

"I'm on sabbatical," I say.

"Uh-huh. You know, if you get lonely, Kevin looked pleased to hear you were coming back to the States ahead of schedule."

"Kevin Drew?"

"The one and only. Come to think of it, he's been looking over-worked lately. Maybe he could use a little R&R of the S-E-X variety."

I laugh, but I can't help but remember dreamy Kevin Drew and his five-thousand-dollar suits and perfectly veneered smile. He's my financial advisor, and also a bit of a player, but he's put all that practice to good use. We hooked up while I was home, and though we always had a good time, it hadn't been enough to stay. And, incidentally, when I wanted to leave Thailand, I didn't want to go to Boston. Not for Kevin and not for Stanley—it was home, but it wasn't.

"I'm breaking my habits, Stanley. No more being reckless. You said you'd support me."

"Kevin Drew is not something to give up so easily!"

I laugh, but he's wrong. Because that's the thing with traveling nonstop: it's hard to have relationships, but it's easy to have flings. It's easy to keep my heart separate from my head.

"Maybe in September," I make myself say, if only to get him off my back.

"You won't last that long."

"Thanks for the support. I'm hanging up now. It's lunchtime, and I have to go meet the staff I haven't already accosted."

"Remind me why you're doing this?" he pleads. "Working as a maid?"

"I'm the kitchen/cabin manager," I clarify. "Not a maid. And Hank and Mary are the kindest people I know. They were short-staffed, and I wanted to come back."

"And you want to hide."

"Starting now." I hang up and head for the dining room.

The typical Saturday workday ends the moment the guests drive off the property, but today Hank and Mary have forced everyone to gather in the dining room (now tidy), to greet the newest member of their ranks. Chefs Alec and Mark have made lunch, and once Hank and Mary have embarrassed me, we all sit down.

The four kitchen/cabin girls sit together, as do the wranglers. Brandon is joined by two other similarly hulking, plaid-shirt-wearing men, though when I ask Mary which one is Shane, she looks around, perplexed.

"He's not here," she says after a minute. "Not sure where he's got to."

"What do you need?" Hank asks.

"A ceiling fan. I'm in the sweatshop again."

They laugh, no doubt remembering my complaints from long ago. "Shane's the guy to ask about that," Mary confirms. "We hired a handyman, but he couldn't change a light bulb. Still, nice guy."

We make small talk for the rest of the meal, and eventually people start filtering out, ready to enjoy their brief reprieve from work. Hank, Mary, and I linger to go over the basics of my duties, further verifying my impression that nothing has changed in the ten years I've been gone.

Because the guests have a set schedule during their stay, the kitchen/cabin staff has a pretty fixed routine. The wranglers come in for breakfast at six thirty; guest breakfast is from seven to nine. When the guests go out for morning rides or various activities, we clean cabins, then come back to serve lunch from twelve until one. Once the dining room and kitchen are clean, we have a few hours off—most of which are spent napping—then we set up, serve, and clean up dinner from six until nine. After dinner the guests have the option of hanging out in the lounge or at the pool, but they're normally so exhausted by the day's activities that they just retire to their cabins. The staff, on the other hand, washes up and goes to O'Malley's, the nearest bar.

Sure enough, that evening the Saturday night routine is just as I remember it: around eight I hear the female wranglers and kitchen/cabin girls cramming into the two bathrooms and fighting for space in front of the mirror, gossiping about who kissed who and who hurt whose feelings.

I'm alone in my room with the door open, trying to decide if I should join them. I haven't technically been invited—and given my introduction to the kitchen/cabin girls, I'm not expecting to be—but I was an O'Malley's legend in my old days, and I wouldn't mind checking it out again. Not that I'd be repeating any of my previous shenanigans, but still…It could be fun. And I wouldn't mind showing the girls that I don't have to be the strict schoolmarm my phone booth lecture suggested. We could start fresh.

There's a faint knock on the door, and I look up from my pensive position on the bed.

It's Hailey. "Hey," she says.

I straighten. "Hey."

She steps inside and immediately fans herself. "It's hot as hell in here."

"Tell me about it."

"Christ. Did you want to come out with us tonight? Everyone's going to O'Malley's. It's much cooler."

A bead of sweat winds its way down my spine. "I'm in."

O'Malley's is much the same as I left it: dimly lit with wood-paneled walls, small stage for a live band, busy bar. Only a few couples dare hit the dance floor this early—and this sober—twisting and twirling to the tinny jukebox songs.

There are enough of us that we take up four tables, and I end up jammed at one end with Hailey and sous chef Mark, along with a few of the wranglers I met earlier. Apparently the ranch hands never come to the bar, and rarely socialize.

"So, Kate," Hailey says once we all have beer. "We're dying to know what brought you back."

I look around in surprise. She and Mark are openly attentive, and a couple of wranglers appear to be eavesdropping. "Well…I worked here for three years when I was younger, and I kept in touch with Hank and Mary off and on after that. Then it just happened that this year they needed a kitchen/cabin manager at the same time I was looking for something else to do—"

"What were you doing before?" Mark interrupts.

"Uh, I was working in Thailand. Trying to work, to be more specific. I just couldn't concentrate, and this felt like the right place to escape to."

"You left Thailand for this?" Hailey asks, gesturing to the almost entirely denim-clad population of O'Malley's.

I laugh. "Yep."

"That's the right answer," a voice booms over my shoulder. Everyone jumps. I turn in my seat to look up in pleasant surprise at Zeke O'Malley, proprietor and bartender extraordinaire. I knew him well in my younger days, and he's seen more of my drunken antics than anyone should have to.

"Zeke!" I jump up to hug him.

He's a barrel-chested old man who could probably still wrestle a bear—a story he swears is true—and he hugs me back.

"As I live and breathe," he says when I pull away. He looks me up and down as though confirming that I have, in fact, survived this long.

"I'm here for the summer," I say. "Back at Ponderosa."

"I had a feeling we'd see you again."

"Did not."

"Did too. Not everybody's made for life out here, but some people are. You'd be surprised."

"Zeke!" someone bellows. "Beer!"

He smiles at me, revealing an additional missing tooth since the last time we saw each other. "Be good, Eight-Shot Kate. Assuming you know how?"

"Me?"

He laughs and disappears into the crowd.

When I turn back to the table, everyone is staring. "Wait," Hailey says, wide-eyed. "*You're* Eight-Shot Kate?"

I bury my face in my hands and slump in my seat as absolutely everybody begins to laugh. A gaping Mark points to a glittery bra hanging from a mounted moose head. "Is that your…And that picture…?"

And sure enough, there's a photo of me—from behind, thank God—dancing topless on the bar.

Hailey slams her hands on the table, making the beers jump. "Did you perform a striptease for Zeke's birthday when you were seventeen?"

"On top of a table?"

"While singing an original song?" someone else chimes in.

My face is burning. "I was nineteen," I correct through my fingers. "And very drunk."

Everybody laughs uproariously. The wranglers start to clear the table, and right on cue, Gretchen Wilson's distinctive voice spills out of the jukebox, telling everybody she's here for the party. "Eight-Shot Kate! Eight-Shot Kate!" people start chanting, slapping the table.

"No!" I say frantically, waving them away. "Absolutely not! I'm not nineteen. And perhaps most importantly, I'm not drunk."

"Tequila!" the people shout.

"And I'm not going to be!"

Mercifully they stop their shouting, but everyone is looking at me with new eyes. The ceiling-fan-obsessed girl has been transformed into the face of the pink rhinestone-studded bra and topless photo (from *behind*) that's been hanging around this dingy backwoods bar for more than ten years.

"Those days are past," I say firmly, but they don't look convinced. "Maybe if you'd met me a year ago, but now…no more."

They groan their disappointment.

"You pervs. Drink your beer. It's on me."

And just like that they cheer up again, drinking and dancing the night away until I stand up to go shortly after midnight. Everybody boos me for being the first to leave, but tomorrow is my first official day of work, and I'm determined to set a fine example for the kitchen/cabin girls. I set myself a limit of two beers and stuck to it… plus two shots of tequila. When I stopped there everyone teased me, so to shut them up I finally joined a bunch of people on the dance floor — remaining fully clothed and respectable, but still having fun.

Come to think of it, that's the first time I've danced in a while. I flash back to the last time I was in a bar and immediately shake my head to clear it. That was the reckless Kate. This is the new me. Nothing to worry about.

I rode over in one of the ranch vans, but Randy Cooter and his old cab are parked in their usual spot in front of O'Malley's, so I hop inside and ask him to take me home. Randy's not much of a talker, which I appreciate because I've been talking and shouting all night and need to tone it down a notch. The cab windows are open, and the warm mountain air blows through. I'm told we're experiencing a heat wave at the moment, which explains the uncommonly hot weather for early June.

We make the ride home in silence, and fifteen minutes later I pay Randy and wave goodbye, weaving my way over the gravel to the staircase leading to the bunkhouse. Each step lends a sense of foreboding as I approach my sweltering room. I squint through the darkness as I stop at my door. There's a large box leaning against the wall, but I can't see what it is.

Pushing open the bedroom door I'm greeted with a wall of heat and groan as I instantly start to sweat. I flip on the light and blink as my eyes adjust. I've unpacked a little and made up the bed with its tattered sheets, but it's just too hot to sleep, and I don't want to show up at Hank and Mary's house drunk (just a little) and asking to spend the night.

I reach outside and heave the box into the light, grinning when I see that it's a brand new ceiling fan. *Excellent.* Not quite as good as if it were actually hung on the ceiling, but we've made progress.

I strip out of my jeans and blouse and swap them for shorts and a tank top, then park myself in front of the window, gazing over my shoulder at the ceiling fan. I look up at the metal post protruding from the ceiling. *How hard can it be?* I wonder. I kneel on the floor and open the box, pulling out the brief instruction manual. The fan needs to be assembled, but according to the illustrations, all that's required is a screwdriver. I think we've got a few tools and a stepladder in the supply closet. A bead of sweat trickles down my back, and I make up my mind.

I'm braless beneath my tank top, so I pull on a sweater before slipping into my sneakers to run downstairs in the dark. I let myself into the supply closet and dig around until I find a rusty old screwdriver. I scoop up the stepladder and race back upstairs, weaving a little, but arriving safely.

I cast aside my sweater and sneakers and set up the rickety wooden stepladder beneath the post for the ceiling fan. When the lodge was built, this entire level was one open space, and when they divided it into staff rooms, they built them fairly carelessly. Each room has a window and a light, but not necessarily in the center of the room. In the case of this room, both the light and the fan are at the end of the rectangle, in front of the door.

At length I get the fan assembled. I heave the contraption onto my shoulder and climb the shaky ladder until I can reach the ceiling. I've got the screwdriver clamped between my teeth, and it takes all my strength to heave the fan onto the post. Once it's centered I climb even higher so I can hold it up with one hand while attempting to screw it in place with the other.

The combination of the heat, my proximity to the light, and my unaccustomed exertion makes me sweat even more. I can feel rivulets of water creeping down my back and between my breasts, and my armpits are damp. Much more of this labor-intensive work and I'll—

I shriek as the door flies open and crashes into the ladder. I pitch forward, leaving the ceiling fan dangling precariously from its two screws, and topple onto the massive stranger. He's huge, but thanks to the ladder I'm taller, and when I fall my slick armpit smashes straight into his face. I feel his nose press into my skin, his muffled shout of surprise, and then my entire limp, sweaty body slides down his front until I crumple to the floor. He falls backward, landing on his ass with a thud and a grunt, and then a faint creaking sound has us looking up, just in time to see the ceiling fan come loose and fall to the ground, cracking into several jagged pieces.

Breathing hard, I sit up to stare at the man glaring back at me. Clad in a black T-shirt and cargo pants, he's got tousled dark hair and even darker eyes. He's not beautiful like Brandon, but there's something powerful about him. The smooth plane of his nose suggests it's been broken, there's a hard line to his jaw. Something south of the border clenches instinctively. *What?* It must be the alcohol. And the heat.

"What the hell are you doing here?" he finally asks, dusting himself off and standing. Almost as an afterthought he reaches down and grips my arm, pulling me unceremoniously to my feet.

I jerk away and check myself for injuries. With the exception of my wounded pride and a few bruises, I appear to be fine. "I'm not hurt, thanks for asking," I reply. "And I'm here because this is my room. A great question would be what the hell are *you* doing here?"

His eyes flash, and he reaches into his pocket, pulling out a handful of small papers I recognize as requisition notices. "I came back to this," he says. "Apparently someone named Kate is in *dire* need of a ceiling fan."

Thanks, Brandon. "You're Shane."

"Uh-huh."

"Do you normally walk into rooms unannounced in the middle of the night?"

He smirks. "Never been a problem before."

What an asshole. I gesture to the broken fan. "Well, it's a problem now. I need a new fan. And I need you to knock before you come in to install it."

"Seems like you know what you're doing." He shrugs. "I don't think I need to come back at all."

"Are you always an asshole?"

He raises an eyebrow. "I beg your pardon?"

"You heard me. You barge into my room, nearly kill me, break my fan, and apologize for nothing."

His dark eyes rake me up and down. I suddenly remember I'm not wearing a bra. And I'm pretty sure I'm gleaming with sweat.

"You look all right to me."

"Fine. I'll fix the fan myself. Where do I get another one?"

"I'll bring it up. Put some clothes on."

He's gone before I can reply, but as soon as his heavy footsteps fade down the hall, I dig through my bags for a bra and a top that provides a little more coverage. I don't have a huge chest, but it's enough to make a statement in the tiny shirt I have on. Goddammit. I spent the past hours making a good impression on everybody else, and when I finally meet the guy I've been searching for all day, I slam a sweaty armpit in his face and fight with him. *Oh no.* Speaking of which…I duck my head and covertly sniff under my arm, even as I wonder why I'd care if he thinks I smell. He works in a barn, for crying out loud. *And he* deserved *it,* I remind myself. *He didn't even apologize!*

A few minutes later I hear work boots thump up the steps and Shane pushes open the door—again, no knocking—with a new fan under his arm.

"Thanks," I say, reaching for it. "I'll take it from here."

He ignores me. "I'll do it. It's the last one we've got. I can't have you breaking anything else."

"Nothing would be broken if you'd knocked!"

"I thought you were at the bar. I knocked when I brought the fan up, but didn't get an answer. When I came back with the ladder I assumed you were still out." Behind him I can see a ladder propped against the wall in the hall.

"With the light on?"

"I'm not a detective, Kate. Now move so I can get this hung up."

He uses his foot to clear space on the floor, then crouches down to assemble the new fan. I stand awkwardly for a second, then gather up the broken pieces of the first fan and toss them into the garbage. That takes all of one minute, however, so then I just watch him, and he eventually shoots me a look.

"What?" he asks.

I shrug. "What am I supposed to do? Do you want some help?"

He tries not to scoff. "No."

"I'll go brush my teeth."

"Good idea."

I grab my toiletries bag and squeeze past him out the door. When I'm in the bathroom, I shut—and lock—the door, then lean against it. My hairline is damp with sweat, my heart is beating fast, and my mouth is dry. I tell myself again that it's a combination of heat and alcohol, but something within me has come alive for the first time in a long time, and I don't know how I feel about it. Actually, I know exactly how I feel about it: appalled. Men like Shane are not my type: huge, hulking jerks who don't apologize when they're wrong. I like the Kevin Drews of the world—polished, finessed, accomplished men who know how to order wine and fly first class.

I splash cold water on my face, then hastily brush my teeth and will myself to calm down. I'm tired and jetlagged. It's normal to feel out of sorts. I'm not myself. Older, wiser Kate knows this.

I march back to my room and screech to an abrupt halt. Shane's standing on the stepladder, arms extended overhead, biceps bulging as he fixes the fan in place. His stance on the ladder puts his prominent package directly at eye level.

Oh God. My face burns, and I squeeze past before he sees me looking. I drop the toiletries bag on the dresser and stand in front of the window to cool off. Again. "When is this heat wave supposed to end?" I ask.

"Couple more days."

I groan inwardly. "Great."

Finally he steps down from the ladder and surveys his work. "Give it a shot," he orders.

I flip the switch next to the door, and the fan begins to turn, a blissful, slow spin that sounds like heaven. I sigh and reach up to tug the string that speeds it up. The fan turns faster. I pull it again and it reaches max speed, sending cool air churning throughout the room.

"Thank God," I sigh. I look at Shane in time to see his eyes lift from my chest.

"Need anything else?" he asks. A muscle in his jaw ticks.

I can think of a few things, and while my former self might have given voice to her dirty thoughts, this Kate steadfastly refuses. "No," I say. "Thank you."

He shrugs, smiling faintly. "Suit yourself."

Chapter Three

"**O**h God," I whisper, not sure this is happening, not sure I should let it. I'm definitely going to let it.

I'm lying on my back on top of the blanket, T-shirt and panties discarded, and Shane's kneeling at the foot of the bed. He hooks his big hands around my ankles and tugs me down, down, until my legs are spread wide and my knees dangle over his shoulders.

My body is a live wire. Every part of me is on fire. I press the backs of my hands against my cheeks — I'm burning up. A trickle of sweat makes its way along my hairline and down my neck.

Shane's calloused palms stroke up and down my thighs, stopping occasionally to press his thumbs into the soft skin behind my knees, making me arch my back and thrust my throbbing sex close to his face. His laugh is low and warm, and on one such thrust he catches my ass and holds me there, suspended in space for an eternity. When my muscles are shivering from exertion and I'm sure I'll collapse, I feel his teeth on my inner thigh, biting lightly.

I cry out. And I'm not really a crier when it comes to sex. I don't moan or scream names, and I don't care for guys who do either. It feels forced and pornographic, and I prefer finesse and choreography.

Shane's moves are not choreographed. I don't know what comes next. I know what I'm hoping for, but still, when it happens, I'm not prepared for it. He fastens his open mouth over my drenched folds, and pulls me into his mouth, hard. My body gives out and I fall back onto the bed, his hands anchoring my knees to his shoulders, keeping my thighs firmly spread.

I writhe in a mixture of agony and ecstasy — wanting to escape his searching tongue but also desperately wanting it to find…that… spot. And just like that, my weakened muscles spark to life again, tensing dangerously around his neck. He chuckles, deep and hot against my flaming, swollen lips, and everything tightens low in my belly and prepares to —

The shrieking alarm clock jolts me upright. I look around frantically in the dark room, expecting — hoping — to see Shane kneeling on the floor, mouth damp, ready to finish what my subconscious has started. But he's not there. It's five twenty-five in the morning, and I'm alone, my T-shirt and panties sadly in place. The only carryover from the dream is my heated skin and the unbearable ache between my legs.

I reach over to turn off the alarm and groan in frustration. I can barely remember my last orgasm. In Bali, I believe. Last fall. With Stefan, a Swedish scuba instructor. He was hot. Sleek and sexy. I remember the first time I saw him, leading a group of tourists in a dry run with their scuba equipment. I was on the beach, reading a book, not absorbing a word.

But now, thinking about Stefan, seeing his blond hair and clear blue eyes, I can't remember what it was about him that drew me. Dark hair, brooding eyes, and a mass of muscles — that's the cause of this twinge between my thighs. And the reason for my imminent cold shower.

I'm on the first shift on Mondays, so at six o'clock I flip on the lights in the dark dining room, yawning and blinking as I set up the buffet. I've had the same dream twice in a row now, and I'm not sure how much longer I can take it. Yesterday was Sunday, aka changeover day, which means the kitchen/cabin staff was swamped with work. I haven't seen Shane since he hung the fan, so my reasoning that he'd been in my dream because he was the last person I saw before bed on Saturday went right out the window when I woke up hot and bothered again this morning. He was in my dream because something about him and his awfulness has gotten under my skin. What does older, wiser Kate have to say about that?

Chef Alec is working alone this morning, and he's quiet and focused on his tasks. I'm grateful for the silence, as it lets me stew in peace.

The wranglers show up first for breakfast, surprisingly rowdy for a group that was out drinking until just a few hours ago. When they leave, the girls show up on time for their seven o'clock start and guest breakfast begins.

A little while later I'm making more coffee when Alec asks, "Who's taking this over?"

The girls groan, and I turn to see a row of four plates, heaping with more food than a small family could eat, lined up on the counter. Alec covers each one with a room service lid and stacks them on top of each other.

"Not me," Lisa whimpers.

"Not me," Janie and Becca echo.

Hailey looks at me.

"What's going on?" I demand.

Apparently the ranch hands — Shane, Brandon, and two others — get their meals delivered out to the barn. They bring the dirty dishes back themselves, something we're evidently supposed to be grateful for, but three times a day someone's required to schlep a mountain of hot food out to them.

Everyone votes, and they nominate me unanimously as the best candidate for the job. Hailey helps me collect the heavy plates, and I balance them against my chest, tilting backward a bit before maneuvering my way through the kitchen and out the back door, past the Dumpster, and around the front of the lodge to the barn.

It's still foggy this early, and the trip is a treacherous one. Twice I nearly stumble, cursing furiously when bacon grease burns me through my shirt. I'm in a bad mood when I reach my destination and spot four men sitting at the desks. Only Brandon offers to help as I struggle to set down the precarious stack, then step back to wipe my slippery hands on my jeans.

"You didn't tell me you were Eight-Shot Kate of O'Malley's fame," Brandon accuses, shooting me a smile as he doles out the dishes. "We probably could've found you a fan a lot faster."

"Those days are behind me," I say primly, earning a laugh from two of the other men. Shane sits silently, staring at me. I do a double take when I spot a small bruise on his cheekbone. Well, good. He deserves it. I have bruises of my own. "And I did get a ceiling fan," I add.

"Did it help you cool off?" Shane asks, leaning back in his seat. His fingers are linked over his stomach, and his shoulders are broad enough to completely obscure his chair. Just like that, the dream comes back to me and I feel a flush rising up my chest, threatening to show on my face.

"It was fine," I say, turning on my heel to hurry away.

"Thanks for breakfast," Brandon calls.

"You're welcome," I return over my shoulder. "Brandon."

Back at the lodge we finish breakfast and I offer to sweep the dining room so the girls can get a head start on their cabins. When I checked their work yesterday, it became woefully obvious that while Hailey was okay, the other three were not. The cabins are supposed to be in pristine condition when the new guests arrive, but at four o'clock I was still finding unmade beds, forgotten towels, and even a pair of dirty underwear stuck under a couch cushion.

Today I pop into the cabins sporadically to check their work, which has improved somewhat, though I have to give Lisa a second lesson on how to use a vacuum cleaner.

It's quarter to twelve when I return to the main lodge to start setting up for lunch, and the sun is bright and hot overhead. I transfer the "teaching vacuum," as Lisa called it, to my non-achy shoulder and shield my eyes from the light as I look over at the pool with longing. I've been yearning to go swimming since I got here, but there just hasn't been time. And after the combination of the stepladder fall and lugging ranch-hand food to the barn, my shoulder has started to hurt.

"Howdy." The deep voice interrupts my thoughts, and I stop in my tracks to spot the source. It's Shane, rounding the side of the shack that houses the hot tub.

"Howdy," I reply, the word sounding ridiculous. As a matter of fact, it sounds ridiculous coming from Shane, who—clad as ever in cargo pants and a T-shirt—looks no more countrified than me.

He approaches, sunglasses covering his eyes so I can do no more than take his cocked eyebrow as a signal of his current emotional state: doubtful/amused. "Did you write this?" he asks, thrusting a slip of paper into my free hand. I rest the vacuum on the ground and look at the requisition slip I filed an hour earlier with Pete, the twenty-year-old handyman.

"Yes," I say.

"What does it say?"

I read from the paper: "Please remove bat from cabin nine."

"Bat?"

"Yes."

"As in bat-bat, not baseball bat? Not hat?"

"Bat-bat," I confirm. "Like vampire, like fangs."

Shane shakes his head. "Couldn't find it."

"The guests mentioned it at breakfast," I tell him. "And Lisa says she saw it too."

"Where?"

"In one of the bedrooms."

"Who's Lisa?"

"The blonde with the hang over."

"Any chance she just saw spots, not a bat?"

"What about the guests saying they saw it?"

"People come up here expecting to see wildlife. Sometimes they see it when it's not even there." This is said with more than a little disdain.

"City people are not especially known for imagining things."

"Well, I couldn't find it," he says, taking the slip from my hand and putting it in his pocket. "If you see it personally, let me know."

I roll my eyes. "Will do." I pick up the vacuum and leave him standing there. As if bat hunting is part of my job description.

I meet the other kitchen/cabin girls in the dining room, and we prepare for lunch service. Soon we're so busy that I manage to completely forget about the bat until Lisa corners me.

"Can you have someone look for the bat?" she begs. Seems the guests from cabin nine returned from horseback riding and found said bat still in its position. "They're getting angry."

"Where is it, exactly?" I ask.

"In the window of the master bedroom," she says. "Top…right. No, left. No, right."

I sigh and glance out at the barn. I'm not writing another requisition slip and enduring another inquisition without reason. "Okay, I'll go take a look."

"You're going to do it yourself?" she gasps. "What if it's...poisonous?"

"It's not poisonous," I say, hoping this is true as I slip out of the lodge and back around to the cabins.

I knock as a formality, though of course there's no one inside cabin nine. The doors don't lock, so I let myself in and enter the small master bedroom, which, like everything at the ranch, adheres to an "upscale backwoods" design scheme. The walls are wood planks, the ceiling has exposed rafters, and the bed is covered in a handmade quilt in the tribal design pattern of the local Native Americans.

None of the cabins have televisions or telephones, and there's Internet access only in our main office. When guests come to Ponderosa Pines, they're meant to "rough it"—in the five-star-dining sense.

There's only one window in the room, so I approach tentatively, pretending my steps don't falter as I get near. I've seen bats before, but never right up close, and I don't know how this one will react. The curtains are open but still obscure the top corners of the window, and the bat is, of course, not visible. I reach tentatively for the curtain, then pull my hand back and scurry outdoors. Surely it will be easier to spot the bat through the glass from the outside. Once outside, however, I realize the window is too high to really get a good look, though I think I see a small dark blur in the upper left corner.

I return to the bedroom, whisper a small prayer that the bat will remain sleeping and/or not attack, and very carefully peel back the curtain. Sure enough, there's a bat: a teeny-tiny bat, fast asleep, looking for all the world like a little dark brown frog. *Aww.*

I then realize I have no idea how to get a bat out of a room, so I beat a hasty retreat to the lodge kitchen, pick up the ranch hands' lunch, and take it to the barn. The men are sitting around the desks, so I drop the tower on the closest table and they promptly start attacking.

"Do you still have that requisition slip?" I ask Shane.

He stares at me for a moment, his dark eyes unreadable, then reaches into his pocket and pulls out the tiny folded paper. I take it, re-read it, and hand it back. "Bat in cabin nine," I say.

"You saw it yourself?"

"Yes."

"When?"

"Just now."

He stands, and suddenly we're just inches apart. This close I can feel the heat radiating from his body. Even though I'm hardly small at five foot seven, he makes me feel that way.

"Let's go," he says.

We don't speak en route to the cabin. When we arrive, Shane opens the door and gestures for me to enter first. Not wanting to argue, I go inside and beeline it for the master bedroom, preparing to point to the window. Then I hesitate.

"What are you going to do?" I ask, turning.

Shane, right on my heels, skids to a stop to prevent a collision, then removes his sunglasses to look down at me.

"What do you mean?"

"How are you going to remove the bat?" The way the windows open doesn't allow for simply popping out the screen and pushing the bat through the other side.

"Let me see it," he says, trying to step past me to the window. I move to block his path and he stops, cocking that eyebrow. This time, however, he doesn't look doubtful/amused, he looks annoyed.

"What are you going to do?" I repeat.

"You'll see," he says.

I realize he's chewing gum and watch his jaw work for a second. "Are you going to kill it?"

"It's a bat, Kate." He sighs. "Don't worry about it."

"What's the alternative?" I persist.

"You have a thing for bats?"

"I have a thing for not killing things." I move again to block him from passing me. This time he steps forward so we're nearly nose to nose, but are definitely chest to chest. My breasts press into his ribcage, and I feel his chest contract as he inhales.

"Move," he says softly.

"No," I reply.

"Now."

I take a deep, fortifying breath, put my hands on his chest, and push. He doesn't budge. At all. But this time *both* eyebrows raise and he looks at my hands, suddenly small and futile, on his chest.

"What are you doing?" he asks, his voice deceptively quiet.

"Never mind," I say. "I'll do it myself."

"Do what?"

"Get rid of the bat."

"You will not."

"It's gone," I lie.

"Uh-huh."

"Look, it's small and harmless, and I don't want you to kill it. If that's your only plan—"

He sighs, hooks his big, calloused fingers around my wrists, and all-too-easily uses them to push me away, at the same time turning us so his back is to the window and the back of my knees bump the edge of the bed.

"I'll do it—" I say again.

He closes his eyes as though summoning patience, then tips me back slightly so I fall on the bed when he releases my wrists. In the three seconds that I'm startled and falling he whips a handkerchief out of his pocket, whirls around, pushes the curtain aside, and scoops up the sleeping bat in his cloth-covered fist.

There's a faint squeak, and I'm not sure if it's me or the bat. "Are you killing it?" I ask, leaping up and chasing him out of the room. "Don't squeeze too hard—"

The cabin door is still open, and he flicks his wrist. The handkerchief opens to spill out a tiny, dazed bat that falters for a second before extending its wings and zipping away.

Shane turns to me, sunglasses in hand, and once again I'm too close. My skin flushes at our proximity and maybe because of the look in his dark, dark eyes.

"Satisfied?" he asks.

Chapter Four

We make it through the evening's dinner service without injury or embarrassment. Rather than try to convince someone else, I hustle the ranch hands' food out to the barn. They're nowhere in sight, so I leave it on the desks and return to the kitchen. In between entrées and dessert the girls discuss their plans for the evening: returning to O'Malley's.

"Are you coming?" Hailey asks.

I notice Sous Chef Mark listening in.

"No," I say. "Not tonight."

"Why? Too tired?"

"Ah…" I am definitely not too tired. Like most of the staff, I slept all afternoon, waking only at the insistence of my alarm clock. I have plenty of energy and even want to return to O'Malley's, but I don't want to keep reminding people of Eight-Shot Kate's previous antics. Plus I really want to swim, and the pool will be empty if they're all out partying.

"Tomorrow?" Lisa asks.

"Yeah, maybe," I hedge. "Drink responsibly tonight, okay? You're opening tomorrow."

Lisa grins. "Definitely," she vows. "Whatever you say."

It's nearly ten by the time the staff clears out and I have most of the ranch to myself. From my room I can hear a ruckus in the lounge downstairs as the guests amuse themselves at the pool table and some-one strums a guitar. I step outside to scan the pool: the single security light shines bright and the water is empty. Perfect.

I hurry back to slip into a bathing suit. The only one I can find is a bright blue bikini that's a little on the skimpy side, but no one will be around to see, so I put it on and check myself out in the mirror. I look okay—maybe a little too skinny, but I'm working on that. Eating has never been a problem for me, but I haven't quite been myself for the past six months. The bottoms sag a little in the back, but my boobs look half decent in the bandeau top.

I wrap a towel around my chest, slip on a pair of flip-flops, and hustle to the pool as quietly as I can. The ranch is still and dark, and there are no guests roaming around. The pool is raised up on a wooden deck wide enough to hold a dozen lounge chairs and the small shack for the hot tub. The water gleams in the moonlight, luring me in. I still feel the heat from the kitchen clinging to my skin as I drop the towel on a chair and step out of my shoes.

I nearly have a heart attack when a massive figure steps out of the shadows. "Ahh!" I squeal, reaching behind me for my towel but succeeding only in knocking it to the ground between the chairs. My options are to turn around, bend over, and dig for it—not going to happen—or stand there awkwardly, exposed. Without much choice, I opt for the latter.

Shane steps out of the hot tub shack and closes the door behind him, a towel wrapped around his hips. Even in the weak light I can see the water glistening on his chest. He's built like an ox: his muscles are defined, but he's mostly just big, and though I have no idea what a lumberjack looks like, that's the first word that comes to mind.

"Evening," he says. He's not moving, and I know he's looking me up and down. I definitely don't want to turn around to hunt for my towel and show him my saggy bikini bottoms.

"Evening."

"Cabin nine have any more complaints?"

"None."

"Good."

We continue to stand there. He's got the benefit of the shadows from the shack, but while the security light may not be bright, I'm standing in its glow and know that I'm on display.

"You going swimming?" he asks finally.

"Yes. You?" Dammit. I shouldn't have said yes. Now if he says yes I'll still have to go. I could've said I—Well, what could I have said? That I came out for a nighttime tan?

"No," he says. "I'm done."

I nod uncomfortably. "Okay."

He finally peels away from the shack and moves toward the staircase. This involves coming closer to me, and I watch him from the corner of my eye as I dip my toe in the water. He's twice the size of the guys I usually go for. I like them sleek and refined, not brutally strong. Don't I?

"What's wrong with your shoulder?" he asks suddenly.

I freeze. I hadn't realized I'd been rubbing my sore shoulder. For some reason I don't want to tell him it's from carrying his freaking food. "Oh, nothing," I lie. "Mosquito bite."

Shane hesitates for a second, then nods as he turns down the steps. "Good night," he says without looking back.

"Good night." Without waiting to see him disappear, I dive straight into the deep end.

I've got first shift the next morning, so at quarter to six I reluctantly roll out of bed. There isn't really time, but I still hop in the shower and now I pull my hair up in a wet bun. And, because I'm foolish, I apply mascara and blush for reasons I don't care to dwell on.

I enter the dark dining room and navigate my way through tables and chairs, using the light from the kitchen doors as guidance. Suddenly my shin slams into an out-of-place table and searing pain shoots up my leg. "Fuck!" I hiss, since I'm alone and don't need to set an example. "Fuckity fuck!"

"I can hear you," Alec calls.

I stagger to the light switch and flip it on. The dining room is in disarray. The tables have been cleared but not wiped down or returned to order. Clearly the girls prioritized going out over doing their job, and I foolishly trusted them enough to assume they were up to the most basic of tasks.

I stomp into the kitchen as best I can on one good leg and beeline it to the coffee machine, which, to my surprise, is already brewing. "Thanks, Alec," I say, pouring a grateful cup.

"Wasn't me," he replies, not lifting his head from the batch of biscuit dough he's kneading.

I don't really know how to reply because no one else is around at this hour. I hesitate and sniff the coffee, then utter a quick prayer that it's not left over from the night before. I sip tentatively...It's fresh. And I don't care who made it. I need it. I need this and another cold shower and a whole lot more that there's just not time for.

I take the coffee with me and hastily rearrange the dining room, wiping down tables as I go. I get cutlery and coffee cups on the two wrangler tables just in time and manage to take their breakfast orders without showing my simmering rage/angst/dissatisfaction with everything.

On one return trip to the kitchen I catch a pair of broad shoulders disappearing out back, and I can't stop myself from watching them depart. It's Shane, thermos in hand. Part of me knew he must have made the coffee. That same part knows it cannot dwell on him if I'm expected to concentrate on my job. *Which would make* one *of us*, I think, irritated, as four hung-over girls stumble into the kitchen at two minutes after seven.

"You're late," I snap.

Janie blinks tiredly as she slips the rubber dishwashing apron over her head. "What?"

I bite my tongue. I don't want to go all Mother Hen on their asses, but if I don't, who will? Then again, I remember being seventeen and listening to just such a morning lecture, then promptly discarding it. They're not going to care about anything I say right now. I'll let it go. Just this once. It's not their fault Dream Shane made an appearance again last night, disappearing before he could finish what he'd started. Again.

Too-eager guests are already filling the dining room, and Hailey, Lisa, and Becca are busy taking orders when Alec stacks the now-familiar pile of room service plates on the counter.

"Ranch hands," he barks, in full chef mode.

I'm in no mood to make the trek out to the barn, so I snag Hailey the next time she's in the kitchen and ask her to run them out.

"Absolutely," she agrees.

"What the what?" I ask, temporarily forgetting I'm pissed.

"I danced with Brandon last night," she says under her breath. "Two songs. Slow songs." She raises her brows meaningfully. "And then a little something else."

"I had no idea you two had a thing."

"Me either," Hailey concedes, "but I'm not complaining." She scoops up the plates, sags briefly under their weight, then steps carefully to the back door and beyond. I watch her go, semi-pleased that at least someone is happy.

"More?" Alec half-shouts as Lisa hangs up another order card. "How many fucking people are out there?"

Hmm. If low-key Alec is tense, maybe I'm not the only one having the good kind of bad dreams.

Lisa does not recognize his question as rhetorical and goes to the door to count. Unfortunately she stands in front of the in door, which promptly swings open and cracks her in the face, knocking her down and making her nose bleed.

"Shit!" she cries. "My face!"

Becca, the offending door opener, looks horrified and drops to the floor beside her friend. "Lisa!" she squeals. "I'm sorry! I'm so sorry! It was an accident, I swear! I'm sorry!"

"My face!" Lisa moans. "Oh no…"

I want to kick them both, but I take a calming—okay, it's not calming at all—breath. "Take her to the bathroom, Becca. Check out the"—I lower my voice—"*damage*, and report back."

Becca nods and helps Lisa out through the laundry room and into the cramped staff bathroom. Even over the kitchen noise I can hear her devastated sobs. Part of me feels bad for her, even if she is stupid.

"Janie," I say sharply, breaking her out of her stupor. She's been standing in the same position for the last three minutes, not washing a single dish.

She finally looks at me. I take another breath.

"Take off the apron and go out and take orders," I tell her. "Now."

It's a full ten seconds before she starts to move. When she's finally in the dining room I turn to Alec. "What's happening?" I plead. "What's going on today?"

He shakes his head, mouth tight. "I've got fifteen fucking orders of French toast," he says. "It's going to be one of those days."

I sigh again and peek into the dining room. Janie's come out of her trance and is smiling, moving around semi-efficiently. I'm loath to go out there with my wet hair and simmering rage, so I'm relieved that she seems to have it under control.

"Kate?" Alec says. I get the impression it's not the first time he's said it.

"Sorry," I say. "What?"

"Do you mind making some more batter for the French toast? The recipe's right there." He nods to the counter where a handwritten card awaits. Mark gets two mornings off a week, and this is one. It's all Alec today. I look at the griddle: it's full of about thirty eggs and ten pieces of French toast. He's clearly got his hands full.

"Of course," I say, glancing anxiously out the window. What the hell is taking Hailey so long? Just then I hear what may or may not be banging coming from out back near the garbage cans.

Alec hears it too, and we exchange a look. "Raccoons?" he guesses.

Oh God. I remember the summer we found a bear out there rummaging around. Despite the precautions the ranch takes to discourage wild animals from coming too close, it still happens. I snatch up a heavy frying pan and creep out back to scare away the culprit.

"Hailey!" I'm standing on the steps with the pan raised over my head, watching my only good staffer kick the crap out of a garbage can. "What the hell?"

"He didn't even look at me!" she fumes. *Kick, kick, kick.* The can is permanently dented. And so is her cowboy boot, from the looks of it. "He got to second base seven hours ago, and now he can't make eye contact? Or say thanks for breakfast?" *Kick.* "I lugged eighty billion pounds of food half a mile, and he can't spare me a glance?" *Kick.* "Fucker!"

"You're right," I say—though for the record, it's not that far. I lower the frying pan as I step closer and rub her back. "He's a fucker. But right now we really need you in the dining room. I think Lisa broke her nose."

Hailey stares at me. "No way."

"Way."

"Was there blood?"

"Lots."

She books it inside.

"What the hell are you doing?" Shane asks, appearing from nowhere. I nearly jump out of my skin.

"What are you talking about?"

He looks from my face to the frying pan to the dented, listing garbage can. "I came to see what the banging was and find you taking out your rage in an unhealthy way."

I can't talk to him right now. I'm suffering my own kind of hangover—dream hang over—and all I can see is the top of his head disappearing between my legs. I blush furiously and avoid his eyes.

"It wasn't me," I mumble, returning to the building.

"Who broke their nose?" he calls.

I point over my head in the general direction of the lodge and hear him curse and follow.

"French toast!" Alec cries when I return.

"On it," I answer, snatching up the recipe and a mixing bowl on my way to the pantry.

"Nose?" Shane asks, stopping me with a hand on my elbow.

"Bathroom."

He nods and disappears in search of our victim.

I scramble around in the pantry for ingredients, hastily dumping them into the bowl. I don't cook often, but I know how to follow a recipe, and—with the exception of spilling half a bottle of vanilla extract down my shirt—things come together. I'm soon delivering a gallon of frothy French toast batter to a harried Alec.

"Thank you," he mutters, dropping in half a dozen slices of bread.

"No problem."

Hailey comes in with a stack of dirty plates. "How's everything out there?" I ask.

"Under control," she answers, nodding to show she means it.

"Okay."

I grab a paper towel and pat down my sickly-sweet-smelling chest, then cross through the laundry room to check on Lisa. I find her sitting on the toilet with Shane crouched in front of her, open first aid kit at his side.

"What's the verdict?" I ask.

"Not broken," he says. "And not bent, either," he adds, when Lisa opens her mouth to ask.

"You'll still be pretty," I assure her.

"I will?"

"Uh-huh."

Tears slip down her cheeks. "Good."

Becca's still standing there, wringing her hands. "Go help in the dining room," I tell her. "It was an accident. It wasn't your fault."

"Was too," Lisa mumbles.

"Go," I tell Becca before she can start crying again.

Shane finishes patting down the strips of white tape holding gauze to Lisa's nose and looks at me.

"Can I do anything?" I ask.

"Nope. But you'll be down a cabin girl for the morning. Get some rest," he tells Lisa. She rises unsteadily and weaves her way out the side entrance in the general direction of the staircase to the bunkhouse.

"Jesus," I say. "What a morning."

Shane packs up the first aid kit and rises. I step aside to let him pass, but he doesn't move. "Why?" he asks. "What else happened?"

I watch his lips move. See a flash of pink tongue. *What is wrong with me?* I shake my head. I don't want to get into it.

His eyes lower to my breasts, and I scowl indignantly before realizing he's staring at the brown vanilla stain on my white shirt. He lifts his gaze and smiles, knowing exactly what I thought. He steps close, too close, as he passes, dipping his head to speak into my ear. "Be careful out there," he says softly, and the feel of his hot breath on my neck undoes all my cold shower's hard work.

"Okay," I say to the three remaining girls an hour later. We're standing in the supply closet, each with a basket of cleaning supplies and fresh towels. "Lisa's out for the rest of the day, so I'll be helping with cabins."

The ranch is filled to capacity all summer, which means there are fifteen occupied cabins to get through in just under three hours. "I've been noticing some…oversights in the cabin cleaning, so I dug out the old checklist we used to use when I first worked here." I catch Becca and Janie sharing a look that clearly says *a million years ago*, but I ignore them. "I want you to use it when cleaning your cabins. When you're done, come find me and I'll inspect your work. Anything that's not up to par will be done again—and again, if necessary—until it is. Understand?"

"What about lunch?" Janie asks, a whiny note in her voice.

"What about it?"

"If we have to do all this, how will we have time to prepare for lunch?" She waves the half-page checklist as though it's a giant dictionary. "It's too much!"

"You haven't even tried it yet."

"But—"

"And it's pretty basic stuff. Make the beds, replace the towels."

"We've been doing that."

"On occasion. Let's start doing it all the time."

"But—"

"We're wasting time. Head out."

Becca and Janie offer a split-second evil glare of mutiny before whirling on their heels and storming off. Hailey lingers.

"Sorry about this morning," she says, looking guilty. "I shouldn't have let that other stuff carry over."

"Don't worry about it," I tell her. "I understand."

We're cleaning the farthest cabins, so we walk out together. "So what did happen last night? I thought the ranch hands never went to the bar?" I try to hide my personal interest in the question.

"They don't," she says. "But last night they showed up about an hour after we'd gotten there. They mostly kept to themselves, but I bumped into Brandon when he was at the bar and one thing led to another…Well, to two dances and a bit of groping."

I think about seeing Shane at the pool. He must have gone to the bar right after our encounter. Did he leave when he realized I'd stayed behind? What on earth for? *Dammit, why didn't I go to the bar?*

"Then I guess he went back home and immediately forgot about me," Hailey adds. "Because when I brought in the food this morning he didn't even look up. Didn't say a word."

"They're not much for talking," I agree. "Just eating."

She laughs. "Yep."

We part ways, and I climb the wooden steps to the now-familiar cabin nine. The family staying here isn't particularly messy, so cleanup doesn't take too long. I even double-check that I've completed all the chores on the list, just in case one of the girls decides to verify my work. Before leaving I give the window in the master bedroom a second look, but it's free of bats and other rodents, and twenty minutes later I'm entering cabin ten, which is a disaster. For some reason none of the bedding is on the beds. Or the floor. Upon searching I find it in the bathtub, which is full of water. I don't know if I'm more confused or disgusted. It looks like they emptied the entire bottle of complimentary shampoo into the water as well. Did they think they had to do their own laundry?

I sigh and jog back to the supply room to get a hamper, fill it with brand new bedding, then jog back to the cabin. I shimmy into some new rubber gloves, grimace as I collect the sodden linens, then dump them on the porch and resume cleaning the cabin, which, thanks to my damn checklist, takes forever. *Wipe down windowsills.* Seriously? Like these guys are checking for dust.

An hour later cabin ten is clean, and my face is shiny with sweat. I trudge over to my final cabin with my basket of cleaning supplies, then return to drag the basket of wet bedding behind me. Thankfully cabin eleven is in decent shape and after a quick wipe down and swapping out the towels, I'm done. At least I think I am. Just as I reach the door I hear a faint whoosh, then the telltale flapping of wings. I whirl around just in time to see a tiny dark flash zip into the bedroom.

Nooooooo. It can't be.

I tiptoe to the bedroom door—this time the children's room—and peek inside. Nothing moves. Except—is the curtain swaying just a little bit? I creep over to the window, press my head to the wall, and look behind the curtain. Sure enough, a small dark shadow is pressed into the corner. *Whyyyy?*

One hand reaches automatically for the notepad in my back pocket even as the rest of me knows I'm not going to fill out a requisition form. I'm not ready for another battle with Shane, and I'm ninety percent certain he would have killed the first bat if I hadn't gotten in the way. Not only do I not have time to protect this new bat—or maybe the same bat all over again—I'm still shaking off the vestiges of my dream hang over and don't want him to sense my weakness.

Okay, no problem. I saw him get rid of the bat yesterday—I'll do it myself. I'll just…Well, first I'll take all of my supplies back to the supply closet, and then I'll come back to deal with this. That makes the most sense. I still have twenty minutes before lunch, plenty of time to handle the bat, inspect twelve cabins, and mop the sweat off my forehead.

I stack my cleaning basket on top of the wet linens and groan as I straighten. It's already hot as hell out here, I'm a mess, and my overheated skins seems to be reactivating invisible traces of vanilla. I changed my shirt after breakfast, but I still smell like the victim of a bath shop explosion. I stagger into the supply closet and drop off my basket. Sweat is actually dripping off my brow onto the floor, and I swipe the back of my arm across my face. There are sweat stains beneath my armpits. I'm disgusting. I'm desperate for another dip in the pool, but there's no time. Instead I settle for splashing water on my face, wiping away smeared mascara, and changing into my third shirt of the day.

I toss my dirty shirt into an empty washing machine and grab a rag to snatch up the bat. Except now that I feel the rag in my hand it seems pretty…flimsy. Surely there's a better way—Aha! A cleaning bucket. I'll just…No, this is definitely not going to work well in a corner. And then I spot it: a net! I have no idea what it's used for, but it's covered in cobwebs so I can't imagine it's an essential ranch tool. Well, that's perfect. I've just wrapped my fingers around the handle when I hear—

"Collecting butterflies?"

Shane.

I turn to see him propped up in the doorway, the sun squeaking in past his broad form. Why is he so big?

"Just…No. Just looking."

"Huh." He nods but doesn't move. I let go of the net as though it's of no interest to me. My eyes dart to the clock. 11:46. I have to be back here by noon for lunch.

"Did you need something?" I ask.

He holds up a square of paper. "Broken mirror in cabin five. Fixed now."

"That's great."

He nods again.

"Did you need anything else?"

I can tell he's trying not to smile. He knows he's holding me up, and he knows I want the net. I stare him down.

"No, Kate," he says finally. "That's everything."

He leaves, and I count to ten before sticking my head out the door and looking around. He's out of sight, probably gone back to sit in the barn and act important. But I don't have time to dwell. I dart inside, snatch up the net, and sprint back to cabin eleven.

The bat's still in its resting place. I manage to move the curtain without disturbing it, then stare at the net. I'm not sure how this will work, exactly, because there's no way to actually seal it around the bat. I suppose the plan is to cover the bat as best I can, then hope it flies straight into the net. Then I'll just…run it outside.

I follow my new plan, place the net over the bat, then wait. Nothing happens. The bat remains pleasantly unaware and asleep. I blow on it. Nothing. I tentatively knock on the wall above it. Nothing. "Hey," I whisper. "Wake up." No movement.

A sudden banging on the window from outside scares the crap out of both me and the bat, who shoots out from the window just as fast as I drop the net and duck down, terrified. "Ahh!" I scream.

The bat zigs and zags randomly, equally frightened.

"Oh shit!" I scoop up the net and chase after it. "Come here!" I bellow. "I'm going to help you!"

The bat bangs into a lamp before flying straight at my face. I screech and duck, holding the net over my head in the vain hope the bat might fly in. It doesn't.

I flail wildly, eventually shooing the bat out of the bedroom and into the main room, where at least there's a door it can escape through. I shut the doors to the bedrooms and bathroom so the still-scared bat has no alternative, then run to the front door and turn the handle. The handle turns, but the door doesn't open. "What the fuck?" I mutter. These doors don't even have locks, how can it—

A deep laugh on the other side has me seeing red.

"Shane?" I shriek. "Is that you? Open this door right now."

The door swings open, and we narrowly miss another bloody nose as I dodge both the door and the bat, which is frantically trying to find its way out, but whose only egress is blocked by a lunatic with a net and an asshole with nothing better to do.

"Get out of the way!" I hiss at Shane, first pushing uselessly at his shoulder then giving up and pulling him inside by his forearm. Why he wouldn't let me push him away but lets me pull him in is a question for another time.

The bat circles the room at an impressive speed, wings flapping. The door is wide open but it's not going out, banging instead at the window.

"Stop it!" I snap, running to the window, net outstretched. "Come here! Get in the net!"

The bat zips away from me and straight at Shane, who calmly ducks. I spend another three minutes chasing the bat in circles before it finally finds its way to the exit. I slam the door in case it's tempted to return, then lean against the wall, breathing hard, net dangling uselessly from my fingers.

When I remember, I look at Shane, who is sitting on the couch, red-faced from laughter. I hurl the net at him. It bounces on the cushion next to him, and he stops laughing.

"What the fuck did you do that for?" I demand furiously.

"Language, Kate."

"Why did you do that?" I snap. "Why did you make a difficult situation even worse?"

"Why didn't you fill out a requisition form?"

I stalk toward him but halt when he stands up and comes toward me, stopping when we're a foot apart. I have to look up to see his face, which is no doubt why he stood.

"Because I didn't want you to kill the bat."

"I didn't kill the one yesterday."

"But you wanted to."

"They're rodents. They carry disease."

"They—"

"The best way to free them is to open the door and let them find their own way out. I woke it up because blowing on it wasn't going to do the trick."

My jaw drops. "How long were you watching me?"

He looks like he's ready to answer but stops, sniffing the air. "Are you wearing perfume?"

I take a step back. "I — No."

He sniffs again, then steps closer. He pinches my collar between his fingers and lowers his nose to inhale. I have to hold my breath. I can feel the heat from his skin on my cheek, and I'll never make it out alive if I breathe him in. Already my legs are weak, and there's a telltale tingle between my thighs.

"What is it?" he asks, straightening slightly, but not letting go.

I resist the impulse to whimper and throw my arms around him. Instead I take a step away and answer with a steady voice. "Vanilla extract. From earlier."

His mouth quirks. "You're making me hungry."

Oh God. Very vivid flashes of my dream stab my brain. I cannot think of Shane eating. I won't be able to walk straight.

He taps his wrist. "Guess it's lunchtime."

And then, as if he'd planned it, the dinner bell sounds and he walks out.

Chapter Five

I'm a frazzled mess when I arrive at the lodge for lunch. Thankfully the girls have already set up the dining room, and guests are being seated.

"What took you so long?" Hailey asks. "I thought you were going to look at the cabins."

I recount the story of the linens in the bathtub, and she looks disgusted. "That's the Tall Boys," she tells me, and we peek into the dining room to study a table of five extremely large (both tall and wide) men. Their size gives no indication as to why they'd put bedding in the tub, but I suppose it's nice to put a face to a minor act of vandalism.

"Has anyone checked on Lisa?" I ask, garnishing plates while Hailey fills a tray with drinks.

"I was up there a little while ago," she replies. "She'll be fine. She's bruised, but as long as we keep telling her she's pretty, I think she'll recover emotionally."

I can't help but smile. "That's good."

"Do you really think her nose will be okay? That was a lot of blood."

"She'll be as good as new in a couple of weeks," I say. I learned this the hard way approximately six months ago, but don't elaborate.

"Sorry to break up the gabfest," Alec interrupts, "but we've got food to go out."

Hailey and I sigh in unison as we stare at the familiar stack of plates. "Why can't they come in and eat?" she demands. "Why do we cater to them like they're special?"

Alec shrugs but obviously couldn't care less, since he has to make the food either way. "Beats the hell out of me," he says. "It's been like that since I got here."

I sigh again and grunt as I pick up the stack. "I'll be back."

My shoulder throbs on the way to the barn, and I think I might have to insist on this being a two-person job in the future. If the road weren't so uneven we could put this stuff in a wagon. If the barn were farther we could drive. As it stands, this is the least-bad option, though my shoulder would disagree.

It takes a second for my eyes to adjust when I enter the barn, but I immediately sense Shane. The weight bench is off to the right, and I can see two men standing on either side of it while one does bench presses. What does it say that I can locate the man merely by the sound of his grunting?

Brandon is the only one at the desks, and he helps me steady the stack as I set the plates down. "Thanks, Kate," he says. He smiles, and I have to say, the man is pretty damn beautiful: clear blue eyes, sharp cheekbones, a chiseled jaw that makes the prettiness masculine. If he hadn't blown off my friend, I might have smiled back, but instead I nod curtly. "You're welcome."

A low whistle comes from the corner. "You did it, Shane. You upset her."

"What's wrong, Bat Girl? Bad day?"

This is from the other two men whose names I have yet to learn. At this moment, I'm not sure I want to learn them. I turn on my heel and stride out, waiting until I'm away from the barn to stretch my shoulder. We're definitely implementing a two-person delivery plan from now on, both for delivery and moral support.

"You pissed?"

I pause at the sound of Shane's voice. After a second I turn around. He's leaning against the side of the barn, next to the door, out of sight of his friends.

"No." I start to turn back, but he speaks again.

"What's wrong with your shoulder?"

"Nothing."

"Bullshit."

I glance at him. "What do you care?"

"You're spending the summer in the mountains. It's only going to get worse if you don't get it looked at."

"What would you know?"

He shrugs. "I know."

"Maybe I'll see a doctor."

"Come here."

"Absolutely not."

I hear him chuckle, and every instinct tells me to run, but even as I hear the dull thud of his work boots approach, I stand still. He stops when he's next to me, close enough that I can hear his breathing.

"You mind?"

I look at him out the corner of my eye. "Mind what?"

He raises his hand, and it hovers above my shoulder for a split second, waiting for my refusal. When it's not forthcoming he lifts his other hand, holds my shoulder in his fingers and probes gently, feeling around the base of my neck and down along my shoulder blade.

I stifle a groan. What he's doing feels amazing, but I'll never admit it.

"You've got a knot here," he says, zeroing in on a spot that feels distinctly not-amazing.

I try to shift away but the hand on my shoulder tightens, holding me in place.

"You have to rub it out."

I risk a look at his face, but he's concentrated on his task, presumably watching his fingers rub a hole in my skin — that's how hard they're pressing. I arch my back to move away, but his grip is like iron.

"Take a deep breath," he orders.

I realize I'm holding my breath so he doesn't hear me whimper, and I quickly inhale.

He laughs softly. "Do you like it?" he asks.

"No," I breathe.

"Because it hurts?"

"Yes."

"It'll get worse before it gets better."

"That's stupid."

He presses harder, and I cry out, wrenching away. This time he lets me go.

"I can't do this now," I gasp, one hand wrapped over my shoulder to press on the now-tender spot.

"You have to work it out," he says, but doesn't try to come closer.

"Maybe another time," I manage. "I have to work."

Shane shrugs. "Any time."

"No," I say. "No other time. I'll go to town, find a professional."

He smiles faintly. "Suit yourself, Kate." His gaze lingers for a second before we turn and walk in opposite directions.

After I return, lunch is considerably less hectic than breakfast, and it's not until we're wiping down the tables and sweeping the floor that Mary comes in.

"Kate," she says, "do you have a minute?"

Even though I'm thirty, I flush like a guilty child. Did she see Shane and me near the barn? Did she misinterpret our spontaneous physical therapy appointment?

"Sure." I follow her down the hall to the small suite of offices. I smile at Gina, the lone office worker responsible for taking reservations, processing payments, and pretty much everything else the office might be used for, and she returns the smile.

Mary leads me to the smallest office at the very back, the one I remember finding her in so many times in previous summers. It looks like it hasn't been used much since the last time I was here. The walls are still decorated with pictures and awards, but the calendar is from three years ago and open to September, and with the exception of a dated computer—which is turned off—the desk is bare.

"Have a seat," she says. I sit as she goes to the far side of the desk and gets comfortable.

"What's up?" I thread my fingers together to hide my nerves.

She sighs. "I'm getting complaints from the guests."

I straighten in surprise. I've been here half a week. "What kind of complaints?"

"The same ones I've been getting for the past couple of weeks," she admits. "The girls aren't doing the job. Food orders are getting mixed up, cabins aren't fixed right...They're just not getting it done."

I know how hard it is to get good staff out here. There's slim pickings in the mountains, and most of the staff are from other parts of the country, spending the summer on a ranch just to try something different. Each summer I spent here a handful of the staff quit, and no matter how crappy their work ethic had been, they were still able bodies needed to get the basics accomplished, and they were missed. Mary can't just fire these girls—it'll take weeks to find new ones, and we'll be screwed. Or I will be, because I'll be the lone kitchen/cabin girl.

"I'll talk to them," I promise. "I dug out the old cabin checklist this morning, and I'll start inspecting the cabins to make sure things are getting done. It'll be okay. You'll see."

She runs a hand through her hair, and I'm surprised to see just how gray it is. I realize she's aged—we both have.

"I'm getting too old for this, Kate. Hiring, firing—I just can't be bothered. I want to enjoy this place, not run it."

"You can do that," I assure her. "Don't worry about anything. I'll talk to the girls, and things will get better. I promise."

She smiles and looks relieved. "I'm glad you're here, sweetie. We missed you."

I step around the desk and hug her. It's been a long time since I've hugged someone for reasons other than hello or goodbye. "Me too," I say.

I return to the dining room just as the girls are preparing to leave. "Not so fast," I say firmly. "Have a seat."

They exchange looks and slump into seats around one of the tables. I join them and pull out the list of guest complaints Mary gave me. "Does anyone know what this is?" I ask a sea of blank faces.

"Another checklist?" Janie asks dryly.

"Guest complaints," I reply. "A long list of them. We're going to go over the list one by one and see what we can do to fix them."

Janie rolls her eyes.

"Question?" I ask her.

"Yeah. Why are we being blamed for this?"

I read the first item on the list. "Towels not replaced in cabin four for three straight days."

The girls avoid my eyes.

"You're not being *blamed* for anything," I force myself to say calmly. "But this is your job and it could be done better, so I'm here to teach you how."

"Great."

"You applied for a position as a kitchen/cabin girl." I address the comment to all three girls, but really it's for Janie. "Don't act surprised when that's what you're expected to do."

"So somebody forgot some freakin' towels. Big deal!" she exclaims. "It's not like somebody died."

"If we can't do the small things right—like replace towels—how can guests feel confident about the rest of their visit? How do they know the food is prepared well or the horses are trained?"

"What does this even have to do with us? We're supposed to be off now."

"Well, you're not. We're going to take this list and go over it point by point until I'm confident you understand why it *is* a big deal that a cabin didn't get new towels for three days."

"This is ridiculous."

I bite my tongue before I can tell her it's her attitude that's ridiculous. I didn't come here to be the bad guy, but she's doing a great job of pushing me into it.

"Let's go," I say.

Two hours later Becca and Janie, even Hailey, are on the last threads of their patience. I lost mine some time ago near cabin five when Becca, supposedly in charge of cleaning it for the past week, could not find the vacuum she swore she'd used earlier that morning.

"The checklist was not a suggestion!" I snapped, not for the first time. "None of what I'm saying is optional. Just do it!"

It's after three when I send them back to the bunkhouse and sneak myself into the lounge. One of the rules for the new, wiser me is to drink less, but if anyone needs a shot right now, it's me. Plus, as "management," it's totally fine for me to help myself every once in a while.

The lounge is blessedly empty when I tiptoe behind the bar. It actually is okay for me to be here, but I can't shake the feeling of being seventeen and doing this exact same thing—minus the permission. I've got a shot glass on the bar and have just found the tequila when I hear, "Make it two," from behind me.

I whirl around and nearly drop the bottle when I see Lisa taking a seat at the bar. Her nose is covered with gauze bandages and both her eyes are rimmed with bruises, making her look like a sad raccoon.

"How old are you?" I ask.

She smiles and slumps forward. "Eighteen."

"So...illegal."

"Please?" She bats her eyes at me.

"Wrong gender," I reply, filling my glass and grabbing a lemon wedge from the fridge. "Besides," I tell her, "as rough as you look, trust me when I say my day has been worse."

"That's what I was hearing."

I down the shot. "What did you hear?"

"That you're a slave driver."

I nod and pour a second shot. My last one, definitely. "That's not too far off."

"Why'd you come back here?" Lisa asks.

"To the bar?"

She shakes her head, and I down the second shot, wincing as I bite down on the lemon.

"I came back for a change of pace," I say finally. "I needed things to slow down a little, get my head on straight."

"Why? Weren't you in Hong Kong or something?"

I shrug. "It wasn't really a place I was trying to leave. More like... a pattern."

"Of what?"

That's a hard question to answer. No one likes to hear a rich person complain about how hard it is to be rich. I mean, on paper my life was awesome: free travel, the best hotels, great food, interesting people, shows, and concerts. Then there's the first-class flights, champagne, and designer clothes. And for a while it was awesome. But somehow, gradually, I started to love those things less. I didn't eat a great meal and feel fancy, didn't put on expensive shoes and feel like a queen. I started to feel empty and lonely and old.

Self-pity is unattractive on anyone, but it's extremely unattractive on a wealthy blonde in seven-hundred-dollar heels, so I kept those thoughts to myself and let them fester. Even if I had wanted to share them, I wouldn't have known where to turn. Sure, I had friends—acquaintances, really—but I kept them at a distance. It's only in these past six months that Stanley and I have become close, though I've known him for ten years. I'd made and lost so many friends in my travels that it never seemed worth opening up to anybody. But I can't tell Lisa all this, though I appreciate her asking.

"I just realized I wanted something else," I eventually answer.

"Like what?"

I give a dry laugh. "Good question."

I put the tequila away, and it's Lisa's turn to sigh sadly.

"What about you?" I ask. "What brought you out here?"

"Janie."

"You're sisters?" With their long blond hair and big blue eyes, they're the very image of American apple pie.

"Cousins," she corrects. "We're starting college in the fall, and she wants us to pledge together. I made the mistake of telling her I wasn't sure I wanted to be in a sorority and next thing I know she's handing me a plane ticket and telling me we're working at a dude ranch for the summer. A dude ranch!"

I can't help but laugh at her dismay. "Interesting choice of punishment."

"I don't even know what she was thinking," Lisa moans. "I mean, we don't know anything about horses…or cleaning."

"No kidding."

"And she hates it here. Like, she flirts with the wranglers, but…I don't know. She's not really meant for working."

"What about you?"

Lisa looks around, confused. "What about me?"

"Do you hate it here?"

"Um…I don't know."

What should have been a statement comes out as more of a question. While it's hard for me to relate to someone—anyone—not loving it here, even on days like this, I can empathize with feeling like you don't know where you belong.

"Give it time," I tell her. "It'll get better."

"What if it doesn't?"

"You've got a plane ticket, don't you? It has to end sometime."

Chapter Six

Janie and Becca give me the silent treatment throughout dinner service. Hailey's on dish duty and because Lisa's still upstairs mourning her bruised face (and the lack of tequila with which to drink away her pain), I help run the food.

Carrying trays of five or six plates was hard enough last time I did this, but today I find it positively exhausting. My feet are aching, and I'm bitter as I watch Janie and Becca dart around easily, beaming and laughing with the guests, then turning the evil eye on me when they catch me looking. I sigh. I yelled at them once already today. I'm not going to go overboard.

At least Hailey is still on my side. "How's it going?" she asks when I bring in a load of dirty plates.

I scrape leftovers into the compost bin. "Not bad," I lie. "Tiring." I rotate my shoulder. I've been here less than a week, and while I'd hate to admit Shane is right, maybe I should make a trip to town sooner rather than later. This knot isn't working itself out. If anything, it's getting worse.

I set down the plates and pour myself a glass of water. I didn't have time for a nap earlier—after cracking the whip with the girls and chatting with Lisa I was lucky to squeeze in a shower before dinner. I close my eyes when I hear the familiar sound of covered plates being stacked.

"Sorry," Alec says, instead of "Ranch hands' dinner is ready."

I down half the water and set the glass on the counter. My two-person idea is going to have to wait until we have hands to spare. I have a feeling we're lucky Becca and Janie even showed up for dinner service, so I'm not going to ask them to make the trip.

"I'm on it," I say, sounding more confident than I feel. I hoist the stack of plates, feeling their warmth against my chest, and maneuver out the back door. I've just rounded the corner of the lodge when I hear the rapid pounding of running feet. Big ones. Clad in work boots.

"What's going on?" I shout. I know it's Shane, but if he's running from something, I want to know what and get a head start.

"Here," he says, breathing hard as he stops in front of me. I feel his calloused palm on the back of my hand as he takes the stack of plates from me. I shake out my arms and stare at him. Against his big frame the plates look miniscule.

"What's happening?" I ask.

"You don't have to do this anymore," he replies.

"Do what?"

"Bring the food over."

"Well, there's no one else right now. Janie and Becca hate—"

"Leave it on the counter inside the door, and we'll pick it up."

"Oh. But I thought—"

"Why are you arguing?" He arches that damn brow again.

"I'm not."

"How's the shoulder?"

I whirl around to go back inside. "Just fine."

I hear him laugh behind me.

"That was fast," Hailey remarks when I return for my water.

"They're going to pick up the food themselves from now on," I tell her, and by default Alec, who is standing right there.

"Really?" he says, seeming interested. "That's a first."

I shrug. "I'm not going to argue. Those plates are heavy."

"Yep," Hailey agrees. "No reason to go to that barn. No reason at all."

I smile, and she smiles back. I don't know what Brandon's deal is. Hailey is incredibly pretty, with hair to die for. On top of that she was a college volleyball player and is still enviably fit. And, unlike the other kitchen/cabin girls, she's mature.

"You coming to O'Malley's tonight?" she asks.

It's on the tip of my tongue to say no, but just then Mark enters with a tray of molten lava cakes for dessert. "Say yes," he urges. "I'll give you a free cake."

"Cakes are for guests," Alec points out.

Mark winks at me. "Of course."

"Okay," I say. "I'll come." I can't help but wonder if Shane will be there again. And why he's breaking tradition: going to O'Malley's, picking up the ranch hands' food.

"Come where?"

I turn to see Janie standing just inside the door, half-full coffee pot in hand.

"O'Malley's," Hailey answers.

Janie sighs dramatically and does everything but stomp her foot. "Seriously? Again? Why? Why are you everywhere?"

"Relax," I tell her. "I promise not to speak to you."

"Thank God."

"Hey," Alec snaps. "Like it or not, Kate is your boss and this is my kitchen. If anybody gets to be rude, it's me. Got it?"

Janie looks like she wants to say something else, but merely turns on her heel and returns to the dining room. Becca enters, spots her friend leaving, and quickly follows.

I roll my eyes. "I don't have kids," I say to Alec. "Do you? How long will this last?"

"They're teenage girls." He shrugs. "They're monsters. From what I've heard, you weren't much better."

I gasp, offended. "Me? Never!"

He laughs. "Do you believe in karma, Kate?"

I suppose I do believe in karma. And if I wasn't certain I was in the right for coming down hard on the girls earlier, I'd believe I was being punished right now, because it looks like karma has arrived in the form of Cassidy Reyes, my teenage nemesis.

"I can't believe she's still coming here!" I hiss at Hailey, who sits beside me at O'Malley's, nursing her third "and final" beer.

"I can't believe you're still saying that!" she replies.

"And her dance moves haven't changed at all!"

Mark snorts with laughter and leans past us to see. "Looks all right to me," he says, earning himself a kick in the shin.

"Shut up!"

I glower into my drink as Cassidy continues to dance with four men simultaneously. All are completely entranced, though what they see in bleached-blond hair that has recently seen a crimping iron, I'm not sure. Though when she turns, spreads her knees, and shimmies low to the ground, her enormous breasts nearly fall out of her corset—yes, a corset—and I decide it's safe to assume it's not the hair that caught their attention.

Cassidy's family owns a nearby ranch, and each summer I worked here was spent in some sort of face-off with what we called the Summer Skank. The staff and I would come here most nights after work, and Cassidy would inevitably be waiting with her small posse of friends, ready to sort through the summer workers to pick her next victim. The boys were more than willing to comply. She was a siren none could stay away from.

My first two summers were spent wrapped up with Ryan Parker, one of the wranglers. We were serious and committed when we were together, though when the summer ended we were promptly and seriously single again. My third summer, however, I'd expected us to pick up where we'd left off, only to learn that Cassidy Reyes had gotten her claws into him the day after I'd left the year before, and they were still together. I spent each night after that at O'Malley's, furiously drinking and dancing my ass off, pretending my pride wasn't stung by their coupling. But it was. How could any guy who wanted me want that awful skank? Even now I can't stop myself from judging the four slobbering men grinding against her.

I share my sob story with Hailey and Mark, who nod sympathetically. And neither says, "It was ten years ago, Kate. Move on!" for which I'm grateful. It's much easier to be self-righteous when your friends are supportive.

"Want to dance?" Mark asks.

I shouldn't, I know—not with my scandalous history—but I nod and stand up anyway. I'm not drinking tonight, and my days of dancing like Cassidy Reyes are way behind me. Even if I had planned to try to show her up — which I hadn't — those plans would've been quickly derailed when the band launches into a slow song.

"Lucky me." Mark smiles, gathering me into his arms.

He pulls me a little too close, and I move away gently, putting some breathing room between us. If he notices he doesn't say so, just sways easily to the music. It's nice to be this close to someone, but while I know he's probably got feelings more romantic than mine, my body just doesn't react to his the way it does to Shane. The way it knows when he's in the room. The way his breath on my neck makes goose bumps spring up on every inch of my skin.

I feel something cold on the back of my neck and reach up under my hair, but there's nothing there. I look around to find the source, but spot nothing. And then Mark spins me and I see it: Cassidy Reyes's icy gaze. She's spotted me. She's draped over one of the four men from before, but her attention is focused squarely on me. I smile falsely and give her a finger wave. She hesitates before doing the same.

Her partner twirls her, and I watch her miniscule skirt spin up so high her pink panties are briefly revealed, a fact noted by every man in the room. As soon as she's back in his arms, her gaze returns to mine and I turn away, pretending to be interested in Mark's story about culinary school.

When the song ends he asks me to stay for the next one, but I excuse myself to go to the restroom and hurry away. *How is it that I still harbor so much resentment for that girl?* I ask my reflection a few moments later. Her relationship with Ryan hurt my pride more than my heart — have I really not gotten over it? Or is she just one of those awful people I'm bound to hate eternally?

"Hey, Kate."

I turn to see that she's sidled into the small, saloon-themed bathroom.

"Hi, Cassidy."

"It's been a long time."

"Ten years."

"I heard you were some hotshot writer. What brings you back?"

I shrug. "Just helping Hank and Mary. What are you still doing here?"

It's Cassidy's turn to shrug. "I never left."

Of course she wouldn't leave. Big fish, small pond. I squint at the sudden flash of light on her left hand. A ring.

"You're married?" I splutter. Which of those four men was her husband?

Cassidy hesitates, her eyes darting away. "Widowed," she says, and something in her voice rings true.

"I'm sorry."

She answers the unspoken question: "It wasn't Ryan. I don't know what happened to him."

"Oh. Good." I wince inwardly. What a terrible thing to say. I'm awful in situations like these. I was the good-time girl, not the one you turned to in times of trouble. Unless you needed to be bailed out of jail.

"So how long are you here for?"

"Just the summer."

"Is that guy your boyfriend?"

"Why, you interested?"

She smirks. "Maybe."

The door bangs open and a similarly outfitted blonde bursts in. "Cass, what are you doing? Your song's on!" The familiar strains of an old country song blast in, and I smile thinly. Silly, stupid, and dated: the song describes Cassidy to a tee.

"Better get out there," I say.

She adjusts her cleavage. "Your boyfriend's waiting," she replies.

I watch the door swing shut and scowl, willing myself to calm down. When I get back to the table, however, Janie and Becca are there too, and Janie's in my seat.

"Hey," Mark says, spotting me. I watch Janie take her hand off his leg and look at Hailey, who shrugs.

"I thought you left," Janie says with a pout. "Now this table's no fun."

"Want to sit down?" Mark asks, pushing his seat back as though he didn't hear what Janie just said.

"No, thanks," I say. "I'm just getting my drink."

We all watch in disbelief as Janie reaches across and knocks over my glass, spilling ginger ale over the wooden table. Hailey jumps back before she can get splashed, and Mark quickly throws napkins on the puddle.

"What the fuck, Janie?" he demands.

She ignores him. "Your drink's done," she says. "You can go now."

I glare at her. I'm not seventeen anymore. These games don't work with me. I open my mouth to reply, but Hailey jumps in.

"Maybe we should go," she says. "It's getting late."

"Yeah," Becca echoes lamely. "Get lost."

People have started to stare. Even though Janie's the idiot in this situation, I can't help but feel that because I'm the adult, I'm the one who looks foolish. Like I can't handle an argument with a drunk teenager.

My cheeks flush with anger. "I don't need to go," I say tightly. "Get me another drink."

Janie looks at me, wide-eyed. "I can't get you another drink," she says, the words slightly slurred. "I'm only eighteen. How old are you again? Forty?"

My teeth clench, and I'm aware of Hailey's hand on my arm, just as I'm aware of Janie returning her hand to Mark's thigh, and Mark, who is my age, not removing it. What is it with this guy? I dance with him once and every skank in the bar wants him? "Your shift may be over," I inform Janie, praying my voice doesn't waver, "but I am still your boss. That will never change. Your attitude needs to."

"My attitude?" Janie scoffs. "Please! Your show up here with your uptight checklists and think you know everything! You don't know anything. You're just some old wannabe writer hiding out for the summer. That's what everyone says, and it's true."

I can't hide my surprise. Janie's no natural-born country girl either. She's a spoiled little bitch who's not used to being told what to do, and I tell her as much. Now it's her turn to look shocked.

"You whore!" she swears, swinging a hand at my face and missing by a mile. There's an audible gasp in the room, and I know instantly this thing has gone far enough. I'm the adult, I have to end it. It's obvious there's no point in talking to Janie anymore. I'm so furious my hands are trembling as I snatch my purse off the back of the seat and blow off Hailey's concern.

"I'm leaving," I say tightly. "I'll speak to you in the morning."

"Fuck you!" Janie bellows. Someone laughs.

I ignore the stares as I weave my way out of the crowded space. Hailey and Mark call after me, but I don't stop. I'm infinitely glad I had the presence of mind to be the driver tonight, and I find the ranch van and hop in, twisting the key in the ignition before the door's even closed. I hear someone call my name, but I hit the gas and peel out of the gravel parking lot without looking back.

It's just a short drive back to the ranch, but even with the windows down and the cool night air blowing on my face, I'm still flushed and angry when I arrive. I park in one of the unmarked spots next to the barn and shut off the van. It's after midnight, and the sky is black and quiet. If I listen carefully I swear I can hear my pounding heart. I press the backs of my hands to my heated cheeks and try to calm down.

I've never been somebody's boss before, and I don't know how to deal with things like this. I'm an only child, I don't fight with people. Even in high school I didn't deal with catty girls. The only girl I've ever really battled was Cassidy Reyes, and even though I hated her passionately—still do, apparently—I always considered those battles temporary, like my stays at the ranch. *That's all this thing with Janie is*, I remind myself. *Temporary.* We'll both cool off tonight, and in the morning we'll sit down and I'll tell her...I'll tell her...what a spoiled little bitch she is. No, I already said that. I'll think of something else.

"Hey."

I jump in my seat and twist my neck so hard to look at the open passenger window that my shoulder seizes and excruciating pain shoots everywhere. I cry out and bite my lip to stifle the sound.

I hear footsteps on the uneven ground and know he's coming over to my side. I try to roll up the window, but my still-shaking hands can't seem to manage the motion. I succeed in unbuckling my seatbelt, but that accomplishes pretty much nothing.

"What's wrong?" Shane asks, now at my window. He's so close I feel his breath on my cheek when he speaks. He smells faintly of beer.

"Have you been drinking?" I ask, staring straight ahead.

"Only one. Don't tell."

I know he's smiling, but can't return it. I'm still too upset.

"What's going on? Your shoulder? I told you, I'll help. Get out."

"It's not my shoulder."

"Then why'd you scream?"

"I didn't scream, I —" I take a breath. "Okay, that was my shoulder, but that's not why I'm upset."

"Get out of the van."

"What? Why?"

"Come out and tell me. My trailer's on the other side of the barn. Sit out with me and have a beer."

My mouth opens and closes soundlessly. Truth be told, I don't really know why I'm still in the van except that nowhere else seemed better. Until now.

I get out and follow him around the barn, which, true to his word, has a large silver Airstream trailer parked on the far side. A small porch has been added to the front, and two Adirondack chairs sit to one side, overlooking the paddock.

"How have I never seen this before?" I ask as I follow Shane onto the porch and take a seat. He opens a cooler and pulls out a beer. He twists off the cap and hands it over, our fingers touching a second longer than necessary.

He shrugs and retrieves his beer from the railing, taking a long swallow. "So what happened?" he asks.

I close my eyes and drink. How do I recount the events without sounding like a teenage girl myself? I decide to skip the Cassidy Reyes stuff and just tell him about Janie. I start at the beginning, with her attitude around the ranch, and finish with the missed slap.

"She tried to hit you?" he echoes in disbelief.

"I've never been in this position before," I moan. "I just…I don't know."

"It might explain why you're so tight," he says.

"I'm not uptight! For Christ's sakes, why do people here keep saying that?" My whole life I've been chastised for not being prim and proper enough, and now I can't seem to escape the charge.

"I said *tight*," Shane repeats, "not uptight." The look on his face suggests he might be reconsidering.

I take another swallow of beer. "Sorry."

"Come inside."

I choke. "I beg your pardon?"

"Let me work on your shoulder."

The porch is lit with a tiny string of chili pepper lights glowing red and orange along the perimeter, but it's not enough to show me the intention in Shane's dark eyes. I can guess at his plans, however, and I'm pretty sure going into that trailer will only lead to one thing.

"I can't go in there," I say.

"Why not?"

"You know why. My…reputation."

He laughs. "Your reputation? What is it you want to be known as? The uptight manager or the woman with a loose shoulder?"

I can't help but smile. I don't think it's my shoulder people will be calling loose. But still — each time I lift the bottle to my lips I feel a painful twinge in my back.

"Nothing can happen," I say.

He shrugs. "Nothing will happen. I'll fix your shoulder and send you on your way."

I finish the beer and set down the bottle.

"Promise? I've had a bad night. I don't want to fight with you too."

He extends a pinkie finger, mocking me. "I promise, Kate. No matter how much you beg me, I'm not going to fuck you."

I freeze, pinkie finger halfway extended. "Jesus, Shane."

He wraps his finger around mine. "Pinkie swear," he whispers, and it sounds like a threat.

Chapter Seven

I follow Shane into the trailer. He flips on a light, and I blink to let my eyes adjust as the door closes behind me. It's surprisingly spacious and fastidiously neat—there's not an item out of place. Even the coffee table is bare. Off to the left is a tiny kitchen, next to which is a door that presumably leads to a bathroom. We're in the living room, and to the right is a sliding door, presently open, that leads to a bedroom with a neatly made queen-size bed.

"Come on," Shane says over his shoulder. He sits on the edge of the bed and unlaces his boots. "Get in here."

I take a few steps forward. What am I doing? I know that some part of me desperately wants him to fix more than just my shoulder, but tonight feels wrong. I'm on edge, this is not a smart idea, and I have promised myself that I would be smarter. I know bad things happen to stupid girls. As ridiculous as it sounds, I believe Shane's pinkie promise. It's myself I don't trust. Older, wiser Kate is on shaky ground at the moment.

"This isn't a good idea," I repeat.

"I'm just going to help your shoulder, Kate."

I swallow. "I know."

"Then what's the problem?"

"You know," I mutter.

"Listen…" Shane sighs. "Don't take this the wrong way, but you're not my type."

I stifle a laugh. "You're not mine either."

"So what's the problem? Still worried about your *reputation?*" He's teasing me again.

"No."

"Then take off your shirt and lie down on your stomach."

My heart leaps into my throat, but when I look at Shane he's staring back at me steadily, nothing insinuating in his gaze. He means what he says, and he expects his instructions to be followed. As the foreman, he's used to being obeyed. And everything in me wants to listen.

"Now, Kate."

I unbutton my top before I can overthink it. Just my shoulder. He promised. I'm not his type. He's not mine. Just my shoulder. I push the shirt down my arms so I'm standing in a white tank top and jeans.

"Keep going," he says, standing. When he rises, the room seems to shrink by half. He just takes up so much space. Makes every inch of my skin aware that he's near.

"W-What?" I stammer.

He reaches past me and grabs a small tube of lotion from the top of the dresser. "Take this off," he says softly, fingering my tank top. "It'll make things easier."

His shoulder brushes mine as he straightens, and I avoid his gaze. I'm wearing a bra that covers more than he saw the other night at the pool. *And*, I remind myself, *he promised*. Just my shoulder.

I look straight ahead at the curtains covering the window and pull the tank top over my head. I may be imagining things, but I swear I hear Shane inhale sharply. I hang the tank top on the back of a chair next to my first shirt and stand there in my bra.

"Boots too," he says, close to my ear.

I have to hold his arm as I squeeze the boots off my feet, and it's a sign that something is seriously wrong when the feel of his massive bicep — previously not a turn-on — is the most wonderful and reassuring thing I've felt in months. When the boots are off, he slides his warm, rough palm over my back, fingers squeezing the base of my neck before trailing down my spine and stopping only when they reach the top of my low-rise jeans.

"Now get on the bed."

I move before I can talk myself out of it. The blanket is soft, worn cotton, and it feels wonderful on my heated skin as I stretch out on my stomach and rest my head on my folded arms. Quiet night sounds drift in from outside as my eyes sink shut. I'm vaguely aware of Shane taking my right arm and extending it up and out to the side, elbow bent, lifting my shoulder blade.

The mattress dips as he sits down next to me, the soft fabric of his cargo pants brushing my hip as his knee presses lightly into my side. I hear him squeeze lotion into his palm, then rub his hands together. "Ready?" he asks.

I murmur my assent, somehow nearly comatose already. Maybe it's the potent combination of exhaustion and Shane's no-nonsense demeanor, but all my concerns about this encounter have gone out the window. I'll let Shane do whatever he wants. If I weren't so worn out by the day, I'd be alarmed at this level of trust. I don't even know his last name.

"What's your last name?" I mumble.

His hands, which have been smoothing over my back and shoulders, pause for a moment. "Maddox," he answers.

"Maddox," I repeat. "Got it."

His hands resume their hypnotic circling, and soon his thumbs are pressing into my shoulder blade, under my shoulder blade, finding that knot and working around it. It hurts, no question, but not as much as earlier. He's working slowly, methodically, getting deeper and deeper into the tight muscles until—

"*Jesus Christ!*" I shriek, bolting upright so fast he falls off the bed.

"What the hell, Kate?" He shoots to his feet.

His face looks angry in his surprise, but I'm still gasping. I don't know what he touched, but I have never known pain like that before. It felt like a live wire searing something deep inside.

"What are you doing?" I demand, lower lip trembling. "That hurt. Too much," I add, when he opens his mouth to argue. "Do you really know what you're doing? Is this some…ploy you use to get girls in here?"

His mouth twitches. "Ploy?" he echoes. "Really?"

He sits back down on the bed and puts a hand on my shoulder, trying to push my resisting body back to the mattress. He sighs when

I remain stiff and unyielding, glaring at him suspiciously. I'm suddenly aware that I'm wearing only a demi-cup bra, my chest heaving indignantly. He seems aware of it too, and I watch his gaze drop. It's tempting to let this rage turn into something else, but smarter, wiser Kate knows that that's a terrible idea. I snatch up the pillow and clutch it to my chest.

Shane sighs.

"Lie down, Kate. No one's going to hurt you."

"You just did."

He presses more insistently, and eventually I give in and lie prone on my stomach once more. "That's because we're getting to the root of the problem," he says patiently. "Your muscle is clenched so tightly that pressing on it forces those fibers to start releasing, but in order to do so they clench even tighter first. We have to force it to spasm until it wears itself out."

"You're kidding, right? I'm supposed to lie here while you make *that* happen? We're hoping my shoulder just spasms to death and gives up?"

"Not hoping," Shane corrects. "It will."

"You're used to getting what you want."

"Only because I'm always right."

I roll my eyes as best I can from my position. He's smiling slightly.

"Here," he says, one hand massaging my back, the other going to his belt and quickly unbuckling it. He pulls it free of the loops, and I try to sit up again. This time he holds me down.

"What the fuck, Shane?" I squeal, face pressed into the mattress.

"I'm not going to hit you with it," he says, amused. I don't need to see that eyebrow to know it's arched.

"That's not what I'm worried about!"

"What did you thi—Oh," he breathes, voice low. "I'm not going to tie you up, either, Kate. But nice to know."

I scowl, cheeks burning. "Then what's it for?"

He holds the end to my lips. "Bite down."

"Bite down?" I snap. "I'm not a cowboy! We're not removing a bullet."

He laughs. "Suit yourself. But don't move or I will tie you up."

"I'd kill you."

He laughs again. I'm glad one of us finds this hilarious.

"Stay put."

He shifts on the mattress so one knee is on the bed beside me and the other leg reaches the floor. He uses his considerable weight to apply just the right amount of pressure, starting with wider circles before zeroing his way back to the muscle in question. There's no doubt this hurts, and when he gets closer and closer the pain increases, and I can't help but whimper.

"You're doing great," he whispers.

"Shut up."

He keeps going. I try to distract myself from what his thumbs are doing, but I can't. He's digging into something that feels like it's on fire, and every thrust of his thumbs may as well be him stabbing me with a dagger.

"I can't," I mumble, writhing. "I can't."

"The more it hurts the closer it is to being over," he promises.

"Bullshit."

"I wouldn't lie to you, Kate."

I squeal and try to roll away.

"Stay put."

I roll the other way.

"Nearly there."

I buck upward on the mattress, trying to throw him off, but he's ready, and the next thing I know he's got a knee in my back and his devious hands are killing me. He's killing me.

"Stop!" I shriek.

"Count to ten."

"I can't!"

"Ten…"

"Nineeightsevensix—"

"Nine…"

"Shane!" Tears are pouring from my eyes. My shoulder is a hotbed of pain, like a barbed, flaming poker is being stabbed through again and again.

"Eight…"

I cry out as the pain intensifies impossibly more—then suddenly, somehow, it's extinguished, leaving me with a faint, distant ache, soothed by Shane's awful, wonderful hands.

"Feel that?" he asks.

"What happened?"

He lowers his head, and I can feel his lips on my cheek as he speaks. "You gave up."

I push against him, but he's still got his knee in my back. "Never," I breathe.

He straightens and laughs. "It's better, right?"

"I wouldn't know. I can't move."

"Hang on. Stay put."

I feel the mattress lift as he stands for a moment, then returns. "What is that?" I ask as I hear some sort of adhesive backing being removed.

"Heat pad." He smooths it over my shoulder blade. It's blissfully soothing, instantly warm and penetrating. "That okay?"

I swipe a hand over my damp eyes. "Yes."

He moves away again, then quickly returns. "Here."

I look up to see that he's handing me my tank top. I sit up gingerly and accept the shirt, fully aware that he's watching as I slide it over my head. My shoulder aches, but it's a faint, vague pain, nothing like the shooting agony from before. Shane hands me the second shirt, but I just hold it in my lap. I'm suddenly embarrassed. I cried. And wailed. And writhed like a child when he was just trying to help. With a knee in my back.

"You don't listen," I accuse, for lack of anything better to say.

"To what?" He leans back against the dresser, feet crossed at the ankles.

"To no!" I exclaim. "I told you that hurt."

"Kate," he says, stepping forward and smoothing a wayward hair from my forehead. "I'll listen to no when you mean it."

Chapter Eight

"Noooo," I groan the next morning. At first I think it's my head that's pounding, then I remember I hardly drank last night and pry open my eyes. Someone's at the door, knocking softly but insistently.

"What?" I hiss, and the noise briefly ceases. "Who is it?"

"Luke," a strange voice answers.

I run a hand over my face and look at the clock. 6:08. "Who?"

"Luke. One of the wranglers."

I stagger to the door and pull it open. Wrangler Luke is standing in the dark hallway, hat in hand.

"What are you doing up here?" There are strict rules about boys in the girls' bunk.

"Alec told me to come," he answers. "There's nobody downstairs."

"I—What?"

I fumble for the light, and we both wince as it flickers on. I find the staff schedule I keep on my dresser and scroll over to Thursday's early shift. Janie.

"Okay," I tell Luke. "I'll get her. Tell them five minutes. Sorry."

He leaves, and I feel my way down the dark hall to the room the kitchen/cabin girls share. I can just make out the bulky shape of the bunk beds and hear faint snores.

"Hey!" I whisper-shout, rapping loudly on the wall. "Janie!"

"What's going on?" someone mumbles. I think it's Hailey.

"Janie!" I whisper-shout again, this time louder. "You're supposed to be working."

"Oh God, stop shouting," Hailey groans.

"Cover your eyes," I warn her. "I'm turning on the light."

I hear the rustle of fabric as I feel for the light switch and flip it on. It takes another second for my eyes to re-adjust, then I gape at the nearly empty room. "Oh shit," I breathe.

Moments later, hastily dressed, I hustle into the dining room and face two tables of hungry wranglers and, strangely, one table of hungry ranch hands. I spare Shane a confused glance, and he shrugs. I mutter apologies and hurry into the kitchen where Alec is expertly cracking eggs.

"What's going on?" he demands at the same moment Shane enters with the same question.

I sigh and try not to cry. When I left Shane's trailer last night, I was unduly optimistic. I felt relaxed and hopeful that things around here could improve. But now three of my four kitchen/cabin girls are AWOL, and the fourth one is in the shower, trying to wash away the stench of last night's overindulgence.

"They're gone," I say. "Three of the girls. Their stuff's gone…They left."

"Shit," Alec says.

I grab a notepad. "I'll take orders. Be right back." I move past Shane to the door. "Excuse me."

"You okay?" he asks.

"Never better."

The wranglers are surprisingly understanding. In my previous summers we'd had people abscond in the middle of the night, but never quite like this. I take orders and run food, and Hailey comes in just in time to help clear. She enters the kitchen with a perplexed look on her face, and I know what's prompted it.

"They just showed up," I say, regarding the ranch hands.

"They never eat in the dining room," she replies. "What's changed?"

"Guess they realized it was a waste of time to have us run food out there."

"Whatever. I'm over it." She pours a cup of coffee and drinks it too quickly, then winces, fanning her burnt tongue. "God. Where do you think they went?"

I shake my head. There aren't a lot of options out here. The girls must have hitched a ride into town.

"I can't think about it now," I say. "We've got too much to do. You're not planning to leave, are you?"

"No."

"You can tell me if you are."

"I'm not. Promise."

"Good." I check the dining room. Empty. "Come on," I say, picking up a bus bin. Hailey does the same and follows me. We have about five minutes to get the room reset for the guests, then the two of us will manage the entire service. What a mess. How am I going to explain to Hank and Mary that my promise to fix things resulted in a mass walkout?

"Honestly?" Hailey says as she wipes down a table. "I'm kind of glad they're gone. I mean, Janie was a bitch."

"Totally."

"And Becca was a bitch robot."

I laugh. "Yep."

"And Lisa…"

We share a look. There's no need to say more. Lisa was the vaguely unwilling member of an evil clique—the one who's not sure she wants to be bad but isn't sure how to be good, either. But now she's gone, and we've got a mountain of work ahead of us.

"Hey," Shane says, boots thudding on the wooden floor as he enters. The door swings shut behind him.

Both Hailey and I look up in surprise. "Hey," I reply.

Hailey hurries into the kitchen with a bus bin, and I resume wiping down tables and straightening chairs.

"Tough break."

"I'd say."

"How's your shoulder?" I nearly jump when I feel his fingers pressing on the heat pad through my shirt. I'd planned to take it off before work, but dressed so quickly I forgot.

"Much better. Thank you."

"Any time." There's more than a little innuendo in that statement.

"I think I'm fixed now."

He laughs and drops his hand. "Have it your way. I came to give you something."

I no longer need the sex dream to remind me that I find Shane incredibly attractive. Maybe it's his matter-of-fact personality, the steadiness in his dark eyes that suggests he sees right through my "I'm mature now, honest!" façade and likes me anyway, or the way everyone automatically respects him, but I'm drawn to the man, even when I know I shouldn't be. That's why, even though I wouldn't be entirely offended if the "something" he wanted to give me was in his pants, I keep my voice level and professional and ask, "What?"

"Pete!"

Plodding footsteps thud down the porch and a moment later Pete, the incompetent handyman, enters. "I'm here," he announces unnecessarily.

Shane shoots me a look that says, *See what I have to deal with?*

I look back to say, *So you're giving him to me?*

"Pete here will help you out for the rest of the day," Shane says. "Isn't that right, Pete?"

Pete shrugs. "Yeah. I guess so."

"He's all yours." He gives me one last look that says so many things I can't even begin to interpret and leaves.

I study Pete. He's got floppy brown hair and big puppy dog eyes. He looks like the guy who writes sappy love songs that rhyme, not the guy who fixes things. Which probably explains why Shane's so willing to part with him for the day. Whatever. Beggars can't be choosers. "Let's go, Pete."

Because Pete has no idea how to take orders or even talk to guests, Hailey and I put him on dish duty and handle the dining room. We're rushed off our feet, but no one seems to notice we're short staffed. It's a relief to know the dining room won't fall into complete disarray as a result of the girls' disappearing act.

The cabins, however, are a different story. It was a struggle for four of us to get them done yesterday, and just three people sharing the same load — one of them being Pete — is almost too much to contemplate. But I don't have the luxury of bemoaning my bad luck. I hand Pete a checklist, confirm that he knows the difference between shampoo and conditioner (his soft, shiny hair suggests he does), and send him on his way. I'm going to inspect the cabins today, no matter what — if I spot a bat I'll just look the other way.

Pete and Hailey depart with their cleaning supplies, and I return to the kitchen for a glass of water before following them. Alec is already working on prep for lunch, and the rhythmic chopping is soothing as I gaze out the window at the green mountains and horse paddock. My eyes drift in the direction of the barn, and my mind conjures up the image of the man inside it—the one who so kindly promised not to fuck me, no matter how much I begged. The man who pinned me down and massaged the hell out of my shoulder, who let me rant and rave about my hatred for a teenage girl, who offered help when I needed it but was too stubborn to ask.

I could probably stay on this train of thought for another hour or so, but the sight of a small figure shuffling down the dirt road toward the ranch catches my eye. She's far enough away that I can just detect blond hair and the dark bulk of something she's tugging behind her. *Janie?* is my first thought, followed by a more optimistic, *Lisa?*

I set down my glass and dart out the back door, running to meet her. It *is* Lisa. Her face is still swathed in bandages, but she looks otherwise unharmed.

"Lisa!" I exclaim as I reach her. "What on earth? What's going on?"

She raises teary eyes to meet my stare. "They left," she confesses. "In the middle of the night. Woke me up and said we were going. So we left and then…I don't know. We were sitting at a bus station, and I said I didn't think we should do this, and Janie said shut up, and Becca was like, 'Yeah, shut up,' and at first I did shut up, but then I couldn't help thinking…maybe I shouldn't go. Maybe I should stay. So I came back. I'm sorry, Kate. I'm really sorry."

She's crying in earnest now, and to be honest, I'm more exasperated than anything. I'm glad she's okay, and I'm glad one staff member came back so we're that much less short-handed. But we really don't have time for this teary confessional, and I pat her on the shoulder and say as much.

"Okay," Lisa says, wiping a hand under her nose. "You're right. Definitely. Let's get back to work."

I help her lug her suitcase upstairs and wait in the hall as she changes back into the ranch polo shirt. Because she missed yesterday's checklist lecture and Pete has never had one, we join him in cabin one and start the lesson.

Three cabins later, it turns out Pete's a pretty good student. And with guilt to motivate her, so is Lisa—though it was more than a little difficult to keep their attention focused on my instructions rather than each other. What does it say that even with a hand-sized bandage covering the center of her face, Lisa can still find a way to flirt? And what does it say about Pete? He's either able to overlook the bandage or has an interesting fetish for gauze…I don't dwell on it.

It's quarter to twelve when we finish the cabins and meet Hailey back in the supply closet. "What are they doing in cabin nine?" she demands. There's an enormous wet spot on the front of her shirt, and she's sweating profusely.

"Bedding in the tub?"

"We should shut off their water!" she fumes. "No more sheets! What the fuck?"

Pete and Lisa laugh, and Hailey finally notices her.

"Wait," she says. "What?"

"I came back," Lisa says.

"And the other two?"

"Gone."

"Good."

Lisa nods uncertainly, as though she's not sure she completely disagrees with Hailey, but can't be so disloyal as to openly agree. What she can do openly, however, is ogle Pete, who is returning the favor. Hailey notices, and we both roll our eyes. At least with Pete around we've got something to tether Lisa to the ranch.

Shane catches my eye when he stops in to pick up lunch for the ranch hands. We stare at each other for a moment, though I'm too busy to stop and talk.

When the guests have cleared out and we've cleaned and swept the dining room, Hailey, Pete, Lisa, and I sit down with sandwiches and iced tea.

"You know about Thursdays, right?" Hailey asks.

"Ranch dance?" I guess.

"You betcha."

I sigh. The ranch hosts a dance for the guests every Thursday night, complete with live music from a local country cover band.

Staff attendance is mandatory, and back in the day I spent many hours in the arms of strange men, two-stepping and boot-scooting my way through the night. If we managed to sneak alcohol upstairs, the nights were mildly entertaining. Sober, they were just a reminder that our time was not our own. I'd almost managed to forget all this. "How have they been going?" I ask. Hailey and Lisa have been around for two dances so far. My late arrival makes tonight my first dance of the season.

They shrug and look at each other. "Okay," Lisa says finally. "Just… you know. We'd rather be off."

"No kidding."

"But…maybe this one will be better," Lisa adds. "I don't know."

The way Pete's looking at her suggests that it will, indeed, be better tonight. Even if her face isn't.

"Kate?" I turn to see Hank and Mary lingering in the hallway. "May we see you?"

I force a smile. "Of course."

They disappear down the hall, and I push my plate away, my appetite vanishing. They've no doubt heard about our missing kitchen/cabin girls, and they didn't hear it from me. In my own defense, I've been busy every minute until now, but still…I probably should have made time to see them. Or at the very least left a note.

Upon entering the small back office, however, I discover that Hank and Mary aren't mad. There were no guest complaints yesterday — a season record, apparently — and they didn't really like Janie or "that other one" anyway. Now that I'm here they're more than happy to let me post an ad online looking for new staff, and take over the hiring.

"Just can't be bothered with it," Hank says, kicking back in his seat like life has never been better.

"Nope," Mary agrees. "Who cares?"

I hesitate. As the one picking up the slack, I certainly care. "Okay," I say. "I'll post something this afternoon."

"Great," Hank says.

"Whatever." Mary shrugs.

They exchange a look. "Oh, hey, Kate," Hank says slowly. "Do you mind maybe…rewriting some of the text on the website?"

My eyes dart between them. They're acting especially strange. "What do you mean?"

"Make it newer," Mary explains. "Fresher. Try to attract more people."

"The ranch is fully booked."

"Change is good," Hank says.

"It's time for a change," Mary agrees.

It's like I'm witnessing some sort of strange performance art. Hank and Mary may be a little offbeat, but in the out of touch, old school kind of way, not…like this.

I nod anyway. "Okay, sure. I'll look at it after I post the job ad."

Hank pushes back his seat and helps Mary to her feet. "Great!" he says brightly.

"Thanks, Kate!"

I watch the two of them fairly skip out of the office. What on earth is going on?

There's an hour between the end of dinner service and the beginning of the dance. I'm upstairs getting ready with the girls, and through the floor we can hear the tables being pushed aside and the band setting up.

The Thursday nights I remember involve ten girls crammed into two tiny bathrooms, but there's only six of us today: Hailey, Lisa, and me, as well as three female wranglers we rarely cross paths with due to our concurrent shifts.

Lisa, Hailey, and I peer at our reflections as Lisa asks for the fourth time if curling her hair isn't too "predictable." She's got wavy blond hair, and Hailey and I assure her that the curls are anything but predictable. Neither of us really knows what this means, but it seems to calm Lisa, and she wields her curling iron with confidence.

"What are you wearing?" Hailey asks me.

"Just a skirt," I answer. "Top. Nothing special. Why? You?"

"Can I see your skirt?" she asks.

This conversation is starting to feel just as peculiar as Hank and Mary's stilted performance earlier.

"Of course you can." I look at Lisa, who does not appear to have noticed anything unusual.

I lead the way to my room and Hailey follows me in, closing the door. I turn to ask her what's going on, but she beats me to it.

"So Brandon talked to me today," she says, sitting on my bed.

"He did? When?"

"During one of my countless runs to the laundry room thanks to the Gross Tall Boys."

"What did he say?"

"He asked if I was going to the dance."

"That sounds so…grade school."

"I know, right? I said I was and he was like, 'Good.' Then he tried to give me a seductive smile. I was like, 'It's mandatory. It's my job to be there,' and he stopped smiling. But seriously, Kate, what's his deal?"

I shrug. Apart from our initial encounters, I haven't had many occasions to talk to Brandon. If Shane hadn't completely obscured my view of any other man, I might have noticed him more, but as it stands…I've got nothing.

"Are you going to dance with him?"

"No. If I dance with him I'll let him feel me up and in the morning he'll ignore me again. I'm not about to make it a habit."

"Good idea."

"Are you going to dance with Shane?"

I shrug. "I don't even know if he's going."

"He's been at the last two."

"Seriously?" I have a hard time picturing it.

"The old ladies love him," Hailey says with a laugh. "You should see them. They act so frail and helpless. For such a serious guy, he's pretty good with them."

"Yeah. He's good at a lot of things," I say absently.

"Oh?" Hailey looks intrigued.

"Not like that," I say hastily. "I wouldn't know."

"But you want to know."

"I'm not going to *know* anything," I say. "Those days are behind me."

"What days?"

"You know. Carelessness. No strings. Jump first, think later. I can't do that anymore."

"What, have fun?"

"Hailey, you're the one who dragged me in here to say you weren't going to let Brandon have any fun tonight!"

"I had to!" she protests. "If I don't say it out loud no one can hold me accountable in the morning."

"I bet if Brandon promised to hold you account—"

"Shut up!" she squeals, throwing a pillow at me. "Fine. Fine. You won't *know* Shane, and I won't *have fun* with Brandon, and tomorrow we'll pat ourselves on the back for being spinsters. Deal?"

"Deal."

We finish getting dressed, collect Lisa, and stomp downstairs to the dance. The wood-paneled room and twanging banjo strings lend the night an authentic country air, and already staff and guests are two-stepping around the floor. Most of the guests at the ranch aren't actual country folk. They show up with brand new denim and cowboy boots and plaid shirts and play dress-up. They're charmed by their surroundings and generally find the simple solitude of the mountains peaceful and calming. At least for a week. Then the lack of technology gets to them, and they're itching to leave by the time Saturday rolls around. I can understand. No television for an entire summer was almost unthinkable when I was a teenager. I remember stopping at the airport newsstand and buying every tabloid available to devour on the plane ride home, desperate to catch up on the important news of celebrity hook-ups and divorces.

Tonight everyone is in a good mood. The band is the same one that played ten years ago, and they're playing a lot of the same songs. Pete's already here, wearing a clean Ponderosa Pines polo shirt and jeans, fending off the advances of a couple of tween girls. His eyes light up when he spots Lisa, but he mimes apologetically that he can't come dance with her just yet. She adjusts her bandage and smiles coyly. It's okay. She'll wait.

Hailey and I exchange another look—we're so far beyond all that—and when she promptly blanches I follow her gaze, though I'm pretty sure I know what I'll find. Brandon is dancing with a tiny old lady, his broad shoulders clad in black plaid, a cowboy hat on his blond head. The man could be in a cowboy calendar: Mr. July.

He's just so damn pretty, and Hailey isn't immune, no matter how determined she is.

"Come on," I say. "Let's find guests to dance with."

She sets her shoulders. "Good idea."

We approach a couple of older gentlemen and ask them to dance. Soon we're weaving our way around the room, agreeing with the men that we are so lucky to work at such a beautiful place, asking if they're having a great time. The song ends, and we dance with more guests. Five songs later I'm starting to sweat. I haven't seen Shane yet, but Brandon appears to be particularly aware of Hailey's presence, though he hasn't been able to get to her before the next guest whisks her away.

I slip past a slow-dancing Lisa and Pete and duck into the hallway to catch my breath. Before I reach the outside door, however, my nemesis—Summer Skank—walks through.

"Sum—Cassidy!" I exclaim.

She looks down her nose at me. "Kate," she sneers. Her blond hair is piled on top of her head with "artful" tendrils swirling around her face. She's toned down her outfit tonight, opting for a barely there nude-colored spaghetti-strap tank top and skin-tight jeans, finished with red stilettos. She looks like a *Showgirls* reject.

In comparison, I look decidedly *Little House on the Prairie*, with a knee-length floral skirt, sleeveless white blouse, and cowboy boots. It's not particularly stylish, but at least it's appropriate.

"What're you doing here?" I ask when she makes no move to explain.

She blows a curl out of her eye. "I was invited."

"Invi—?"

My question is answered when Mark enters the hall, two beers in hand. "Oh, hey, Kate," he says awkwardly.

"Hey, Mark."

"Enjoying the dance?"

"I am. You?"

"Uh-huh."

Cassidy looks between us, amused at our awkwardness. We both know she's only here with Mark because she thought there was something between us, which there most definitely is not. But if she's distracted by the sous chef, she'll have less time to bother me, which works just fine.

"You two have fun," I say.

"Thanks," Cassidy replies, her voice dripping with insincerity.

I'm squeezing past them to get outside for fresh air—which I definitely need—when once again the door opens before I can get to it. A tiny brush of cool night air wafts in, but it's limited since Shane's big body is blocking the way. He steps into the hall, and the door closes behind him.

"Hey," he says, eyes on my face.

"Hey."

"Hey, Shane," says a voice from over my shoulder. A stupid, skanky voice.

"Hey, Cass."

Almost immediately I feel my spine stiffen. I suppose it's not crazy that the two of them might know each other, but *Cass?* An abbreviation? That's not something two barely acquainted people would use, is it?

"Thought I might find you here." Summer Skank sidles past me and slips her arms around Shane's neck, pressing her breasts into his chest and her nose into his neck. Even with her heels she has to lift onto her tiptoes, and I watch, unimpressed, as his hands briefly squeeze her tiny waist in return.

I'm doing my best to hide what I know is my bitch face, but it's clear I'm not succeeding when my eyes meet Shane's. He watches me with that calm, knowing steadiness that's starting to find its way under my skin. The man is a rock, unmoved by anything.

Anything except Cassidy Reyes, that is, because when she finally pries herself off of him I notice his eyes drop to her massive cleavage and linger three seconds too long. I dart a look at Mark, who's nursing his beer and pretending not to witness the display. He's a decent-looking guy, but there's no way he can compete with Shane, and it's become obvious that Cassidy used his invite to have access to the rest of the staff, not him in particular.

"Want to dance?" she asks, running her painted nails up Shane's bicep. He watches her nails on his skin and glances at me before looking back at her. She raises onto her tiptoes again to whisper in his ear, her voice loud for my benefit. "It's been too long since you've touched me, baby."

Ugh. I nearly gag. *Baby?*

And Shane—what is his problem? He doesn't look quite as pathetic as the devoted, slathering men from the night before, but he doesn't look put off by her blatant come-ons, either. It's clear these two have a history, and the knowledge is akin to having a bucket of ice water thrown on my head. I know without question that I do not, under any circumstances, want Summer Skank's sloppy seconds.

"Have fun, *baby*," I say, pushing past them and out the door.

Shane starts to say something, but I let the door slam shut and hurry around to the side of the lodge, darting through the gate to the back kitchen access. This is where the garbage is kept, so I feel pretty confident no one else will be dropping by.

I sink onto the steps and put my head in my hands. *What is wrong with me?* I ask again and again. Why do I let skanky Cassidy Reyes get under my skin? I'm not up for a replay of last night. Though my instincts urge me to get back in there and pull her hair out by her dark roots, I know the best thing to do, the mature thing to do, is keep my distance. From both of them. I'll let Mark be the mooning idiot who watches the pair of them mate on the dance floor. I'm don't care. I won't.

"Kate?" comes a whisper. I recognize Hailey's voice and sigh. I want to be alone, but I don't.

"In here," I whisper back.

Moments later the gate swings open and she steps through, shutting it behind her. "I saw the summer skank," she says. "She was drooling all over Shane."

"No 'the,'" I correct her. "It's just Summer Skank, a proper name."

"Summer Skank. Got it."

"What is she even doing here?" I ask, trying to keep the whiny note out of my voice. "I thought she thought I wanted Mark, but the second she saw Shane she put on this disgusting show, and he totally fell for it."

"Is she even wearing a bra?" Hailey demands. "Who wears flesh-colored shirts?"

"Skanks."

"Skanks, indeed."

We sigh in unison.

"Did you dance with Brandon?"

"No. After I saw Cass—Summer Skank and Shane, I spotted Mark, who told me what happened. It was just as well. The way Brandon was looking at me I knew I couldn't hold out much longer."

"I wonder what changed."

"Probably three days without feeling any breasts."

I laugh out loud. "Poor guy."

Hailey smirks. "Yeah. Let's feel sorry for him."

We're silent for a moment.

"I owe you an apology," she says after a moment.

I look at her in surprise. "You do?"

"I'm the one who told Summer Skank you and Shane kinda sorta had a thing."

"We don't have a thing."

"I know. But I sort of implied that you did."

"What? How?"

Hailey runs a hand through her hair. "Um, by saying you were a couple."

"What?!"

"Last night after you left she came over and was gloating about how you took off and left your boyfriend behind—meaning Mark—and how he couldn't keep his hands off of her. I said Mark wasn't your boyfriend, you hardly knew him, and she said, 'So who *is* Kate's boyfriend?' and I kind of…"

"Hailey!"

"I don't know. She was trying to make it sound like you were going home to cry your eyes out, and I just thought it would be better if you were going home to be ravished by a hot guy."

I snort with laughter. If only she knew. "Well, thanks for trying."

"So much for good intentions. Now she's over here getting her claws into him any way she can."

I shake my head. "Any guy that finds someone like that attractive is not the man for me."

"I hear you. You'd have to dip his dick in bleach."

"Hailey!"

She laughs. "Sorry, I may have made a few trips to the bar in my efforts to avoid Brandon."

"All in the name of duty."

She hiccups. "Yep."

We're silent again.

"He's so pretty," she sighs.

"It's not fair," I agree.

"Dammit." Then she pats my knee, stands up, and leaves.

I watch her go, smiling ruefully. Lisa and Pete, Hailey and Brandon…Cassidy and Shane. Matches made in summer-fling heaven, I guess. I give myself a mental slap in the face. I didn't come here to fool around. I came here to feel safe and comfortable, to get back to being myself. And I can feel it working. I can't let those plans be derailed by hurt feelings over some imagined connection to a guy I know next to nothing about.

"How long are you planning to hide?"

I sit up straight as Shane comes through the gate. This is the worst hiding place ever.

"I'm just getting some air."

"Next to the garbage?" he asks.

"So?" It's on the tip of my tongue to add, "I thought you liked trash," but I keep it to myself. Just barely.

"Come back inside."

"No, thanks. I think I'm done."

"I thought you loved dancing, Eight-Shot Kate."

"Don't call me that."

"Okay."

He comes forward and sits next to me on the steps. I try not to move, but I can't help it. It's like I can see her skanky germs oozing over his skin. I jump up and take a few steps away. When I turn back Shane is looking at me. He looks pissed.

"What was that for?"

"What?"

"Don't play dumb, Kate."

"What do you want me to say? I didn't feel like sitting."

"You didn't feel like sitting next to me."

"So?"

"So last night I had my hands all over you, and today I can't sit beside you?"

I shrug but don't speak.

"What changed?" he demands.

He must know I have a problem with Cassidy. I didn't launch into the story last night, but tonight's awkward encounter should have told him enough.

"Cassidy?" he guesses.

"Don't play dumb, Shane." A mocking note creeps into my voice.

He stands up, and I take a step back. I have to look up to see his face—he's got to be at least six foot three. He dressed up for tonight: dark pants and a white button-up, the top buttons undone to reveal a swath of tanned chest. He looks so damn dangerous—sexy and strong. And contaminated.

"You're not mad about her, are you? Some girl I dated years ago?"

"You dated?"

"You didn't know?"

"How could you date her? She's so gross and desperate!"

His face tightens. "Don't insult her."

"Oh God. Spare me. This—this is why I'm getting some fresh air."

"What?"

"To get away from her! I knew her years ago, and we didn't get along. Nothing has changed. She's a disgusting slut and if you—you *fucked* her, then you're disgusting too."

He takes a menacing step forward. I back up again. I don't have much farther to go until I'm at the fence.

"I'm disgusting?"

"Don't take it personally."

The faint porch light is at his back, casting his face in shadows, but there's a full moon, and I can see it glint in his furious dark eyes.

"Which part? The part where you call me disgusting or dumb?"

"You know what? Take everything personally. Or don't. I don't care. We don't know each other, and we're not going to."

"You realize you're overreacting, right? You're acting like the spoiled bitch everyone says you are."

I look at him sharply. "I beg your pardon?"

"I'm supposed to apologize for dating someone years before you ever showed up? What business of it is yours?"

"I didn't make it my business! You two did when you groped her in the hallway!"

"No one groped anyone!"

"Please. I know what I saw. *Baby*."

Shane heaves an exasperated sigh and runs a hand through his thick hair, leaving it standing on end. It only makes him sexier. *Dammit.*

"It was two years ago," he says.

"It was ten minutes ago," I counter.

"I don't even know why I'm explaining anything to you."

I shrug. "Don't expect me to guess. You followed me."

"What do you want, Kate?"

"I wanted to be left alone."

"You want Mark? That's your type?"

I scoff. "Mark can have Cassidy too. Assuming he hasn't already."

Shane takes another step forward. This time I don't back up. I can smell the faint scent of his aftershave and realize this is the first time he's worn any. He cleans up nice. And he fucks Cassidy Reyes.

"I'm not like her," I say finally.

"I know you're not." He steps forward again, but I hold up a hand and he stops.

"I used to be," I say, flashing back to last night, to her grinding away on the dance floor. "I used to be that girl. But I'm not anymore."

"Okay."

"And I can't — I know it's unfair, but I can't see myself being with someone who could ever be with someone like that."

"Like you? Like you were?"

"I know you don't get it — "

"No," Shane interrupts, stepping close, then pushing past me to the gate. "I get it. You're too good for this place — "

"That's not what I — "

"And for the people in it. Don't worry, it's crystal clear, Kate."

And then he disappears through the gate, slamming the door so hard behind him that the entire structure shakes. I hear his footsteps fade in the darkness and can't tell if it's guilt or regret that makes my chest ache.

Chapter Nine

"So the day started with someone running away from you..."

"And ended the same," I confirm, slumping onto the overturned milk crate in the ranch phone booth. "It's been two weeks, and he hasn't spoken to me since."

"That's rough," Stanley says.

"Rough doesn't cut it," I moan. "Everybody hates me."

"I thought you said the redhead and the girl with the broken face—"

"Don't call her that! Her nose has healed. And okay, they don't hate me, but I'm their boss so they—"

"Hey, self-pity called. It found your pride and wants to trade."

"Stanley!"

"If it's that bad, why don't you leave? I'm never going to understand why a girl with your money and resources is cleaning toilets for a living."

"I told you. I'm helping Hank and Mary."

"Uh-huh."

"What?"

"You're hiding."

"We covered that. I thought we were adding to the list."

Stanley sighs. "Do you want me to come down there?"

"You would do that?"

"Oh, you'd take me up on the offer?" He sounds worried.

I laugh. "No."

We're quiet for a moment, and when he speaks next the joking tone is gone.

"Seriously, Kate, I know I wasn't there for you before, but if you're really stuck, I'll get on a plane, come to that ranch, and kick some cowboy ass for you."

"That's sweet, but unnecessary."

"You're not alone."

"I know. We have fifty-plus guests demanding something different every minute."

"You know what I mean. You're not alone in the world. You're my best friend, and I'd do anything for you."

"Same here."

"I know you would. And you have. But I haven't, and I'm telling you that from now on, I would. I will. I'll never turn off my phone again."

"You were on your honeymoon! Stop beating yourself up."

"I can't."

"You must. I'll stop pitying myself, and you do the same."

Stanley takes a deep breath. "Okay."

"Okay."

"I love you. Call again soon."

"I will."

"And send me a picture of this guy."

I laugh. "I'm not taking a picture of him!"

"Come on. The first guy in a million years to get under Katharine Burke's skin…"

"He's not under my skin."

"You just talked about him for ten minutes straight."

"About how much he hates me! And how much he loves the silent treatment."

"So he knows how to commit."

"You're such an optimist."

"Take a picture and get it to me."

I laugh again. "I'll get right on that."

"Bye."

I hang up, feeling a little better.

But that's where things stand. Shane hasn't said two words to me since our fight at the dance. I'm pretty sure the last time I got into a fight with a boy at a dance I was fifteen, and he spilled punch on me. How did my promises to be older and wiser transport me back in time?

The ranch hands still come in with the wranglers for breakfast, but on the days I open and take orders, Shane just eats from the buffet, refusing to so much as look at me. He and Brandon send Connor, one of the other ranch hands, in to pick up lunch and dinner and return the dishes, because, in addition to Shane not speaking to me, Brandon, who couldn't get enough of Hailey at the dance, is now avoiding her like the plague.

Is it the heat? The isolation? Maybe it's something in the water that's making everyone act like hormonal teenagers. Speaking of which, I've had to rearrange the cabin cleaning schedule to ensure that Lisa and Pete are working on opposite sides of the ranch, otherwise they'd never get anything accomplished. I haven't been able to find one without the other since they met, and while even jaded old me has to admit their puppy love is kind of sweet, it's also disgusting. Particularly since the only guy to warrant a sex dream in the past five years now only looks at me when he thinks I don't notice. Maybe I'm making it up, but I swear I feel Shane's eyes on me when I haven't realized he's around. And when I turn to locate the source of the feeling, he's somewhere near, focused intently on a task that doesn't involve interacting with me.

So he's pissed, I get it. But Cassidy hasn't been back to the ranch since that fateful night, so if he's getting laid, it's not by her. And if it's not her I'm not sure who it could be, because Hailey has her ear to the ground and reports faithfully on any comings and goings from his trailer, of which there have been none. According to ranch gossip, he never lets anyone in his trailer, ever. Even Cassidy. Hailey and I have become great friends and confidantes, but even with her I omit the fact that I've been in that trailer, in that bed, without my shirt. Some things I need to keep to myself.

The point is, my frustration — professional, emotional, sexual — hasn't lessened since the night of that painful massage, and no matter how stubborn or stupid he's being, I know Shane's feeling the same way. He has to be. Right?

I exit the phone booth when I see Hailey, who has just finished her last cabin of the morning, and we walk to the laundry room together. With practice, our morning routine has become somewhat streamlined, and we're back with a full half hour to spare before lunch is due to start. We peer out at the cabins, and watch as Pete slowly makes his way back with his basket. Shane is mad at me, but not so mad that he's taken back Pete, which is a blessing since I've only had one response to my job posting, and it was from someone in Nigeria who promised to split seventeen million dollars with me if I wired him two grand.

The problem with hiring somebody now is both our remote location and the fact that most seasonal workers have already found jobs. Most people aren't going to come all this way having already missed a month of work. It's just not worth it. But I'm still trying. And in the meantime I've been helping Hank and Mary modernize the website, fancying up the writing to better sell the features of the ranch. They seem happy with it, though I'm still not sure what has prompted their sudden desire for change.

Outside, Lisa comes darting across the grass to join Pete, flinging her arms around his neck and kissing him passionately. Her nose has healed, and with the exception of some faint yellow bruising on her cheeks, she's as good as new. And Pete still doesn't seem to care one way or the other. He drops his basket, and tiny bars of soap scatter everywhere. Lisa finally releases him and hurries back to her cabin to finish cleaning.

We watch Pete crouch down to collect his wares, and Hailey props her chin on her hand. "Why can't I find love like that?" she moans. "What am I doing wrong?"

He straightens and resumes walking toward us, though he's staring so hard over his shoulder at Lisa's retreating form that he bangs right into a utility pole and falls down.

"Oh," Hailey says. "I see. I set the bar too high."

I laugh. "I'll go set up the dining room."

"I'll start on the laundry and meet you in there."

"Sounds good."

I leave her and pour myself a glass of water in the kitchen before scooping up a tray of cutlery. I'm exactly halfway through the out door to the dining room when Shane passes through the in door. Our eyes lock, and he immediately looks away. I scowl but don't stop, though it's possible that I bang the tray of cutlery on the closest table with a little more force than necessary. Dessert spoons bounce out and clatter to the floor, and I squat to pick them up.

The out door swings open, and I recognize Shane's heavy steps as he enters the dining room and stops. I immediately wish I were wearing different jeans. These are low cut, and I'm pretty sure I'm flashing my underwear. I snatch up the spoons and straighten, sticking them in my pocket so I don't mix them with the clean ones. I wait for Shane to leave, but he doesn't. Finally I turn around.

He's staring at me.

I stare back, stone faced. Is this some new form of silent treatment? Instead of merely ignoring someone you purposely encounter them so you can force them to acknowledge that you hate them?

"The guys need Pete back this afternoon," he says finally.

I want to ask why, but I refuse. "Okay."

"Now, actually."

"He should be in the supply room."

"All right."

He's still not moving. The dining room is large and empty, but it feels the opposite — like the walls are closing in, pushing us closer and closer together. He's six feet away, but I can feel the energy pulsing off of him in waves. I haven't had that sex dream in a while, but I remember it well, and two weeks of the silent treatment have done nothing to diminish its effects. Nights now are long and lonely, and I haven't returned to O'Malley's for fear of bumping into Cassidy. It's dull, but it's better this way. It's the right thing to do.

Speaking of the right thing to do, I owe Shane an apology. I put my own issues on him that night and insulted him, blamed him for things that are none of my business. There are plenty of things in my past I'm not proud of, and I wouldn't welcome anyone else's judgment, either.

"Shane, I know I —" I break off when I see his face contort. I don't know how to explain it, exactly, but it looks like two dozen emotions cross his face at the same time. He looks like he knows what

I'm going to say, like he wants to hear it, like I'm forgiven, like he hates me, like he's sad, like he's turned on. But finally he just takes a deep breath, those dark eyes heated and cold at the same time, and backs through the door, leaving without a word.

I sigh and start setting tables. Stanley is definitely not getting a picture.

"Would you calm down?" Hailey says, more than a little irritated. "He'll be back by dinner."

"I know," Lisa whimpers. "But what will I do until then?"

She's bemoaning Pete's absence, the way she did all through today's lunch service. Apparently the ranch hands have to repair a section of fence—a fact that has Hailey singing "Desperado" on repeat—at the edge of the property, and they need four sets of hands. As the general manager of everything around here, Shane has to stay close. The wranglers will be out with guests, and there won't be many other staff members on hand on the off chance that something requires urgent attention.

"Come to town with me," Hailey suggests.

Lisa perks up. "Really?"

"Yeah. I need a break from this place. You in?" she asks me.

"I wish. I have to re-post the job ad and write up a few more things for Hank and Mary."

"You sure? We could all use a break."

"I couldn't," Lisa sighs.

Hailey rolls her eyes. "Trust me," she tells her. "You could."

"Get a head start," I tell them. "I'll finish up in here."

"You sure?" Hailey asks again.

"Positive. You'll need all the time you can get if you're going to be back by dinner."

"We will. Promise. Let's go, Lisa."

"Bye, Kate!"

I wave them off. Lunch went fine, the dining room is clear, all that's left to do is feed a few more trays of dishes through the sterilizer and wipe down the counters. Alec left a while ago, and Mark has the afternoon off, so I'm all alone. Without its usual hustle and bustle, the kitchen is a warm, quiet space—all smooth metal counters and white subway-tiled walls.

Ten minutes later the final load is in the sanitizer and I'm emptying out the clean trays. I saw Hailey and Lisa drive off, and there can't be more than five or six people left on the ranch. It's impossibly hot out and this is the perfect opportunity to spend some quality time by the pool. I've gone swimming twice since the night of the dance: once I was completely alone, and the second time I surfaced just in time to see Shane going down the stairs. He must have been in the hot tub shack and waited until I was underwater to leave. The man knows how to hold a grudge. And I get it—I was petty and stupid and insulting, and I'm sorry for it. But it's not easy to say those things to someone who's going so out of his way to make his point.

I'm rounding the prep counter with a colander in one hand and a sauce pot in the other when I slip. My arms cartwheel, and both the colander and the pot go flying, clattering across the floor. I manage to catch myself before I fall too hard, grunting as I land in an enormous puddle of water.

"What the fuck?" I mutter. Almost instantly my jeans are soaked from ass to ankle, and I pull myself up cautiously, looking for the source. The entire floor is wet, I realize. I hadn't noticed while I was doing the dishes, because we stand on raised rubber mats, but the kitchen floor is covered in a fine sheen of water.

I check the sink, but it's off, and the sanitizer, which is working overtime but most definitely not leaking. I pick my way over to the fridge, which is surrounded by water but is not the problem, and finally spot the source of the leak: the ice machine. And *leak* isn't the right word. A pipe must have burst, because a steady stream of water is spraying out from the wall behind it.

"Oh shit!" I exclaim, slipping again. I kick off my socks and sneakers, hoping it will improve my traction, and make my way over, not entirely sure what to do. The room is full of water, and there a ton of appliances plugged in, the ice maker among them. There's no way I'm touching that thing without turning off the power, and damn if I know where the fuse box is. Or what I'd do with it if I found it.

I hurry through the dining room, bare feet squeaking over the wooden floor, and turn down the hallway to the main offices. "Gina?"

I call. "Gina?" She'll know what to do. Gina has worked here for eight years and is everybody's stern but lovable mother. She'll know. If I can find her. "Gina?" Nothing. "Dammit!"

There's nobody upstairs. The wranglers are out with guests, Hailey and Lisa just left, and Pete's off with the ranch hands. Alec and Mark share a cabin out back near the boys' bunk, but I know what they'd tell me to do: First, go to hell for interrupting them on their time off, and second, get Shane. *Goddddd.* I do not want to do that. But there's no time. I cut back through the dining room, and water is starting to spill out from the kitchen and cover our freshly cleaned floors. I pick up the pace and push through the front doors, onto the porch.

"Shane!" I holler in the general direction of the barn. "Shane!"

No response. Not unexpected.

I left my wet socks and shoes in the kitchen, so I hoist up my sagging, soaked jeans and dart down the steps, across the gravel road, and down to the barn, hissing when I step on a particularly pointy rock. "Shane!" I call again when I'm near the barn. "Stop ignoring me! This is a work emergency!"

Still nothing. No way he left with the ranch hands, right? If he's not here I'll have to get Hank and Mary and explain that not only did I cause several staff members to quit, I have now flooded the place. Confessing is a last resort.

"Ow, ow, ow!" I grunt as I hurry across the grass around to the back of the barn and Shane's trailer. I pound on the door. "Shane!"

No answer.

"Shane! I know you're in there!" I know no such thing. "Please come out. This is a work emergency! A pipe burst in the kitchen, and I don't know how to fix it!"

I try the handle but the door is locked. I'm ready to cry. I can only imagine the disaster zone the kitchen is and how I'll spend all afternoon cleaning it up. I'm so hot, and I'm so tired, and I stepped on a super sharp rock, and my foot really hurts.

"*Shane!*" I bellow, pounding hard. "Open this fucking door! I'm very sorry for what I said at the dance! I don't think you're dumb or disgusting. You're very kind, and you helped my shoulder, and I'm sorry I never thanked you, but please come help me in the kitchen! I don't know who else to ask. Alec's cabin is so far and—"

"What the hell happened to your pants?"

I whip around to find Shane fast approaching from the paddock. He's got an open plaid shirt over a white T-shirt and cargo pants, and it's hard to say whether I'm so happy to see him because I think he's gorgeous or because I'm so desperate.

"Burst pipe in the kitchen," I manage, trying to compose myself. "Please help me."

Shane hops the fence easily and jogs around into the barn. I follow as quickly as I can, which is actually incredibly slowly because my foot hurts, and then I just watch as he exits the barn with a tool belt and runs into the lodge.

"Be careful!" I holler after him. "It's slippery!"

He doesn't look back.

I limp across the road, onto the porch, and into the dining room, half of which is now covered with water. *Shiiiiit.* What a brilliant day to send my two remaining employees away early.

I enter the kitchen and find Shane crouched in a pool of water, pulling the ice machine away from the wall. The familiar hum is absent, and I assume he's turned off the power. He's removed the plaid shirt and his white T-shirt is already sodden, water dripping from his biceps as he pulls the heavy machine away from the wall.

"Can I help?" I ask. I'm promptly rewarded with a spray of water straight to the face as he finally dislodges the ice maker and the pipe twists my way. I gasp and nearly fall down, blinded. I feel Shane's hand on my ass as he steadies me, though just as quickly he takes it away.

Water drips into my eyes, and I'm grateful I skipped makeup this morning. Mascara tracks would be the perfect addition to my edgy new drowned-rat look.

Shane's got a wrench in hand, but he's just using it to beat a stubborn, rusted valve that refuses to turn.

"Is there anything I can do?" I offer again. "Tell me how to shut off the water. Or maybe you need another tool? Or I could get someone else?"

"Get a towel," Shane mutters, dodging the water. "Hold it over the spray."

That's a great—and very obvious—idea. I have to put a hand on his shoulder as I squeeze past him, my feet sloshing in the water. I make it to the laundry room—also flooded—gather up two towels and return, pressing them to the busted pipe and finally staunching the flow.

"Thanks," Shane says after a moment.

"Do you know what happened?"

"I was going to ask you."

"I don't know. One minute everything was fine, the next I fell down and found this."

"Pipe's old," he says finally. "Probably just gave out. I shut off the water, but the pipes are full. That's why it's still spraying."

"Thank you for coming," I say. "There was no…Everyone else was gone."

"It's my job."

He gives the valve a final (and, in my opinion, unnecessarily hard) bang, and it snaps off and rolls away. He pulls out a pair of pliers and twists the now-exposed metal threads. There's a hiss and a groan and right before our eyes a new hole appears in the pipe and filthy water sprays directly into our faces.

"Fuck!" we cry in unison, belatedly covering our eyes.

"Goddammit!" Shane curses, punching the ice maker.

I use the free towel to wipe gunk off my face and turn so Shane can't see me as I spit. I hear him do the same and feel a faint pull on the towel as he uses it to wipe his own face. I look back and his dark hair is gleaming with water, a piece of unidentifiable black goo is stuck to his forehead, and his white shirt clings transparently to his chest. If this were a porno I'd invite him upstairs to clean *my* pipes, but of course I can't say that. Though I want to. All the frustration of the last three weeks is gathering between my thighs, and I just want some relief. Relief I know those strong hands can provide. If the distance in his eyes is any indication, however, he is not feeling at all pornographic.

I look away and pull my pink polo shirt away from my chest, wringing it out.

"The machine will be out for a couple of days," Shane says. "We'll have to go to town for parts."

"Okay."

"Just make ice in the freezer."

"Got it."

I pull myself up and limp past him to find the mop and bucket.

"What happened to your foot?"

"Nothing."

"Kate."

"I stepped on a rock."

I see him stare at my foot, and I want him to pick it up and inspect my wound and tell me it'll be okay. But he doesn't. He stands up and wrings out his shirt before using the hem to wipe at his face. He succeeds in smearing the black goo over to his temple. I don't laugh, but I want to.

He gestures to the mop. "Got another one?"

It takes an hour to sop up the water. We empty the mop buckets sixteen times. I'm grateful for the water by this point—it hides the copious amount of sweat my body has produced. With the electricity turned off we have no fans to rely on, and the sodden mop is heavy.

Finally we pour the last bucket of filthy water down the drain and wheel the mops and buckets back to their places in the corner.

"God," I groan. "I'm disgusting. I need a shower." I freeze—*disgusting* is not a good word to use around Shane. But when I shoot a tentative glance his way he's simply running the back of his arm over his brow, forehead shiny with sweat.

"It'll have to wait," he says.

"What?"

"Connor knows more about plumbing than I do. I shut off the water, and it's off until he gets back to fix it. It's well water, and he'll have to turn the pumps back on. I don't know how to do it."

"You're kidding."

"Nope."

"What am I supposed to do? Air dry? I can't go in the pool like this, I'm gross."

Shane looks me up and down. "Yep," he agrees.

I scowl. "Thanks."

He sighs. "Come on, then. Put your shoes on." I watch in surprise as he goes into the laundry room and picks up two more towels, but I don't argue. I squish into my wet sneakers before following Shane outside and down the dirt road.

Oh. I quickly realize his brilliant plan. The river that divides the ranch from the road is too shallow and fast-flowing for swimming, but it will rinse this sticky, sweaty, gunky mess off our skin no problem.

It's about four hundred yards to the river, and Shane doesn't speak on the way. He walks too fast for me to keep up, even if I weren't limping, so he gets there before me and has already stripped off his shirt and shoes and has his hands on the button of his cargo pants when I arrive.

He stares at me, then undoes the pants and pushes them to his ankles. He's wearing black boxer briefs that strain against his hips, and again I wonder why I never found men with muscles that sexy before. I mean, this man is pure physical perfection, and if he didn't hate me so much, he'd be ideal. But Shane does hate me, and he turns away and climbs into the river before I'm done looking.

The river is lined with trees, so the only way people would spot us is if they were trying to find us. I hesitate, then decide to keep my shirt on anyway. I shimmy out of my jeans, uttering a thankful prayer that I opted for boy shorts this morning and not a thong.

I step into the water cautiously, feeling the strong current around my knees, and curl my toes around the slippery rocks below. I can't stifle my moan as I sit down, letting the water rush around my shoulders. It's cool and clean and wonderful. My eyes sink closed, and I dip my head back and run my hands over my face, washing away the stress and black goo of the past hours.

When I resurface Shane is watching me. He's about ten feet away, also seated, but this time he doesn't look away when our eyes meet.

"I'm sorry," I say.

He stands up and makes for the bank.

"Don't leave," I say. "Please. I know you're mad, and I'm sorry about what I said. I'm not good at apologizing. Believe it or not, I don't fight with everyone I meet. I'm just…I'm sorry. It's none of my business who you dated…or who you date. I shouldn't have said anything. You're not disgusting or dumb or any of that. You're very nice. You listened to me, and you fixed my shoulder, and I didn't even—"

"I heard you," Shane sighs, sitting back down. He's about five feet away now.

"Wha—"

"When you were beating my door down. I heard you. Stop apologizing."

"How long do you normally stay angry?"

He smiles faintly. "Forever."

"Uh-oh."

"Let me see your foot."

"Pardon?"

"Now." He arches that imperious brow, and while my instinct is to stick out my tongue, instead I stick my injured foot out of the water and wiggle it in his direction. He slides closer and wraps one hand around my ankle, his thumb pressing into my arch, avoiding the sore spot.

"Gahhh," I gasp, half ecstasy, half horror. What he's doing feels fantastic. I'm horrified that I can't quite hide my response.

Again he smiles briefly. "You'll live," he decides, lowering my foot back into the water but not letting go. I feel his thumb pressing along my toes, bending them backward, stretching the muscles, letting them ease back into place. He's got the hands of a masseuse, the body of a lumberjack, and the grudge-holding stamina of a sixteen-year-old girl. Almost perfect.

"Do you forgive me?"

He's not looking at me. "Yeah."

"Are you going to talk to me again?"

His searching fingers are making their way up my calf, pulling me closer, pressing deep into the aching muscles and making me groan inwardly. Pretty soon I'm sitting next to him, our legs stretched out side by side, my feet at his hip, his just past mine. The hair on his legs rubs against my skin.

"Shane," I gasp as he presses something tender behind my knee. My muscles feel like they've turned to lava, hot and liquid. The water is clear enough that I can see his tan skin move over my pale flesh, and he's watching it too — watching as his hand inches its way over my knee and up my leg, spanning my thigh and massaging my quad.

"You like it?" he asks, voice low.

I know he's looking at me, but I can't meet his eyes. "You'll have to do the other one," I joke to ease the tension. "I won't be able to walk back. This leg will be putty."

His fingers clamp down and tug me closer. With the current at my back I float forward easily. His hand disappears between my legs, squeezing my inner thigh, making me bite my lip.

"I can't be your boyfriend," he says.

I stiffen in surprise. Hell, surprise doesn't begin to cover it. I'm startled, confused, desperately curious. I've certainly never had any-one tell me he couldn't be my boyfriend when I hadn't — and would never have—asked. But strangely enough, the statement doesn't offend me. I get it. And even though I'm pretty sure I know what he's going to say, I want to hear him say the words. I *have* to hear them. I need to know I haven't been alone in this...thing we've got between us, whatever it may be. I need to know Shane feels it, too, boyfriend material or not.

His thumb strokes the crease at the top of my thigh, demanding—and getting—my attention. "And people can't know."

"Know what?"

"About what's going to happen."

My eyes fly up to meet his.

"I want you, Kate, so damn bad."

I swallow thickly, and my eyes drift back down. I can't seem to stop watching his hand.

"Just once," he says quietly. "We'll get it out of our systems and things can go back to normal."

"There's nothing normal about this."

Shane smiles faintly. "I don't make promises I can't keep." His fingers wiggle higher now, pressing against the flimsy, wet gusset of my panties, tracing the seam against my pussy.

"Ah..." I try and fail to form a word.

"But I promise to make you come," he whispers. "And come and come and come. Until you can't take any more."

"Shane..."

"And then I'll make you come again."

Oh God.

"And when you can't walk tomorrow, it won't be because of your leg."

I'm dying. I feel like I'm disintegrating, and pieces of me are washing away in the river.

When I speak, my voice is hoarse. "That's a lot of promises."

"What do you say?"

I'm not crazy.

Or perhaps I am.

But I know what I want.

Chapter Ten

We get out of the water and walk wordlessly down the trail, towels wrapped around our waists. This time Shane waits for me. I try to walk naturally, but we're at a near-run. My foot doesn't hurt anymore. The only thing I can think about is the burning ache between my legs and the fact that my heart is pounding so hard I might pass out. *This is happening*, I tell myself. *It's happening, so don't overthink it.*

We reach the trailer, and Shane digs through the pockets of the cargo pants slung over his arm until he finds the key. He pushes open the door and waits for me to pass through. Maybe later I'll tell myself I should have thought long and hard about what I was going to do, that I should have counted to ten and waited until I regained my sanity before stepping over the threshold, evaluated the pros and cons like a thoughtful, rational adult. But I do no such thing. Shane's eyes are on mine as I step out of my wet sneakers, drop my damp clothes in a ball on the porch, and walk inside. He follows right behind me, and even through my wet shirt I can feel the heat radiating off his bare chest. The man is a furnace.

Every warning about playing with fire zings through my mind, but I dismiss them. I want this. I'm not playing games, and neither is Shane as he grips my shoulders and turns us so my back is to the door and he's pressed up against me. He lowers his head so our eyes are inches apart and looks at me more closely and thoughtfully than anyone ever has. He's checking to make sure I'm okay, that my expectations are in line with what today is about. And they are. *Just once*, we agreed. And that will be enough. It's like what I tell myself before polishing off a family-size bag of potato chips: *I shouldn't do this, but if I eat them all now, it'll take care of the craving and I won't want any more later.*

"Kate," he says quietly, then grips my chin in his hand, tilts my face to his, and kisses me. It may sound melodramatic, but just for a second, the world stops. I can't decide if it's more impossible to believe we've only known each other three weeks or that I've lasted three weeks without the delicious pressure of his lips on mine. For such a hard, rough man, his lips are impossibly soft. They're warm and sure, and his calloused fingers stroke my jaw before tugging enough that my lips open and he pushes his tongue into my mouth.

Okay, now the world definitely stops. I am not a moaner and a groaner, but *damn* if I can keep this one inside. This puts everything I thought I knew to shame. His mouth, his tongue, his fingers on my face — this is all I can think about. All I can feel. I'm consumed by him, and we're just getting started.

Shane seems to feel it too, whatever this is — this desperate rush of lust that changes my definition of *now and forever*. I want him right now, but I want this to last forever too. I wrap my arms around his neck and pull him impossibly closer, molding our wet bodies together. He pushes a knee between mine, and he's so tall that his big thigh immediately presses into my pussy. I wantonly spread my legs so he can grind against my swollen clit, and he obliges with rough nudges.

I moan and twist my head away, eyes squeezed tight as too many feelings flood through me. I thought the dream was good, I thought the dream was hot — the dream was a dish of soft serve. This is the whole fucking sundae.

"Kate," he says again, something hard in his voice. His fingers turn my face back to his, and he ravages my mouth like he'll die if he doesn't. It's the first break in his no-nonsense façade, a tiny glimpse inside the man who comes across as serious and domineering, but who, I'm discovering, is just someone who knows what he wants and takes it. With a man I wanted less I might feel alarm or concern, but with him I'm simply willing. Sex with Shane isn't a game or a story to tell my friends, it's a need. A basic, elemental craving that won't go away with time or denial.

I lower one hand between us, finding his straining erection against my stomach, and stroke him with my fingers. He hisses and pulls back, his hands going to the hem of my wet shirt and pulling it over my head. He undoes my bra like a pro, tossing it over his shoulder, and flashes me a quick, dirty smile as he drops to his knees and pulls my wet panties down to my ankles. I step out and he tosses them aside. I wait for him to stand and lose the boxer briefs, but instead he stays on his knees, studying me. He's looking so intently that I start to squirm. I nearly combust when he leans forward and presses his mouth between my thighs, lips parting, tongue darting out to lick my folds, one hot, long swipe after another.

"Shane." The word comes out garbled. I twist my fingers in his hair and try to pull him away. It's too much, and I definitely want this to last longer—the *now* can wait. At least a little bit, anyway. The sight of his eyes lifting up to mine while his mouth continues its assault nearly makes me come. A hot rush of desire floods my sex, and I can see him smiling, eyes crinkling at the corners.

"Shane," I repeat, tugging on his hair with one hand, pushing at his shoulder with the other. "I don't—I'm going to come. It's too soon. Not yet."

If anything, he picks up the pace. My legs are splayed awkwardly, his shoulders pinning my thighs in place against the door, feet turned out. I'm flailing weakly as my stomach clenches and something over-powering takes over. He uses one hand to sling my leg over his shoulder, opening me even more, then snares my wrists in his fingers and holds my hands away from his head. He's not going to stop. I give in. I can't stop either, at this point.

"Sha—" I start to warn him, but he exposes my clit with his teeth and fastens his lips around it, sucking hard. I explode. I cry out and curl forward. He frees my wrists and I catch myself on his shoulders, muscles seizing and releasing, juices gushing. I have no words. Bent over like this I can hear the gentle sucking sounds as he eats me, his tongue plunging deep inside then flicking again and again over my clit.

I struggle to catch my breath as the last spasms ebb away. I have climaxed before. I have even had great oral sex. I have known wonderful lovers, men who enjoyed giving pleasure as much as they enjoyed receiving it. But I have never felt like someone wouldn't—couldn't—stop tasting me, and it's intense and overwhelming. I cry out when he latches onto my clit again—I'm too sensitive. The ache that's been gnawing at me for weeks has somehow only intensified.

I straighten and push his face away, and this time he lets me. He looks up from the floor, keeping his eyes on mine as he wipes a hand across his mouth. He's so fucking hot it's ridiculous, and when he stands up and pushes the boxer briefs down his legs I inhale audibly. He's enormous. Of course he is. Everything about him is too much for me. I'm so wet I can feel the moisture cooling on the inside of my thighs, but thanks to that orgasm I'm also tight and swollen—there's no way this will work. But there's also no way I'm leaving this trailer without having felt that thing inside me.

I start to drop to my knees to return the favor, but Shane stops me with a hand under my arm. "No," he says. "I'll never last."

He pins me to the door and lowers his face to my breasts, focusing that talented mouth on my nipples, one then the other until they're hard and aching. I've never really cared for having my nipples sucked. Some of the guys I've slept with have been into it, so I've tolerated it, but it doesn't do much for me. I love watching Shane's head bowed so reverently, though, feeling those big hands holding me so gently, feeling the same tongue that just did unspeakable things below, now laving so sweetly. He pulls back and blows lightly, the cool air making my nipples tighten even further.

"You're so beautiful," he mutters into my skin, and something inside me breaks. A tiny piece of the wall comes down, even if it's just for a little while. I'm used to men who are cultured and experienced, men who have been with women far more beautiful than me. I accepted their compliments the way I was taught: with a smile and a thank you, and usually one in return. But right now I can't think of anything to say. I believe Shane. Even covered in river water and dust, I believe him.

He straightens suddenly and gathers both my hands in one of his, raising them above my head so my spine is arched and my breasts press into his chest. He looks into my eyes as his other hand reaches between my thighs, cupping my pussy in his palm, like he's holding my whole world in his hand. Slowly his fingers press higher, three squeezing into me. I'm stretched so taut that I can't move away, can't look away. I can only bite my lip and close my eyes while I acquiesce.

"Open your eyes," Shane says.

I do.

"Look at me."

His dark eyes are fathomless, unreadable, as always. If not for the tick in his jaw, the telltale movement of his throat as he swallows, the searing heat of the tip of his erection on my stomach, I wouldn't know he wants this as much as I do.

When his fingers can't get any deeper he pulls them out and slowly pushes them back in. I groan. He does it again. And again. A slow finger fuck that's eventually joined by his thumb on my clit, circling the swollen bud with merciless precision.

"Shane, please," I gasp after several long minutes of sweet torture.

He chuckles and leans in to bite my neck, hard enough to make me tighten around his thick fingers. "Please what?" he asks.

"Fuck me," I whisper into his hair.

He pulls back and kisses me. Hard and thoroughly, tasting every inch of my mouth. I suck on his tongue and try to pull more of him into me. I want him inside, every huge, hot inch, but his fingers aren't slowing and neither is his mouth.

"Come again," he orders. His voice may be soft, but the note of command is there. The same tone that would outrage me any other time but now only makes me wetter. Being ordered to come is hardly something to complain about, but even if I wanted to argue, I couldn't, because I can feel my internal muscles clasping his thrusting fingers, pulling him deeper, higher, until there's nowhere left to go and I come again. My legs fail me, and it's just Shane's hand inside me and his grip under my arm that hold me up as I let the pleasure have its way.

When the contractions have ceased, I open my eyes to find him watching me. "What are you doing to me?" I whisper.

He smiles and leans in to kiss me, his tongue tracing my lips. "Anything and everything."

Again I reach for his straining cock and again he takes away my hand. If I couldn't see it for myself, I'd think he was hiding something. "I'm going to come the second you touch me," he murmurs against my mouth. "It's too soon."

"I was thinking about the 'just once' thing," I begin, interrupted by his searching tongue.

"Oh yeah?"

"I think *just one* might be more appropriate," I get out on a groan. "Like, just one afternoon."

He chuckles. "Okay."

"So you don't have to worry if you come right away," I continue. "You can come again after. And again after that. And again…"

I wriggle my hand from his grasp and wrap it around his cock. He's smooth and hot against my palm. Shane hisses out a breath and buries his face in my neck, lips and teeth seeking and finding a tendon, biting down lightly. It's my turn to hiss and tighten my grip, twisting my wrist and jerking my hand up and down roughly.

"Shit, Kate, that's it," he grunts, thrusting into my palm. "Like that."

"Back up," I whisper, still pinned to the door. "I want to suck your cock."

He stills. "You sure?"

"Of course I am."

He leans back slightly. I don't know why he's hesitating. Blow jobs aren't my favorite thing, but I've never had a guy turn one down. Plus I really do want to suck Shane's cock. He's controlled both of my orgasms so far. It seems only fair.

"I'm close," he warns. "I don't want to hurt you."

I sink to my knees before him, his massive erection bobbing in front of my face. A dot of pre-come rests on the end, and I lick it off. He braces his hands on the door, and I look up to find him watching me. I stick out my tongue and trace the length of him, root to tip and back. The muscles in his neck are bulging with the effort not to pound into my mouth. I wrap a hand around the base of his cock to control the depth, then open my lips and take him in.

"Ah, shit…" he groans, punching the door with one hand. "Kate…"

"Mm-hmm?" I ask, mouth wrapped around his cock. I feel his body shake, like the vibrations are traveling up his spine.

"Suck it harder," he orders, fighting for control.

The thought that I could have this big, stoic man at my mercy makes my pussy spasm, and I suck him in deeper, harder, twisting my hand, feeling him bump against the back of my throat. I control the pace for a while, then one of his hands finds its way into my damp hair and curls into a fist at the nape of my neck. Soon he's setting the pace, thrusting his cock into my mouth, holding my head still to receive him.

I open my mouth wide and slowly look up. The second our eyes meet, his snap shut, and he starts to come. I grip his ass and hold him inside me when he tries to pull away. I suck until he groans desperately, my tongue working the underside of his shaft. When the last drops are spent I let him go, and he flops back against the door then sinks down to the floor beside me.

"Fuuuuuck." He runs a hand over his face. I see beads of sweat on his brow and smile to myself as they trickle down his temple. Our eyes meet, and he shakes his head ruefully. "You shouldn't have done that," he says, eyes dark.

I'm too limp to be alarmed. "Why not?"

He leans over to kiss me, pressing his lips to mine for a long, quiet moment. "Because now," he says finally, "when I fuck you, it's going to last forever."

"Promises," I say dismissively.

"Get on the bed."

My eyebrows lift in surprise. "Are you—"

"Now."

"Shane—"

"I'm a very patient and understanding man outside the bedroom—" he begins, straight-faced.

"That is not true."

He ignores me. "But in the bedroom, I'm the boss."

"Who's boss in the living room?"

He smirks. "I am."

"The dining room?"

"Me."

"The kitchen?"

"Me again."

"You're the boss of everything?"

He leans over and slides his hand back between my legs, slipping his rough fingers through my swollen folds. "Yes, Kate," he says. "I'm the boss of everything."

As far as I'm concerned, Shane will never be the "boss of everything," but at the moment I'm willing to let him have his silly little illusion. Seconds later I fall back onto the bed, and Shane lowers himself on top of me. The blankets feel as soft as they did the first night, but there's little time to think about that when I finally feel the weight of his magnificent body on mine. He's hot and hard everywhere, his chest crushing my breasts, his thigh between mine.

He braces one arm beside my head and lowers his face to kiss me. There's something so sweet about this bossy man closing his eyes as he kisses, something gentle and hard all at once. His other hand finds my nipple and pinches it between his fingers, easy at first, then tighter, then tightly enough that I arch my back and cry out, trying to pull away.

"I'm the boss, Kate," he reminds me, silencing me with his tongue.

I twist my head away. "I'm not into kinky shit," I warn him. "No pain."

"No pain," he agrees, releasing my breast and using that hand to turn my face back to his. "But don't say no unless you mean it."

"I mean it."

He kisses me. "I hear you."

I keep my eyes open as his tongue finds mine, and he does the same. He holds out longer than I do. We're too close, the intimacy too heightened, and finally I close my eyes. He returns his hand to my breast, stroking the sensitive flesh, eventually circling back to my nipple, pinching it between his fingers.

I inhale sharply, but he merely switches hands, using one to hold himself above me while the other works over my left breast. Again he twists my nipple in his fingers, tighter and tighter, until I'm clenching my knees around his massive thigh, trying not to say no if it's not what I really mean.

"Shane."

"Kate."

"I don't—"

He sits back on his knees and there's the fleeting worry that he's mad, but he merely rearranges our legs so he's between my splayed thighs, staring down at my shiny pink sex. He looks back up at me and licks his finger and thumb, then reaches between my legs and unerringly finds my still-sensitive clit. He pinches it lightly, then harder, mimicking the previous treatment of my nipples.

My hips squirm as the grip tightens and soon I'm all out writhing, especially when his second hand joins the first and one finger rubs my still-tormented clit. "Shane!" I shout finally, jerking my hips away.

"Give me everything, Kate."

"What do you want?" I cry, covering myself with my hands.

"I want you to trust me."

"I do."

"Put your hands on the pillow."

"Please don't ask me—"

"I won't do anything you don't like."

"I don't—"

That damned eyebrow cuts me off. "Are you sure?"

I close my eyes and try to calm down. Am I sure? I'm not a child, of course I'm sure. I'm a thirty-year-old woman who knows…Who is certain…

My hands drift to my breasts, my fingers finding my throbbing nipples. I bite my lip when my fingertips flutter over them. Heat shoots directly from my breasts to my clit, making it swell. What the hell is happening? I have never been aroused by someone touching my nipples, but now…I test the theory again, flicking the tender tips of my breasts, and again a corresponding well of lust opens at my core. What the hell has this man done to me?

"Kate," Shane interrupts dryly. "You're killing me."

I open my eyes to find him crouched between my legs, condom-clad erection pointed in my direction.

"I want you to fuck me," I say, putting my hands on the pillow.

"I will," he promises, gripping behind my knees and pushing them up and out, making me gasp. I can feel my pussy spreading, displaying all the tender pink pieces inside. I'm more vulnerable and exposed than I would ever care to be, but all I can really think about is the fiery need that threatens to consume me.

I close my eyes and expect to feel Shane's cock at my entrance, but instead I feel his teeth on my inner thigh, then his tongue pushing inside my swollen folds.

"Shit!" I hiss. My hips jerk up reflexively, but he's ready, big hands holding me open, keeping me in place for his questing tongue. He licks all around, teeth tugging gently, until finally his lips circle my clit and he begins a pulsing, rhythmic suction.

"I want you inside," I groan, feeling his damp hair slip through my fingers.

"Hands on the pillow," he orders.

"Why?"

A muffled laugh. "Because I said so."

I grunt my dissatisfaction with his answer but return my hand to the pillow. All of my energy is concentrated between my legs, on the tiny bundle of nerves this divine, brutal man knows just how to torture. My hips move of their own volition, thrusting into Shane's face, his teasing tongue, but he's pressing me into the mattress so firmly that it's just my stomach muscles moving, quivering desperately as something deep, deep inside starts to tremble.

"There it is," he whispers, pushing two fingers back into me, curling them up toward the ceiling, finding just the spot.

I cry out, giving in, giving everything, as Shane sucks and strokes me all the way to hell and back, freeing me enough to let me arch up when I explode. His mouth and fingers follow as I try to squirm away, extending the pleasure, the agony, until I beg him to stop, swearing I can't take any more.

"No more?" he asks, rising above me, using one hand to guide his cock to my still-clenching entrance. "Not even one?"

"Not even—ohhhhh." I groan as he pushes inside. Shane's not waiting for permission. He already knows he has it. Tender flesh parts, and I moan and stir to accommodate him. I've never felt something like this—never been with someone so big. So strong. So determined. So in control. I remember watching his face contort as I sucked his cock, and I appreciate now what it must have meant for him to let go that way, however briefly, knowing the power he keeps on such a thin leash.

"All the way," he whispers against my neck. His elbows rest on the mattress on either side of my shoulders, and my hands are still on the pillow, if only because I'm too weak to put them anywhere else. My thighs are spread to accept him, and I feel him everywhere, in every piece of me, deeper than anyone has ever been when he finally seats himself to the hilt.

"Oh God," I breathe, feeling my pussy squeeze him, testing out the invader.

"You're so perfect," he mumbles into my throat, sucking the soft skin in between his teeth until I tug away.

"You're so big," I reply.

I'm rewarded with a laugh I can feel rumbling through his chest, and I can't help but smile. Shane lifts his head and threads his fingers through mine, holding my hands to the bed as he begins to move—slow, dragging thrusts that rasp against too-tender tissues.

I recall his promise/threat to last forever, and my heart pounds. *Now and forever*, I think. I'm ready for the now. When he's pushed deep inside, I force my sore muscles to clench down on his cock, and Shane arches his back, face tightening in pain and pleasure.

"Kate," he warns.

"*Shane*," I return.

"I'm going to fuck you now."

"It's about time."

And he does. He rears those broad hips back and slams into me, again and again and again. I slide up the bed and he releases one hand so I can brace myself against the wall. I give him everything, thighs wide, meeting and accepting each brutal thrust. Sweat gathers on his brow, and his mouth mashes against mine, teeth clashing, tongues mating, until finally—*finally*—the pressure that's been building for weeks finds the outlet it's been looking for. Everything in me converges in that one place, clamping down tightly and refusing to release until Shane lets go too, until he goes rigid above me, eyes locked on mine, and we both give in. I moan into his mouth as I come, and he swallows my cry and answers with a strangled sound of his own, hips pulsing against mine, dragging every last ounce of pleasure from our exhausted bodies.

When there's nothing left, he collapses on top of me. I stroke his back, fingers tangling in the ends of his dark hair, needing to both give and receive assurance that what just happened was very much real, very much shared.

Eventually he pulls out, disposes of the condom, and drops back onto the mattress beside me. I'm grateful for his return, for the feel of him next to me. I'm startled when he laces his fingers through mine, but say nothing. We lie naked on the bed and watch the dust motes float in the muted afternoon sunlight as we wait for our pounding hearts to slow.

I don't know how long we lie there, but I'm not anxious to move. I haven't done anything this rigorous in a long time, and my body is going to punish me for it. *Thank God it was a one-time thing*, I tell myself. I might not survive a second round.

"It's four thirty," Shane says finally.

If I had the strength I'd sit up in shock, but instead I just lay there, surprise on my face. "Seriously?"

"Seriously."

"Oh no." I have to get up. *Move, legs. Move.*

"If you hadn't made all the staff quit, you could take the night off and stay put."

I laugh. "Shut up."

He squeezes my fingers but doesn't speak.

"I need to take a shower," I say finally. "Fine day for the pipes to burst."

There's a pause.

"You can take a shower."

"In the river? I don't think so."

"The water's back on."

I turn to look at him but Shane's eyes are closed. Deliberately.

"How do you know?"

Another pause.

"I turned it on."

"When?"

"Earlier."

"Earlier than when you had told me you couldn't turn it back on?"

"Yes."

"You lied?"

"Yes."

"To get me to go to the river?"

"Yes."

"But you hated me!"

"I don't hate you."

"I said past tense."

"I didn't hate you."

"You didn't speak to me for two weeks!"

"What should I have said?"

"Oh, I don't know…*Kate, I'm not mad at you?*"

"Kate, I'm not mad at you."

"Knock it off. Why did you lie about the water?"

"You know why. To get you to come to the river. If I'd said, 'Why don't you hop in my shower?' would you have done it?"

I hesitate. "I don't know. Maybe."

"Well. Now we'll never know."

I look at the clock. It's four forty, as he said.

"I have to go." I peel myself up and crawl over Shane, then hurry into the living room to find my damp shirt. I pull it on and peek out the window to see if the coast is clear to collect my wet things from the porch.

"You pissed?" Shane asks, standing naked in the bedroom doorway.

"You asked me that before," I say. "After the bat incident."

"And?"

"I said I wasn't."

"Were you?"

"Yes."

"And now?"

"No."

"You sure?"

I roll my eyes. "Shane," I tell him. "This is the one and only time I will ever be glad you lied to me."

I risk another peek out the window. All clear. I put my hand on the knob but stop when Shane strides toward me, his naked body pure, rippling perfection. He gathers my face in his hands and kisses me. Slowly. Thoroughly. I feel the tip of his cock nudge between my legs and force myself to pull away.

"I really have to go," I say.

"I know."

I open the door and bend down to collect my wet belongings. I feel Shane's gaze on my bare ass and wrap the towel around my waist, sneakers and jeans clutched in one hand.

"Well," I say, straightening.

"Well."

"See you."

He nods. A muscle twitches in his jaw, and I think he's going to say something, but he doesn't. Finally I turn and hurry away, back to the bunkhouse, back to reality.

Chapter Eleven

Despite being short-staffed, we're now handling dinner service like seasoned pros and make it through the meal that evening with just two broken plates. Lisa and Hailey came back from town with magazines and chocolate—the things we've been missing most—promising to share with me, and Pete has returned from his outing with the ranch hands. Connor comes in to pick up the ranch hands' dinner, and offers a polite "Thanks" as he goes. I don't see Shane, but then again, I rarely do at this hour.

Once the dining room is swept and ready for the dance, Hailey and I head upstairs to change. She snags a dress from her closet and follows me to my room so we can get ready together. I root around in the pile of clothes at the foot of the bed for something to wear. With the day almost over, I can no longer stifle my yawn.

"No nap today?" she asks.

I freeze. "I—No. The burst pipe kept me busy."

Hailey yawns too. "Dammit. You're contagious."

"Sorry."

She groans. "I really don't want to go to this dance tonight."

"I hear you. I'm aching all over." Let her think it's from the endless mopping and my lack of overall fitness.

"Brandon came in to change a light bulb in cabin fourteen today and turned around and ran back out when he saw me."

"He did not."

"He did. Like a frightened deer. What does he think I'm going to do, shoot him and strap him to the roof of my car?"

"Would you?"

"I'm very tempted."

Hailey continues to rant about Brandon's ridiculousness, and I keep yawning while we change. "Are you going to make it?" she asks when a particularly strenuous yawn sends me reeling backward.

I drop onto the bed. "I don't know."

"Why don't you stay up here and get some rest?" she suggests. "You're working too hard. No need to force sleepy small talk with a bunch of old men."

"They'll know," I mumble into my hand.

"Who will know?"

"Everyone." I'm already slumping back onto my soft pillow, the mattress molding to my achy spine.

"Shh," Hailey whispers, tugging the sheet over my legs. "I'll check on you later."

"Are you going to dance…"

"Hmm?" she asks.

But I'm out.

"Kate!"

My eyes open, and I look around, confused. The room is dark and cool, and I can hear the faint rattle of the ceiling fan as it spins overhead.

"Is she awake?"

"I can't tell."

"Don't turn on the light. Kate!"

Hailey and Lisa are the loudest whisperers ever. "I'm up," I mumble, looking at the clock. 11:15.

"Can we come in?"

"Aren't you in already?"

"Um…yes."

One of them switches on the light, and I blink until they come into focus. They're standing there in bikinis and towels, hair piled on top of their heads in sloppy buns.

"What's happening?" I ask, still groggy.

"Come hot tubbing with us!" Lisa urges. "It will help you relax."

I look at my comfortable, beautiful bed. "I *was* relaxed."

"Even more," she insists.

I look at Hailey. "Please?" she tries. "The pool area is empty. We checked. The guests are in bed, the boys are at the bar…"

"You can have first dibs on *Cosmo*," Lisa promises.

"Dammit. Okay." I swing my legs to the floor.

They wait in the hall while I change, and a minute later I join them, similarly attired in bikini and towel. We creep quietly down the steps and around back to the pool, where we slide open the door to the hot tub shack and step inside. The room is dark and damp, and Hailey switches on the light to its lowest setting, just enough to prevent us from accidentally falling in.

I turn on the jets and we drop our towels, alternately moaning and squealing as we slowly immerse ourselves in the steaming water. This was a good idea, I realize immediately. Oh God, do I need this.

The pounding jets knead my aching joints from top to bottom. My head lolls back, and I may even drool a little.

"Heaven," Hailey announces. "It exists."

"How come we haven't done this before?" Lisa asks.

I'm too weak to reply, so Hailey answers. "Because we're always at the bar. And you're always with Pete."

"Where is Pete?" I pipe up.

"Sleeping," Lisa sighs. "Mending fences is exhausting work."

Hailey sings the opening bars of "Desperado" for the ninety-first time. "Are you two in love?" she asks when finished.

I open my eyes to see Lisa's bony shoulders rise and fall in a shrug. "I don't know," she answers. "I mean, I really, really like him, but…I don't know if we're in love. I've never been before. Have you?"

I stay silent. My longest relationship was with a handsome hotelier I met on my frequent travels. We dated for two years, but I never told him I loved him. I certainly liked the man, found him attractive, and enjoyed his company when we had occasion to be together, but love has never been in the cards for me.

I take a deep breath. The heat is getting to me. The longer I stay out here trying to be older and wiser Kate, the more I realize that the only thing I am is older. I have no more answers than I did a year ago. I'm more responsible, drink less, and keep better hours, but I'm no smarter than I was. I'm just more aware of the fact.

I tune back in to hear Hailey talking about her first love, a high school boyfriend she dated through college. "Then we graduate," she's saying, "and we're in the freaking robes and everything, diplomas in hand, grinning like idiots, ready to face the future—as if—and he turns to me and says, 'I've had enough, haven't you?'"

Lisa's listening, riveted, as Hailey continues.

"So I'm like, 'Had enough what?' and he gestures between us and says, 'This.' Meaning *us!*"

"*What?*" Lisa gasps.

"That's right," Hailey affirms. "He broke up with me minutes after we graduated. Our lives are supposed to begin, and *we're* ending. I was shocked. We'd been together nearly six years, and all of a sudden he's 'had enough.' I didn't know what to say, so I just nodded like he was making perfect sense, and then he shook my hand—"

"*He shook your hand?!*"

"And wished me the best of luck."

I cover my mouth and stare at my friend. With the exception of naptimes, we talk almost all day, every day. How could I have not heard this story?

"So I took my degree, got a job teaching second grade at a fancy prep school, and two years later realized I hated teaching and hated kids and had to escape. So here I am."

"Hailey," I say. "I had no idea."

She shrugs and leans her head back, closing her eyes. "Why would you?"

"What about you?" Lisa asks me. "Have you been in love?"

"I guess so," I lie, squirming at the thought of admitting I have no idea what love would even look like.

"What was his name?"

"Andre," I say, thinking of the hotelier. He was seven years older than me, richer than God, exotic and handsome with the faintest trace of an accent that made everything he said sound seductive. Everywhere we went he knew somebody more glamorous and fabulous than the last, and I always felt like they were all staring at me, wondering what I had that he wanted. And maybe I wondered too.

I change the subject before lovesick Lisa can ask me to elaborate. "So what happened at the dance?" I ask. "Why aren't you guys out with everybody else?"

"Ugh," Hailey groans. "I've had enough of everybody else."

At the same time, Lisa says, "Because Pete's still here."

"Lisa," Hailey intones, and I get the impression she's been saying this all day, "you can do things without Pete. It won't kill you."

"I know, but I don't *want* to do things without him."

Hailey shoots me a look that says *Danger! Danger!* but I just smile and shake my head. Lisa's eighteen. Let her get her codependence out of her system with a summer fling. Hopefully she'll see more clearly in the fall. Maybe we all will.

I feel a twinge in my chest at the thought of autumn. Summer will be over, and I'll return to Boston and my "normal" life, ready to pack my bags and travel again.

But back to the dance. "Why have you had enough?" I press. "What happened?"

"Nothing happened," Hailey answers with a sigh. "It was just... ugh."

"Yep," Lisa agrees. "*Ugh.* Shane didn't come, so all the women were hanging on Brandon, and he spent the whole night dancing with them and not paying attention to Hailey."

"Lisa!"

"What?"

"I don't want him to pay attention to me!"

"You don't? What about all the stuff you said in the car?"

"I said I *had* wanted him to pay attention to me — past tense — but now I don't! I don't care anymore."

"Oh. My mistake."

This time it's Lisa who shoots me the *Danger! Danger!* look, and I smother a smile.

"Where was Shane?" I ask uber-casually.

"I don't know," Lisa says. "I saw him walking toward his trailer at one point, but he wasn't dressed up, and he never came in. He looked tired."

"Huh," Hailey says. "He didn't go out mending fences, there was hardly anybody left on the ranch for the afternoon, and the two people who were here are now uncommonly tired…"

I feel around for her leg under the water and kick it, but Hailey only laughs.

"What?" Lisa asks. "What am I missing?"

"Nothing," I say before Hailey can embarrass me. "Shane helped me with the flood cleanup. He's probably just sick of being in the dining room."

Hailey is the only one who knows about my attraction to Shane, and while I'd like to think of myself as an open and forthcoming person, I already know I'm not going to tell her about today's inter-lude. And not just because Shane and I agreed to keep our one-time thing a secret, but because I want it to be private. Because I've never had sex like that, and I don't know how I feel about it. I mean, I feel good — sore all over, in a great way — but it's vaguely disappointing to know that the man responsible for these pleasurable aches and pains has made it clear he doesn't want to do it again.

The next morning I wake up like a tug boat slowly emerging from a wall of fog: slow, cautious, and determined. I'm on the "late" shift today, which means I start at seven, and it is now six thirty. Counting my three-hour nap last night, I have had nearly nine hours of sleep, and I feel better. Rested.

I climb out of bed, splash water on my face, and brush my teeth before dressing and going downstairs. Outside, the actual wall of fog is cold and invigorating, and if I didn't know better, I'd swear there was a little pep in my step. I needed yesterday: the sex, the nap, the hot tub. Things here have been go-go-go since my arrival: the long trip over, the fights with Janie, the next-to-no days off to compensate for the staff shortage, the tension with Shane. Yesterday was an outlet for all of the frustrated feelings I'd been bottling up for weeks. My well-used muscles hurt pleasantly, but not unbearably, and I feel lighter.

"Good morning!" I call to Hailey as she wipes down the wranglers' breakfast tables.

"Hey," she says. "What's got you so cheery?"

Lisa stumbles in. "Who's cheery?"

"Kate."

"What the hell for?"

"We've been working too hard," I announce.

Lisa and Hailey roll their eyes. "No kidding."

"Well, that's about to change. We're going to get another employee. Not that Pete's not great," I add before Lisa can defend his honor. "The next person who applies is hired, even if they're a barrister from Spain via Nigeria who wants to make me a millionaire."

"Jesus," Hailey says. "Maybe I'll take another nap if I'm going to wake up like you."

Lisa is restocking the buffet.

"Where'd all the food go?" I ask. Since our staff losses we've had to compensate with more buffets to make sure we don't get overrun in the dining room. At breakfast people have the option of ordering off our small menu, and the wranglers usually leave the buffet alone, knowing we'll have to restock it.

"Shane ate it all," Lisa answers. "That man was hungry."

"No idea why," Hailey mutters. "He didn't have to go to the dance last night."

"Pete said the guys were talking while they were out fixing the fences —"

Hailey prepares to sing.

"Don't!" Lisa interrupts. "I said *fix* so you wouldn't sing."

Hailey shrugs, and I wait impatiently for Lisa to finish her story.

"Anyway," she continues, "they said Shane used to be really laid-back and quiet, but this summer he's been different. Meaner. Biting their heads off for every little thing."

Hailey and I exchange a look. She knows about our fight, but not the making up. "Well, some guys are just jerks," she says.

"Yeah," I agree half-heartedly.

The first guests arrive, and we get back to work. Pete's on dish duty, so the girls work the dining room, and I'm in the kitchen helping Mark with prep work, since he had to do extra to restock the buffet.

"How are things?" Mark asks, cracking eggs onto the griddle.

"Good," I say, somewhat surprised. "You?"

Our burgeoning friendship quickly became awkward after he brought Cassidy to the dance. Things have been cordial, but we've exchanged no more than pleasantries for the past two weeks.

"Pretty good," he answers. "Alec's taking the next two nights off, so I'll be running things in here. Finally."

"Nice. I know you've wanted a chance to be in charge."

Mark smiles. "I'm looking forward to it."

His stare lingers a little too long, and I look back at the strawberries I'm slicing. "Well," I say. "Good luck."

Breakfast is drama-free — though I nearly slice off a finger when I see Shane pass by — and after cleanup, everyone goes out to start the cabins. I'm about to enter cabin four when a silver SUV rolls down the road and parks next to the lodge. I'm too far away to discern faces, but two men in suits climb out and look around. I'm debating whether or not I should go over to meet them — Are they late arrivals? Early? — but I stop when Hank and Mary enter the picture, shaking hands. They seem friendly but formal, and I have no idea what's going on.

I tell myself to mind my own business and enter the cabin, sighing when I see that someone has tracked mud across the carpet. I drop my basket on a chair and get to work.

Twenty-five minutes later, the carpet is wet but clean, and my right arm is sore from scrubbing — not to mention that crawling around on my hands and knees created extra friction between my legs, reminding me that my out-of-use muscles need some serious recovery time. Or more practice.

"Kate?" calls a voice from outside.

I climb to my feet and pull open the door. "Mary?"

"Oh, good, there you are," she says. She's alone, no suited men in sight. "There's someone here to see you. I left him in the office."

"Him?"

She shrugs. "He asked for you specifically."

"Okay," I say. "I'll be right over." I'm about to ask her who the visitors were, but she's already hustling back to the lodge.

I pick up my basket and drop it in the laundry room, washing my hands and smoothing my hair before walking to the office to meet my mystery guest.

"In there," Gina says, jerking a thumb over her shoulder and shooting me a look that says my visitor has not made a good first impression.

I enter the small back office and find a boy—well, a man, technically—sitting on the far side of the desk. My side, to be precise. He's tall and lean, with long limbs and shoulder-length blond hair tied back in a ponytail. He's got a goatee, piercings in both ears, his fingers are covered in at least six rings, and he wears a bright yellow button-up shirt with faded jeans and skateboard shoes. I've never seen him before in my life.

"Hello," I say, stopping in the doorway.

"Hey," he says, standing. He towers over me and could be intimidating if not for his surprisingly genuine smile. "You're Kate?"

He extends a hand that I shake, somewhat comforted by the fact that Gina is right outside and knows how to use a gun. Who the hell is this guy? And what is he doing at my desk? Well, I suppose it's not my desk, but it's definitely not *his* desk.

"Yes. You are?"

"Matthew Bacon. Your new employee."

Chapter Twelve

" I beg your pardon?"

He pulls a folded up piece of paper out of his pocket and smooths it to show me the job posting he must have printed out from one of the countless websites I submitted it to.

"I'm here to be a kitchen/cabin girl."

Huh. I may have made the posting a little gender-specific. But while I'm completely in favor of erasing the lines between gender roles, in all my years here I have never seen — or even heard of — a kitchen/cabin *boy*. Well, except for Pete, who doesn't count because people still refer to him as the handyman. "You're applying for a job?"

"Yes, ma'am."

"Then get out of my seat."

Matthew blinks in surprise, then quickly recovers, scooting around the desk and politely gesturing for me to sit. I shoot him a look that says I'm not fooled by his faux chivalry, and he laughs, dropping into the chair.

"Why do you want to work at Ponderosa Pines?"

"Why not? I think it'd be fun."

"What are you doing in the mountains?"

"Traveling. Taking in the sights."

"For how long?"

He taps the job posting. "Until the end of the summer."

I lean forward on the desk. "We start early, Matthew."

"Call me Matt."

"We clean dishes."

"Yep."

"Bathrooms."

"Got it."

"We make beds."

"No problem."

"Where's your stuff?"

He points to a backpack sitting on the floor behind my chair. "Ready when you are," he says.

I figure, *What the hell?* Matthew Bacon can't be any worse than Janie and Becca. Plus, we're desperate. I hire him, he signs a tattered old contract Gina finds in a drawer, then I give him a polo shirt and have him follow me out to cabin four for lessons.

Matt is intelligent, outgoing, and willing, and we breeze through the cabins easily. He tells me he grew up with four siblings and a single mother, and he knows how to clean. He's just looking for an adventure, not trouble.

We'll see. Again, my standards have been lowered. As long as he's not worse than Janie, he'll do.

We meet Pete, Lisa, and Hailey back in the supply closet before lunch, and I make the introductions. "Hailey?" he repeats, holding on to her hand. "I love your hair."

She's momentarily speechless. "Ah, thank you." I can see she's now struggling not to touch her hair.

"You bet."

He turns his back to refill his basket and everyone else shoots me questioning looks. "Wash your hands and find us in the dining room when you're done," I tell Matt.

"Will do."

The four of us shuffle through the kitchen — passing Mark, who looks at us oddly — and into the dining room where we ostensibly set tables but really just gossip. I fill them in on Matt's strange but timely arrival, and they're equally torn between wondering what the hell he's doing here and just being grateful somebody showed up.

"He's kind of cute," Lisa muses.

Pete looks affronted. "Excuse me?"

She strokes his back. "But not as cute as you."

He sulks, and she follows him to start filling water glasses, apologizing for daring to voice her opinion. Though I have to agree. If long hair and piercings are your thing—or even if they're not—Matt's got bright blue eyes, the bone structure of a model, and is good-looking in a decidedly non-ranch way.

Hailey and I roll our eyes and start arranging silverware. "He just showed up out of the blue, huh?"

"Well, I did post a million job ads, so it's not like it was without prompting. I practically begged someone to apply."

Matt enters through the in door, and I explain the principle behind the doors, recounting the story of Lisa learning the hard way. "All right, cool," he says.

"Have you ever served before?" I ask.

"Never."

"Okay, come with me. I'll go over things with you." I grab two glasses of iced tea and an order pad, and we go out back to the steps to sit down. It's Saturday, so the guests are leaving after lunch. I give Matt a quick lesson in order taking and soon we're just killing the last five minutes before the lunch bell sounds.

"There's an actual bell?" he asks, looking doubtful.

"Yeah. One of the wranglers rings it."

"I cannot wait to hear this."

I laugh. "It's just a bell."

There's a pause, then Matt says, "I have to tell you something."

I close my eyes, expecting the worst. What could it be? He's a thief? A killer? On the run from the law?

"I'm a fan," he confesses, watching his sneaker-clad feet.

I don't move. I don't know what the hell he's talking about.

"What?"

"I'm a fan," he says again. "I swear I didn't know before I came up here, but I just thought you'd find out sooner or later…"

"What are you talking about?"

"Your book. *The Sunshine Schools*? I've read it, like, a dozen times. I have a copy in my bag. I just wanted to tell you I'm a fan because

I'm a fan, but also because I don't want somebody to see the book and think I came up here to stalk you. I like to be upfront about things. I recognized you from your picture—and, well, your name, obviously."

"I—Oh. Wow. Well." A pause. "Thank you."

It's important to note that I'm not a novelist. Though I do have a book out there with my name on the front cover and my picture on the back. It's called *The Sunshine Schools*, and it was written almost entirely by accident.

Several years ago I was traveling in Vietnam when I met two young Australian teachers who told me about the schools where they were working. Built and funded by villagers tired of seeing their children trek miles to a crowded school for a poor education, the community had taken matters into their own hands. I followed the Australians to a school still under construction and spent a month helping (if barely managing to use a wheelbarrow counts) with the work and documenting my days.

One night I was on the phone with Stanley when he asked to see some of my notes. I sent the journal along, expecting nothing more than a get-back-to-your-real-job response, and was shocked to learn he'd passed my poorly written pages on to a publisher who'd expressed interest in a book.

A year later *The Sunshine Schools* was published and became a sleeper hit, even spending a few weeks on the bestseller lists. It earned me a surprising bit of money and—coupled with my trust fund and personal savings—meant I no longer had to work unless I wanted to.

All that being said, I haven't encountered many fans outside of the book tour and rarely get recognized. There's a black and white photo of me inside the back cover, but that's the glam me, in a designer little black dress and diamond earrings. It bears little resemblance to the sweaty, dirty me Matt met two hours ago. At least, I didn't think it did.

"Anyway," he says, "I hope that's not too weird."

"No, I—" I pause as I hear something. Or someone. It sounds like footsteps on the opposite side of the fence, moving very slowly, as though someone is trying to either approach or escape unnoticed.

"What is it?" Matt whispers.

I hold a finger to my lips and tiptoe to the gate, pulling it open and peeking out. Nothing. I creep around the corner toward the front of the ranch, but it's also empty. And, I notice, the silver SUV is gone.

I return to the steps and shrug. "Thought I heard something," I say. "But I guess I didn't."

Just then the lunch bell rings, and Matt roars with laughter as he stands to go inside. I hesitate on the steps, looking around. I swear I heard something. Or maybe I just wanted to. Finally I follow him in, hand him a pitcher of water, and tell him to start pouring.

Lunch is busy, but Matt fits in well, especially considering he's already better than Pete, who has been doing the job for two weeks. It helps that Matt's not tripping over himself to be near Lisa at all times, though I do catch his gaze lingering on Hailey once or twice. She doesn't seem to notice, and I'm about to corner her to mention it while she refills the iced tea, but Matt beats me to it, arriving with an empty jug and asking her about the ratio of ice to tea.

They have their backs to the door so they don't notice Brandon come in to collect the ranch hands' lunch, don't see the dark look that crosses his face when he sees Hailey laughing at something Matt said. I decide to mind my own business. If Brandon doesn't know what he wants, then neither do I, and if Matt's interested in Hailey, I'm all for it.

We finish with lunch and everyone departs to clean up and nap, leaving Matt and me behind. "You guys take naps?" he asks, looking perturbed.

"Daily," I say, a little defensive. "You'll see. Plus it's Saturday. People need to rest up for tonight."

We take a brief tour of the ranch, starting with Hank and Mary's house, since they should probably meet their new employee. I expect them to react to his piercings and ponytail, but they don't bat an eye, just shake his hand and welcome him to Ponderosa Pines.

"Happy to be here," he says politely.

Mary gives me a thumbs up as I go. Maybe I'm cynical, but she and Hank look a little too happy with my new hire.

I point out the barn but steer clear of the door so I don't catch a glimpse of Shane and learn that I still want him as much—if not more—than I did before I knew what he could do to me.

I show Matt the pool area and the cabins, then leave him at the boys' bunkhouse with Mark, who promises to show him to an empty bed. It's hotter than hell out, and with most of the staff fast asleep, it's quiet and peaceful. I stop at the pool to debate whether I should go for a quick swim before my nap.

"You found somebody."

I spin around to find Shane standing inches away. "You almost killed me," I gasp, clutching my chest. "How do you move so quietly?"

He laughs. "You were distracted." His eyes drift to the tiny patch of bare skin visible where the top buttons on my shirt are undone, then lift to my face. "Who's the new guy?"

"Matthew Bacon," I reply.

"Bacon?"

"Yep."

"Huh."

"Huh."

Be cool, I remind myself. It was one time. You agreed not to make things awkward afterward. Just be normal.

"You weren't at the dance," Shane says.

"I fell asleep," I admit.

He arches the eyebrow I now find damnably sexy. "Oh?"

I shrug. "I've been overworked."

"Really."

"It should be okay now that Matthew Bacon is here."

"Well, you know what they say: Bacon makes everything better."

"Shane Maddox. Was that a joke?"

He's trying not to smile. "Never."

He's staring at me again, those dark eyes burning into mine and making everything that shouldn't be wanting him want him so damn badly. It's like running a marathon, collapsing, then somehow wanting to get up and run again. I can't—can I? But Shane isn't moving, isn't speaking, isn't doing anything, and the sun is unbearably hot. Yes, that's it. It's the sun that's making my skin flush and my spine prickle.

"Well," I say. "It's naptime." I start to move past him.

"Wait."

I look at him.

"Come up here a minute," Shane says, climbing the stairs to the pool deck. "There's something in here. Tell me if you know what it is."

He disappears into the hot tub shack, and my mind races. Did we leave something in there last night? But what? We brought nothing more than our bathing suits and towels, and those came back with us.

I step into the dim, warm confines of the shack and squint, trying to see this mystery item. "I don't think—"

"Kate."

I turn to see Shane slide the door shut, trapping us in the dark.

"What?"

"Don't think." He kisses me, big hands starting at my hips and sliding up, thumbs grazing my breasts. He tugs the elastic from my hair and threads his fingers through the loose strands, cupping my head, holding me in place even though I'm not resisting.

I make a small, questioning sound in my throat, but Shane's tongue prevents any real words from forming. He takes three steps forward, and my feet are forced to move with him, stopping only when my back meets the warm wooden wall. He presses the length of his body against mine, and I feel a familiar hardness against my stomach.

We pause for breath, and I look away to hide both my confusion and my arousal. "We agreed—"

He kisses me. I turn the other way.

"You said—"

He kisses me again.

"—one time—"

I try to free my mouth, but now his hands are holding my neck, his thumbs pressing into my jaw, trapping my mouth beneath his. Not that I'm really trying to get away, I just want to understand.

"I don't remember that," he says against my lips.

"It was very clear…"

His chest rumbles against mine as he laughs. I smell mint on his breath, like he just brushed his teeth.

"Do you want this?" he asks.

I feel like I should hesitate, act uncertain or coy, like I don't desperately and immediately want Shane every time I see him. But I do. "Yes," I say.

In a split second he has my damp shirt off and one hand under my bra, fondling my breast.

"You're great," he says, kissing my neck.

"I know."

He laughs, and I unbuckle his pants as he pushes a hand down the front of my jeans, finding me wet and ready.

"Is it hot in here or is it just me?"

"It's hot," I gasp as he pushes a thick finger inside.

"You want it slow?"

He adds a second finger and thrusts gently, stretching me. I unzip my jeans and he helps me shove them down.

"No."

"Thank God."

He kisses my shoulder as I wrap a leg around his waist, then his gaze locks on mine as he forges his way inside me. I make myself look back, though instinct tells me to close my eyes. I'm not good at intimacy, and despite our agreement to not do this again—to keep things casual—this feels intimate.

Shane buries himself to the hilt, then holds still as I adjust, his thumb slowly circling my clit.

"Feel good?" he asks after a moment.

"Yes."

"You ready?"

"Yes."

"Kate." He kisses me, long and deep, then grips my ass. "Hold on."

Twenty minutes later I stumble into a cold shower, rinse off the sweat, and shuffle down the hall to my bedroom. Shane and the other ranch hands are driving the guests back to town, and thank God for it—if he hadn't had to leave I'd no doubt be on my back in his trailer doing all the things we promised not to do again.

I collapse naked on top of the covers and fall fast asleep, waking at the sound of knocking on my door. It takes me a minute to figure out why I'm chilly. "Hang on!" I call and quickly slip into jeans and a T-shirt before opening the door. It's Hailey.

"Oh good, you're awake," she says.

"Ha ha."

"Are you coming out tonight?"

She uses her sixth sense to determine that I'm about to decline, and her voice turns wheedling. "Please? I'm tired of talking to the wranglers about horses."

One of the first things Hailey and I bonded over was the fact that though we both work at a dude ranch, neither of us cares for horseback riding. I've gone countless times in the past, but it's just not my thing. I'm not very good at it, I can't shake the feeling that the horse is going to fall down and crush my leg, and the horses seem to sense my ineptitude and take full advantage, basically ignoring my every command or plea.

"I'll buy," she adds, when I hesitate.

I shake my head. "You don't have to buy anything. I'll come. I could use a change of scenery."

"She's in!" Hailey hollers to Lisa, who's down the hall in the bathroom.

"Sweet!" she shouts back.

Hailey elbows her way into my room and shuts the door. "Now let's do something about your hair…"

"You're kidding," Matt says again.

"No joke," Hailey answers, tossing back another shot. "Another three inches and it would've been a different story."

I flush and sip my beer. Lisa, Hailey, and Pete have been regaling Matt with tales of ranch life before his arrival. The more they talk, the more I see Matt's impression of the ranch as an idyllic and simple place disintegrate. Every now and then he'll look to me for confirmation, and I have to nod. They've just finished the story of Janie trying to slap me, and I tap my toes impatiently.

"Want to dance?" Mark asks from across the table. He's been sitting with us for the past hour, but hardly talking. Because he and Alec spend most of their time in the kitchen, the only staff they really cross paths with are us. Hailey's still pissed at him for bringing Cassidy to the ranch, and Lisa pretty much fails to notice anyone who isn't Pete, so Mark doesn't have a lot of friends.

"No thanks," I say after a moment.

He shrugs and returns to his drink. I feel a bit bad for him, but if he really wants to dance, Cassidy's grinding away on the other side of the bar in a skirt that covers less skin than my underwear. I know she's seen me, but so far she's kept her distance. I'm purposely avoiding eye contact, hoping she stays away. If I stir up any more drama—my fault or otherwise—I'll never be allowed back in O'Malley's. We don't get cell reception this far up, but it's become a popular pastime to use one's phone to film the goings-on here, and in addition to the drunken shenanigans of the other staff, there's footage floating around of my showdown with Janie.

"How about you?" Matt says to Hailey. "Want to dance?"

Hailey's finishing another shot, her sixth of the night if the row of empty glasses is any indication. Brandon's not here, so I think she's just relaxing after a week of million-hour days, but still, she seems to panic. "Um," she says, avoiding his eyes, "I—"

I kick her under the table and push back her chair. "She'd love to," I tell Matt. "Have at it."

The band launches into a popular song, and the dancers line up. Matt tugs Hailey into place, and she glares at me over her shoulder as they start trying to follow the moves. They're both equally good or equally bad, depending on how you look at it. Lisa and Pete join in too, but they've had a lot more practice and look happy and comfortable.

"That used to be me," I tell Mark, watching them. "My first summer here, I memorized every step to every song."

He nods, not looking at me.

"Think you'll come back next year?" I try.

This time his eyes drift my way. "Doubt it," he says.

"Why not?"

He shrugs. "It's my third year. It's probably time to move on."

"I thought you liked it."

"I did. I do. But even being here with people I like, good music, lots of beer, I can't shake the feeling that I'm supposed to be somewhere else."

I nod again. I know exactly how he feels. Everything around me is great, but all I'm thinking about is the hot tub shack, Shane's trailer, Shane's bed, Shane's hands, Shane, Shane, Shane.

After the encounter in the shack, Shane kissed me on the forehead, zipped up his pants, and apologized for leaving so quickly but said he had to drive the guests to town. I nodded as I casually forced my jeans back up over sweaty thighs and pretended I wasn't wondering what had just happened and what—if anything—it meant. Or what I wanted it to mean.

"I'm going to go," I tell Mark.

"Already? You've had one beer in three hours."

"I know. I'm old and boring."

"You're neither!"

I laugh. "I'll see you tomorrow."

I'm halfway to the door when a pair of nails digs into my arm. "Don't even think about it," Hailey hisses in my ear. "Get your ass out on that dance floor and have fun!"

"Actually, I'm just—"

"Now," Lisa says, popping up on the other side and mimicking Hailey's firm tone. Matt's kicking up his heels in the background, waggling his eyebrows in what's probably supposed to be a tempting way.

"Just do what they say," Pete sighs, appearing in front of me. "Trust me when I tell you it's easier to boot-scoot boogie than argue."

I relent, and it's nearly two when we return to the ranch. I park the van and Mark, Pete, Matt, Lisa, and Hailey topple out. I stopped at one beer, so I'm the only person walking steady, and we watch the guys slowly wind their way back to their bunkhouse before starting up the stairs to our own.

"That was so much fun!" Lisa crows as we reach the top. I tried to keep an eye on her and Pete all night, but they obviously still found a way to sneak in a few drinks.

"It was fun," I agree. "My feet hurt so much I'm going to know I had a blast for the next two days."

"I like Matt," Hailey sighs as I help her into her bed. "I didn't think I would, but he's really funny. It was nice to think about someone other than Brandon for a change."

"And it's nice to hear you talk about someone other than Brandon," I say, earning a laugh from Lisa.

Hailey may or may not scowl at me, but she passes out a split-second later, so it doesn't matter. I wedge the boots off her feet and arrange them on the floor, then make sure Lisa safely scales the ladder to her bed before wishing them a good night and backing out the door.

I wash my face and brush my teeth, then pull my hair on top of my head so it doesn't tangle while I'm sleeping. When I open the bathroom door, the hallway is an impenetrable wall of black, and I have to feel my way back to my room. I'm nearly at my door when a hand clamps over my mouth, stifling my scream.

Chapter Thirteen

"Shh," a low voice murmurs. "It's me." Even if I didn't recognize the tone, I'd know the steely chest at my back.

My promise not to scream is muffled by calloused fingers as Shane releases me. I turn to give him the stink eye, but it's so dark I can see little more than the outline of his head and shoulders in the moonlight coming through the open door behind him.

"What are you doing up here?" I whisper. "No boys allowed!"

"I won't tell if you won't."

"It's two o'clock in the morning."

"It's Sunday."

"Uh-huh."

Technically, this is true. With Matt taking up some of the slack, we each have fewer cabins to clean, so I told everyone we could start at ten o'clock tomorrow, giving us the rare opportunity to sleep in.

"So you get a late start tomorrow. Come outside for a second. I want to show you something."

"Is it the same thing you showed me in the hot tub shack?"

I can feel Shane smile. "Uh-huh."

I hesitate. This is what I've been thinking about all morning, afternoon, and evening, but now that it's being offered, I can't help but wonder if I'm getting in over my head. I've spent more time thinking about Shane in the past three weeks than I have any other guy in my life, ever, and I'm not ready to worry about what that might mean.

While I'm contemplating he sighs, steps forward, and kisses me. He doesn't wait, just pushes his tongue past my teeth, presses us together from lips to toe, and trusts that I won't say no. And I don't. I can't. Already there's a tension low in my belly that will keep me tossing and turning all night if it isn't addressed. And he's got just the thing to remedy that problem pressing into my hip.

"What happened to just once?" I ask, pulling back and gasping for breath. My heart is pounding from both arousal and the threat of being caught.

Shane kisses me again. "I wasn't expecting to like it so much," he admits.

I pull away, offended. "I beg your pardon?"

"Come outside," he says, tugging my hand.

"You weren't expecting to like it?"

He pulls me down the hall to the door, to the stairs, across the road, through the moonlight. "Come inside," he continues, opening his trailer door and ushering me in.

"What did you think you wouldn't like, exactly?" I demand.

Shane undoes my jeans, shoving them down to my knees along with my underwear, then turns me around and presses my hands to the wall. I feel a broad hand squeeze between my thighs, higher and higher, until he's sawing gently back and forth along the most sensitive part of my anatomy. He pulls my hips back to give himself better access, and we both groan when his tongue begins a leisurely inspection of my damp folds.

I'm done arguing.

I wake up groggy, confused, and weak. My muscles feel like limp noodles. The sun is shining in my eyes, so I cover my face with a pillow and stretch, vaguely registering that my back doesn't feel like it's going to snap in half at the movement.

Then a familiar feeling comes over me: that moment when I wake up and realize I have no idea where I am. I'm not in my bed in the bunkhouse. This isn't my pillow. The light that's shining on my face is too close, too—I whip off the pillow and look to my right. Nothing. Nobody.

This is Shane's bed.

I'm in his bed, in his trailer. Alone.

I twist my neck to look at the clock. 9:08.

"Shane?" I call cautiously.

No answer.

I swing my legs over the edge of the bed and search for my clothes. Not here. I'm buck naked in a trailer on a ranch with dozens of people milling around outside. What the fuck was I thinking, falling asleep? What was Shane thinking? "Keep it casual" doesn't mean *spend the night* (after I've exhausted you beyond the point of intelligent thought).

Crap. I find my clothing in the living room and dress quickly. I knock on the closed bathroom door, not expecting a response and not getting one, then step inside to splash icy water on my face. Where the hell is Shane? Why did he leave me? And why did I not notice him going?

Well, I may have the answer to the last question. The man is a machine—an exhausting, amazing machine that just keeps going and going and going, like that damned pink drumming bunny. And just when you think it's over, when you're ready to drift off to a beautiful, comfortable dreamland, you'll feel a finger or a tongue or—in the best instances—the head of his cock probing you. And then you're awake again and ready to go, meeting that rabbit beat for pounding beat.

I splash more water on my face. *Enough, Kate. Get a grip.* I have more pressing issues right now, namely how in the hell I'm going to get from this trailer to the lodge without anyone noticing. I don't have to go to the window to hear the telltale signs of life outside: voices, laughter, footsteps. I'm surrounded.

The bathroom is small but, like the rest of the trailer, anal-retentively clean. There's a tube of toothpaste (I squirt some on my finger), a toothbrush, dental floss, and a bar of white soap. The stand-up shower looks barely big enough to contain Shane, but it's equipped with the basics: a bottle of two-in-one shampoo and another bar of white soap. I shudder and close the door. I miss my products already. I miss my sweetly scented soap and separate shampoo and conditioner. As compatible as Shane and I may be in some areas, we differ in this one.

I ponder this as I return to the bedroom to hunt down a brush, finding only a tiny comb, and fix my hair as best I can with the small scrap of plastic. I don't think I've ever dated a guy who didn't have a bathroom arsenal to match mine. Andre, the hotelier, had such a wonderfully diverse supply that I didn't even have to bring anything with me when I spent the night. That was heaven. This…I look around the small room, the rumpled bed, the white T-shirt and cargo pants hanging from a hook on the wall. Well, this might not look like heaven, but for a few hours it sure as hell felt like it.

I cross the room, ducking beneath the curtain-covered window when I hear voices pass by, then crack open the door an inch to look outside. Unfortunately Shane's trailer is completely exposed to the horse paddock, which is now full of horses and a few wranglers, and the road, which has a disturbing amount of foot traffic.

I listen carefully and when a full ten seconds of silence passes, I whip open the door, step onto the porch, and turn around to knock. "Shane?" I call, pounding harder than necessary so someone will notice me "arriving." "Are you in there?"

I hear heavy footsteps and turn to see Brandon rounding the side of the barn. "He's not in," he tells me. I try to look surprised. "He had to take Connor to the emergency room a few hours ago."

Now my surprise is genuine. "Why? What happened?"

Brandon rolls his eyes, unconcerned. "Nothing a few stitches won't fix. Connor's real trouble begins when he gets back."

I can tell Brandon wants to talk, so I gently encourage him. "Oh?"

"Shane's running a tight ship this summer," he says. "Like, really strict. More than normal. We're supposed to work, sleep, eat, and get back to work. But Connor had a few too many last night, went streaking through the paddock, and cut open his knee on a piece of barbed wire trying to hop the fence."

I don't know much about Connor, but this seems extremely unusual. The ranch hands have always come across as stoic and un-fun. "That sounds…"

"Out of character? Oh yeah. Pressure's building, you know? All work, no play. All that."

I notice his gaze drifting to the bunkhouse. I'm starting to wonder if his hot-and-cold relationship with Hailey has a little something to do with Shane's mood swings.

"Maybe you could talk to Shane," I suggest. "Tell him people would work better if they had a way to blow off steam."

Brandon gives a bark of laughter. "Yeah. Right. That guy's been waiting to go off on someone for weeks. That's why I've been walking the line. I'm just glad it's Connor, not me."

I know Shane's been…difficult…for the past several weeks, but he's been better these last few days, and I can't imagine him being a hypocrite. If he's "blowing off steam" with me, why shouldn't the guys have the same opportunity?

"I guess it's none of my business," I say, stepping off the porch and turning toward the lodge.

Brandon's voice stops me, and I turn around. "Hey," he says, too casually. "Who's that new guy you hired?"

"Matt," I answer. "We needed a worker and he showed up, so…"

He squints like the sun is too bright and adjusts his baseball hat on his forehead. "He doesn't seem like he fits in here, does he?"

I shrug. "I don't know. It's only been a day. Everyone seems to like him."

"Everyone?"

Maybe it's mean, but I answer anyway, with emphasis. "Everyone."

This time I succeed in walking away and hurry upstairs to my room where I switch into changeover-cleaning clothes — my rattiest, most bleach-stained jeans and an equally splotchy, formerly black tank top — and zip over to the kitchen. Alec and Mark leave out cold cereal for the staff on Sundays, and the remains of a loaf of bread sit by the toaster. I pop in two slices and pour myself a cup of coffee, staring out the window at the sunny morning while I wait.

The past few Sundays have been a stressful, unpleasant barrage of work. Changing over fifteen cabins is too much for four people, and while a few of the wranglers pitched in, helping us swap out towels and bed linens and running supplies, we were still barely able to finish in time. Today, however, I feel upbeat, optimistic, like everything will be okay.

"What was that?" a sharp voice demands.

I jump, hot coffee splashing over the rim of the mug and scalding my hand. "Ow! Shit!"

I turn to see Hailey standing just inside the door, hands on hips.

"What were you two talking about?" She jerks her chin toward the barn.

"I just burned myself," I inform her. "Apologize."

"Sorry." She doesn't sound sincere, but she does snatch an ice cube from the repaired ice maker and extend it like an olive branch. My hand hurts, so I accept it.

"He was telling me about Connor," I say when she taps her toe impatiently. "And how Shane's been rough on them all summer. Why? What's got you so on edge?"

"Matt kissed me," she says.

"What? When?"

"Last night. During all the dancing. He two-stepped me into the corner and kissed me. We'd only known each other for twelve hours!"

I stare at her. Her cheeks are flushed, but I'm not sure it's righteous indignation that has her so worked up. "How was it?"

She covers her face with her hands. "Good."

"Good-good?"

"Yeah. Good-good. Oh God. What am I thinking?"

"That you want to get laid, and Brandon's not up to the job?"

A pause. "Yeah."

"And Matt is?"

"But he just got here! And he turned up out of nowhere. And… and he's not my type."

"So —"

"Okay, fine, he is my type. He's exactly my type. Add a couple more piercings and he's my ex."

"The one who dumped you at grad?"

"Yes."

"Wait. Is this why you like Brandon? Because he's so unlike your ex?"

"Because he's not like Andy, because he's incredibly beautiful, because…I don't know. I do not know." She fixes her gaze on me again. I'm still rubbing the rapidly melting ice cube on my pink hand, while simultaneously trying to eat a piece of toast. "So that's all you two talked about? Connor and Shane?"

"And Matt."

"Other men?"

"Okay, fine. I don't want to make this harder on you. But he seemed jealous. Yesterday he saw you and Matt talking, and he looked jealous."

Hailey covers her face with her hands. "I kissed him."

"I know. You told me."

"Not Matt. Brandon."

"You told me that too."

"No. *Again*."

"When?"

"This morning."

"What?" I'm starting to regret sleeping in.

"Despite my copious drinking last night, I woke up without a hang over. In fact, I had a million mega-bolts of energy zinging through me, so I decided to go for a run to burn some of it off. Then when I was coming back, who the hell did I pass on his morning run?"

"Brandon?"

"That's right! It was just the two of us and nature, and I was sweating, and he said I looked so hot, and I was like, 'What the fuck are you talking about?' and he came really close, and I knew what he was going to do, and I knew what I should do, but I didn't. I let him kiss me. And I liked it."

My jaw is open. I have given up on eating the toast.

"This is not like me," Hailey moans, staring at me desperately. "I've only been with two guys in my whole life: awful Andy and a rebound guy. I don't know what I'm doing. For six years I thought I knew where everything was going, and now? Now I have no idea. How did ranch life get so complicated? It was supposed to be simple!"

"What are you going to do?"

"Beats me. I mean, odds are Brandon will stare right through me the next time we meet, acting like nothing happened, and I'll be super strange and awkward around Matt, because if he actually likes me, I'll feel like a monster for lusting after Brandon."

"I don't want to sound cold and mean," I say, drying off my sore hand, "but don't do anything to make Matt quit. We need him. Keep him happy."

"What are you, a pimp?"

"Do whatever it takes," I say seriously. "Nothing's off limits."

Hailey laughs. "You're evil."

A few minutes later we meet Pete, Lisa, and Matt in the laundry room and I hand out the changeover day cleaning assignments, purposely keeping Matt and Pete on one side of the ranch, Lisa and Hailey on the other, and myself in the middle.

"I'm going to inspect everything when we're done," I say. "So don't cut corners or you'll be back to clean them."

"Aye-aye," Pete says, saluting.

Lisa giggles, and I shake my head, following them out the door. Because the cabins form a semi-circle and I'm in the middle, I have the longest hike. Some guests love cabin eight for its seclusion, and others hate it for the same reason. There's enough space between cabins that you can't hear rowdy neighbors, but not so much that you don't see them coming and going.

Fortunately for me, cabin eight housed a sweet elderly couple this week, and they haven't left any nasty surprises. I strip the beds, collect the towels, and heft them back to the laundry room, tossing the dirty linens into a machine before gathering up new ones.

I'm about to make the return trip when I hear Mary's voice coming from the kitchen. "...recently renovated..." she's saying. "Totally modern, new wiring, equipped for everything."

"Dining room seats eighty and holds twice as many...great acoustics..." This is from Hank.

Suspicious—and, fine, nosy—I set down the clean sheets and creep around to the kitchen entrance just in time to see Hank and Mary lead a couple into the dining room. Like the strangers from yesterday, these two are dressed in fancy suits.

I peek through the crack in the door and try to hear more, but they're already halfway down the hall toward the offices and are soon out of earshot. If these people are guests, they're about seven hours early. And I've never seen guests get a personal tour of the kitchen before. I don't know what Hank and Mary are up to—and maybe it's none of my business—but I can't shake the feeling that despite their perplexingly chipper demeanor, something is not right.

Chapter Fourteen

Two hours later I've kicked Pete out of Lisa's cabin, twice, and am putting the finishing touches on cabin eight. I'm in the bedroom, making sure I've crossed everything off my checklist, when I hear the door swing open and heavy footsteps cross the room. I've been fielding mostly work-related (and a few Hailey-related) questions from Matt all morning and anticipate another one.

"Shoes!" I call. "Take them off. I just vacuumed!"

There's a pause, a rustling noise, then a well-used black work boot sails past me to crash into the wall. I jump and find Shane standing in the doorway, one booted foot, one socked.

"What the hell?" I demand, scrubbing off the scuff mark with a rag.

"Sorry about this morning," he says, leaning against the doorjamb.

"It's fine." I toss back the boot. I'm in the far corner of the room and he's near the foot of the bed, blocking the exit. Given our extra-curricular activities — and his willingness to take off a boot — I'm pretty sure I know what he's here for. Just like I know I don't have time for any distractions.

"You heard about Connor?" he asks.

"Yeah. Brandon told me. How is he?"

"He'll be fine."

I pause, not sure if I should inquire further, but can't bite my tongue. "And after the hospital?"

"What do you mean?"

"I mean, were you...did you..."

Shane arches that brow.

"Well, rumor has it you're really tough on the guys. I'm just wondering if you were...mean...to Connor."

"Mean?" He's mocking me.

I square my shoulders. "Yes. Mean."

"Me?"

"Shane."

"Mm-hmm?"

"If you're not going to answer my question, I really have to get back to work. I have two more cabins to clean and barely enough time to finish."

"I wasn't *mean*, Kate."

"Okay. Good. Glad to hear it." I push past him out the door. He could refuse to budge if he wanted to, but after some effort—and more than a little friction—he lets me by.

"You're sure you're not mad about this morning?" he asks.

"Yes, I'm sure. You had an emergency. No big deal. I didn't mean to fall asleep. It won't happen again."

Shane hasn't made a move to put his boot back on. I watch him out the corner of my eye as I collect my array of cleaning products and stuff them back in the basket.

"I don't care that you fell asleep."

"Well, I do."

"Why?"

"Because I had to get back to the lodge unnoticed this morning!"

"Did anyone see you?"

"Just Brandon. But he thought I was coming, not going."

"If only he'd stopped by earlier."

I'm not easily embarrassed, but my cheeks flush red. "*Shane.*"

"What?"

I'm so not getting into this right now. "I have a lot of work to do. What are you doing here?"

"I just got back from town with Connor. So after I kissed him on the forehead and put him to bed—"

"Ha ha."

"I thought I'd find you before I had to get back to work."

"Well, you found me, but I'm very busy."

"You're sure you're not pissed?"

"I'm definitely not."

"Because you're acting that way."

"I'm just busy! Plus, you threw a shoe at me."

"Not at you. Past you."

"Because you missed."

"I never miss."

I turn to pick up a fallen rag and next thing I know, a boot hits me in the ass. I whip around, jaw dropped in disbelief, and stare at the boot on the floor at my feet. "You did *not* just do that."

Shane smiles, daring me to do...something.

I pick up the boot, march to the door, and hurl it outside. "You need to leave," I say. "Go get your boot."

He glances at his watch. "I have three hours before I leave to pick up the guests. Take off your clothes."

Again, my mouth opens in shock. "You can't be serious."

Shane keeps his eyes on mine as he reaches down to unlace his boot.

I hold up a hand. "If you throw that at me, you'll regret it."

"I regret leaving this morning," he says, stepping out of his boot. "I regret having Brandon pound on my door at five o'clock telling me I needed to drive Connor to town. What I do *not* regret is finding you alone in a cabin without your cleaning posse around to interfere."

"Shane..." I say in weak protest. "I don't have time for this. I have so much to do."

He comes forward, unbuckling his belt. "I'll help you," he promises.

"You'll help me clean cabins?"

"Yes."

I press a hand against his chest to prevent him from coming any closer, biting my lip when I feel the heat from his skin through his shirt. But back to business. I've had plenty of experience bartering in foreign countries with merchants more devious than Shane. I need help, and if he's offering, I'm accepting. "Fine," I say.

"Fine?"

He tries to come closer, but I stop him.

"Cabins first."

The eyebrow shoots up. "You want me to *work* for it?"

"I want you to *clean* for it." I can almost see the wheels turning inside that handsome head. Then he smiles and presses his lips to mine, letting his tongue work its magic, making me damp and soft all over until I almost change my mind.

"Fine," he whispers, then pulls away.

We walk over to cabin nine, keeping an eye out for witnesses. No one's around to see us step inside and close the door. This cabin housed a family of four and is in general disarray, but nothing out of the ordinary.

"What's first?" Shane asks, slapping my ass—hard—as he strides into the room.

I stare at his back. "First," I say firmly, deliberately, "we strip."

He turns. "What?"

"The beds," I add.

He gives me a hard look. "That's what I thought."

I smirk and enter the first of two bedrooms. I expect Shane to take the second room, but instead he follows, standing on the far side of the king-size bed and tossing the quilt to the floor. I shake out the pillows and tug at the flat sheet while Shane wiggles the fitted sheet free.

We stuff everything into a pillowcase. "Now what?" he asks.

"More stripping."

He follows me into the second bedroom, and we each tackle a bed, filling a second pillowcase.

"Grab the towels from the bathroom," I order, "and take everything to the laundry room. Then bring back fresh stuff."

"Okay." I wait for him to leave, but he lingers, blocking the door. "Come here first."

I step forward. "Why?"

His mouth twitches as he fights a smile, then twines his free hand in my hair and holds me still for a kiss I feel straight to my toes. I know from prior experience that this man knows how to use his tongue, but I enjoy being reminded. Finally he pulls away, clears his throat, and goes into the bathroom for the towels.

I grab a garbage can and fill it with the random items left littering the room, and after a minute I hear Shane leave with the laundry. I watch him out the window and take a deep breath. *Jesus.* What was I thinking, going up against that man in an erotic battle? He'll take me down, every time. Then again, I suppose I want him to.

I toss the garbage bag onto the porch and start dusting the windowsills. I hand Shane a rag when he returns and tell him to dust the baseboards.

"Baseboards?" he echoes with a frown. "Who checks the fucking baseboards?"

"I do."

He gets down on his knees. "Then I'll do a very thorough job."

Dusting is a straightforward chore, just wipe-wipe-wipe, but it's damn difficult to do with an ass like that pointing in my direction. My dusting strategy is now more of a wipe-wipe-peek, followed by a stern internal reminder that I have work to do. Each cabin changeover takes about two hours, and I'm less than halfway through.

With the dusting done, I pick up the king-size sheets and go into the master bedroom to start making the bed. Shane follows, wordlessly picking up a corner of the fitted sheet and helping me put it on. The flat sheet comes next, and I watch, bemused, as he painstakingly smooths every wrinkle.

"So," I begin, "you're very neat."

He catches me watching, and I swear he blushes. "That a problem?"

"Just an observation."

"I prefer the term *detail-oriented.*"

"Sorry, did you say *anal retentive?*"

He smirks. "If that works for you."

Now I blush. Fiercely. Note to self: do not say *anal* in front of this man.

"How long have you worked at the ranch?"

"Changing the subject? Very smooth."

"Thank you."

We stuff pillows into clean cases.

"I've been here eight years."

"How long do you plan to stay?"

"Until I own it."

"Excuse me?"

"You heard me."

"You want to buy the ranch?"

"Sure. One day. When it's for sale."

"Isn't that…expensive?"

"That's what savings accounts are for."

"How long have you been saving?"

"Eight years. Why the third degree?"

"I'm not grilling you, Shane. It's called conversation. That's what 'works' for me."

Now he smiles. "Then we'll talk."

An hour later cabin nine is sparkling. When properly motivated, Shane is a decent conversationalist, in addition to being an ass-grabbing, French kissing, sexually deviant cabin cleaner. The same deviant whose hand I pry out of my jeans forty-five seconds after we arrive in cabin ten.

"Clean first," I gasp.

"Screw later," he affirms, holding up his slick fingers. "Got it."

I watch him lick off his fingers and nearly expire. "Jesus."

"You can call me Shane."

I snicker and turn toward the master bedroom to strip the bed. Shane helps, and when we're left with a bare mattress he presses it with his hand as though inspecting the springs. "What are you doing?" I ask.

"Just trying to decide where I'm going to fuck you."

For the second time in fifteen minutes I almost melt. I already knew I wasn't a romantic, and apparently neither is Shane—we're the perfect match.

I opt not to speak and move into the second room to strip the twin beds. Shane's behind me, and after a quick ass grab he's jamming sheets into a pillowcase. If I'm not mistaken he's breathing just a little bit harder than he was a few minutes ago. So am I, for that matter.

When the beds are bare he turns to stare at me.

"No mattress inspection?" I ask.

"Not big enough."

I hand him my pillowcase. "Get the towels and take these—"

"To the laundry room. I know." He steps forward so quickly that I have to scurry backward, stopping when I bump into the dresser. Even with nowhere to go he doesn't stop coming, and soon he's hoisted me onto the edge of the hip-high dresser, knocking the alarm clock to the floor. He drops the pillowcases and twines his fingers through mine, pinning my hands to either side of my head as he kisses me up against the mirror. I groan into his mouth. I know we have to stop, but I don't want to. But I must. But how can I when he grinds his massive erection against me, bumping just the right spot over and over again? The past two hours have been vicious foreplay, and my body is primed and ready. But there's work to do. But I'm about to come. But—

Shane pulls away before I can reach a conclusion. "A master and two twins, right?" He confirms the sheet order, voice strained.

"And towels," I breathe. "Four sets. Plus a bath mat."

His dark eyes rake me from top to bottom. If possible I grow even wetter.

"Take off your pants," he orders.

"We have to work—"

"Work with them off."

He backs toward the door.

"Someone might—"

"Pants off, Kate. Don't make me repeat myself."

Shane leaves, slamming the door behind him. I have never been into domination before, but try telling that to my lady parts. Can I really take off my pants? What if someone comes in? What if—

I put an end to the internal argument by kicking off my sneakers and shimmying out of my jeans, then putting my sneakers back on so I'm left wearing my tank top, pink boy-cut underwear, socks, and shoes. I look ridiculous. And if I weren't so turned on, I'd feel ridiculous. But the thought of one less barrier between me and Shane's cock—tongue, fingers, anything—is all it takes to assure me that I have made the right decision.

When Shane comes back I'm on my hands and knees dusting the baseboard, ass deliberately pointed in his direction. I'm hoping the execution looks sexier than the preparation: to avoid any awkward encounters I'd been crouched beneath the window, one eye peeking over the ledge to keep an eye out for Shane. When he was ten feet away I'd made a mad dash to the opposite side of the room, snatched up a rag, and fallen to my knees, hoping desperately to appear sexily absorbed in my work.

The door opens and closes, and then there's silence. After an agonizing minute I risk a look over my shoulder. Shane is standing in place, eyes locked on my ass, stack of clean linens still in his hands. Beneath that I can see a distinct bulge at the front of his pants. My panties get a little wetter.

"Kate," he growls.

I turn back to my task. "Dust the windowsills," I order.

I hear a thud as he drops the linens on the couch, then his pacing footsteps as he decides whether to get to work or get to *work*. In the end, however, he picks up a rag and starts dusting windowsills.

When I finish the baseboards I stand up and glance down at my knees, which now bear a distinct rug pattern. I look up to see Shane watching me. He drops the rag, and I hold up a hand, heart pounding. "It's not fair that I'm halfway undressed and you're not," I say sternly. "Take off your clothes."

"Why?"

"Because I said so."

"But you're much prettier."

"Even so, do as I say."

Shane laughs and pulls his shirt over his head. My mouth waters as I watch the muscles in his abdomen stretch taut, his broad chest rippling. *Rippling.* Like on the cover of a romance novel. The man is sex personified. He bends over to unlace his boots, then pushes down his pants and steps out so he's left in black boxer briefs.

I bite my lip.

"Take off your shirt," he says.

"That's enough for now." My voice is thin and unconvincing.

"You do it or I will."

I hesitate long enough that he closes the distance between us and tugs my shirt over my head in one determined movement. Now I'm left in my bra, panties, socks, and sneakers. He looks me up and down. I resist the urge to cover myself.

"You're beautiful," he says.

"Stop saying that."

"Why?"

"Bec—"

"Why?"

How do I tell him I don't want him to make this harder than it is? That this thing, whatever it is, is finite, and as much as I love having him in my body, I don't want him in my head. His unexpected sweetness, the honesty with which he delivers a compliment—these things are working their way inside me, into a place that promises to scar when I leave all this behind at the end of the summer.

Shane slides his hands up my sides, fingers slipping under my bra, finding my tight nipples and pinching them lightly. I remember the rough treatment of our first night and tense up.

He seems to read my mind. "You liked it," he reminds me, fingers tugging gently, insistently.

"I don't know how I feel about it," I correct him.

He releases my nipples and swipes back and forth over them with his thumb. There's an echoing twinge between my legs.

"Okay," Shane says, taking away his hands. "Let me know when you decide."

I back up a step. My heart is pounding, and I feel dizzy. No one has ever made me feel this turned on before. No one has ever appeared this turned on by me, when I haven't even done anything.

"Let's make the beds," I say.

Shane picks up the sheets. "After you."

We make the twin beds first, and I return the alarm clock to the top of the dresser. When the room is finished I step back to admire our work. "Looks good," I say.

Next we tackle the master bedroom. I take the far side of the bed and wait for Shane to unfold the fitted sheet. For a moment nothing happens, and when I glance at him I see he's got a strange look on his face. "What is it?" I ask.

"I'm remembering the day with the bat," he replies.

"Which day?"

"The first one. How you stood between me and the bat like your life depended on it."

"His did."

He sets the linens on the bed and comes around to my side. "You're right," he says. "It did."

"I knew it."

"You put your hands on my chest."

"You pushed me onto the bed."

"I had to."

"You did not—"

"If you'd come any closer you'd have felt my hard-on."

All the air leaves my lungs.

"I had to get that fucking bat out so I could get back to my trailer, take my dick in my hand, and jerk off, thinking about you dancing on tabletops."

I lick my lips. I can't breathe. I can barely stand.

"The next day I saw you get the butterfly net and sneak up to the cabin…I couldn't stay away."

"You scared the crap out of me."

"You were scared for the wrong reasons, Kate. I didn't give a fuck about the bat. I wanted to bend you over the sofa and drive into you so hard you'd forget your own name."

My clit pulses dangerously. I squeeze my thighs together.

"After watching you run around, tits bouncing, smelling like vanilla, I thought I would come in my pants."

"Shane…"

"Are you wet?"

"You know I am."

"I'm going to bend you over now."

"The sofa?"

"Right here's fine." He turns me so I'm facing the bed and presses between my shoulders until I'm kneeling on the floor. "Ass up," he says, swatting me lightly.

I shift so I'm lying over the bed, knees not quite on the floor, ass in the air.

"Let's get these off…" Shane murmurs, fingers working under the edge of my panties and peeling them down my legs with painstaking care. He makes a sound low in his throat, and I know he can see how wet I am, how desperately swollen.

"Shane—" I start to twist around, but he splays one big hand across my back and holds me in place. I kick off my shoes and socks so my toes can find better traction on the carpet.

I don't know where the condom comes from, but I hear him rip one open. The tattered package falls on the mattress near my head. He pushes my legs apart, so wide I whimper and my toes strain to hold me up.

Shane drops to his knees behind me, and I feel his cock on my thigh. His hands stroke up and down my legs, first my calves, then my thighs, up to my ass. His thumbs delve between my cheeks and open me. I shiver at the thought of his gaze on my darkest, most secret place, and when I can't take any more I reach back and cover myself.

He chuckles and removes my hand. "No hiding."

"That's off limits."

He bites my ass in response, then fits his cock at my sopping entrance, pushing in easily. "Fuck," he grunts. "You're so wet."

I bite my fist to stifle a cry. He feels so perfect, like the only solution to a very personal problem. He strokes carefully at first, then harder and harder. Soon I feel his pubic bone slamming into my ass with each thrust. My fingers scrabble for a hold on the smooth mattress, and my legs spread wider as I struggle to hold myself up. Each thrust of his cock reaches somewhere deep inside, deeper than anyone has ever been, and it's so good it hurts. I'm crying out, and my eyes are shut tight.

I want to reach between my legs to touch my clit, to answer this burning need, but I need both hands to keep myself from sliding all over the place. "Shane," I gasp. "Please."

He doesn't ask what I need. He curls forward so he's covering my back and reaches one hand around, rasping down my stomach with his calloused palm. I can hear his rough breathing in my ear, feel his teeth on my neck. But he doesn't touch my clit. Instead he spreads his fingers wide over my lower belly and pushes in, pressing against something inside me so each push of his cock feels impossibly tight. Now he's nudging that perfect spot, the one that makes me clamp down and moan as the need and pleasure escalate.

"Oh God," I groan, turning my face into the mattress so he can't see the tears leaking from my eyes. I've never cried during sex before.

I've never wanted to. But now I can't seem to control myself. Every part of me is raw and exposed, every thrust takes me to the brink but not over.

I lower a trembling hand between my legs, trying to touch myself, to finish what Shane has started, but he whispers soothing words in my ear and takes my hand away, returning it to the mattress. "I've got you," he says, breath tickling my neck.

"I can't take any more," I moan. "What are you doing to me?"

He pounds into me harder and harder, stroking over that spot again and again until everything in me converges in one place, then finally dips his fingers between my legs, rubbing roughly and grunting, "Come," in my ear.

I've been called stubborn most of my life, but not now. My body's not listening to me anyway. It's found a new master, and his name is Shane. I come. I come harder than I've ever come in my life. My pussy spasms so tightly it hurts, and I hear Shane cry out, biting my shoulder as he explodes inside me. I feel an incredible wetness on my thighs and realize I'm still coming, the waves taking me down, holding me under. My nails scratch the mattress, and my toes curl.

Eventually his thrusts slow, drawing out the pleasure, bringing us back to earth. His body is draped over mine, crushing me, but I don't mind. It means he's as weak and winded as I am.

"Kate," he groans when several minutes have passed. "You okay?"

I smile into my hand, though my smile fades when I feel my wet cheeks. I quickly scrub away the tears and nod into the mattress. "I'm okay. You?"

We both moan when he pulls out, suffering the deliciously torturous slide of his softening cock on my very well-used muscles.

"I'm fine." He kisses my shoulder blade before standing and leaving to get rid of the condom. I use the alone time to hunt for my composure—what was I thinking, crying like that? But even as I try to chastise myself, I know I had no say in the matter. In any case, the tears are gone now, and I grab my panties, wincing as I pull them on.

When Shane doesn't reappear I pad slowly into the living room, reluctant to face him. What just happened was the most intense thing I've ever experienced, and he was responsible for it.

I find him sitting on the couch, pants back on as he ties up his boots, all business. He looks up and his eyes seem flat and distant.

No-nonsense Shane is back, and I can't help but flinch at the sudden change, turning away as I get dressed.

"What's left?" he asks after a minute. "Just the bed?"

"The bathroom. Vacuuming."

"Which do you want?"

My face is burning. I'm normally the one who's cool and casual after sex, but now the tables have turned. I feel like a fool. I spot the clock: we still have half an hour left before we're supposed to finish, and that's more than enough time to complete the cabin by myself.

"You know what?" I say, smiling. "Don't worry about it. I can do the rest."

Shane stands and tugs on his shirt. "A deal's a deal."

"You were a big help," I answer, pulling my hair into a ponytail. "Thanks."

The look on his face switches from cool and collected to murderous in an instant, but I'll never know what he was going to say or do next because at that moment I hear Lisa's voice calling, "Kate? Which cabin are you in? Kate?"

"You should go."

Shane's fists are clenched at his side. "What just happened?" he demands.

"What do you mean?"

He comes toward me, but stops halfway. "Don't play dumb, Kate."

"What would you like me to say? I came back out here to find you getting dressed."

"So—"

"And then you ask me what chore is next. Well, you're all done. Thanks."

"Hey, Matt, have you seen Kate?" Lisa's getting closer.

"All done? Like a fucking stud horse?"

"You were the one getting ready to leave!"

"I couldn't clean with my fucking dick hanging out!"

I take a breath. "I don't want to fight with you. I didn't mean thanks for the orgasm. I meant thanks for helping with the cabins."

"You're welcome."

He's looking at me so intently I want to squirm. I settle for avoiding his gaze.

"Hailey, is Kate in the laundry room?"

"Haven't seen her."

Now Shane comes close, pinching my chin lightly between his thumb and forefinger. "You want to be done?" he asks.

I could pretend not to know what he's talking about, but I know he means us, and I can't lie. "No."

"Kate?" I hear footsteps crossing the porch. Lisa.

He nods. His eyes are dark and cool again. "Good." He lets go and steps away just as Lisa knocks on the door and pushes it open.

"There you are!" she exclaims. "I've been calling you. I'm done with my cabins."

"That's great," I say, drawing a deep breath. "I'll come check in a minute. I'm almost finished."

"Okay. And Shane, there's a drip in cabin fourteen. Pete couldn't fix it. Can you look?"

"Yeah. I'll be there in a minute."

"All right." Lisa leaves, and the door slowly closes behind her.

Shane turns back to me, ready to say something, but there's a second voice from outside.

"Is Kate in there?" It's Matt.

"Yep."

More footsteps approach.

Shane purses his lips. "I'd better go."

"Yeah."

Matt appears at the door. "Hey, Kate, do you know if we have more twin-size flat sheets? I can't find any."

Shane squeezes past Matt and leaves without a backward glance.

I run a hand over my face. "Let's have a look," I say.

Chapter Fifteen

Freshly showered and beaming, Hailey, Lisa, Matt, and I—Pete has the night off—stand on the porch and watch as the guests arrive that evening. Shane holds the van door and helps the women out, but he never glances my way. To be fair, I'm trying my very best not to look at him either.

"How long?" Hailey asks, the smile never leaving her face.

I wave at an elderly couple. "How long what?"

"Until this gets old. Same thing, week after week. How long?"

"I don't know. It's different for everyone. Plus it's just for the summer."

I glance at her out the corner of my eye. She's watching Brandon load suitcases onto the tractor wagon that will drive them to the cabins. He catches her eye and smiles. I see Hailey flush, then deliberately look away.

"It's kind of fun," Matt says, failing to notice the exchange. "I feel like I'm in a parade, waving at everybody like this."

We laugh. "You do seem to be having a particularly good time," I agree.

The final van pulls up, and the last batch of guests begins to pile out.

"God," Hailey groans. "How many are there?"

"Be positive," I order. "We know the routine. Nothing has changed."

"That's the problem!"

"Be careful what you wish for," I warn. And then, as though designed to illustrate my point, Stanley hops out of the van.

Dressed in an expensive suit with a bright purple tie, my agent and friend of ten years waves frantically, a huge smile stretching his handsome, Botoxed face.

"That guy's really excited," Matt says worriedly. He stops waving.

I'm momentarily speechless. Then I wince when I see Stanley press money into Connor's hand—and Connor look perplexed—before running toward me.

"Kate!" he shouts.

Hailey turns. "What the—?"

"Excuse me," I mutter, darting down the steps. Stanley envelops me in a massive bear hug, swinging my feet off the ground. He smells like lavender and home, and when he pulls away and clasps my hands in his, I feel the soft skin of his palms and note how clean and carefully buffed his nails are—the very opposite of what I've been learning to love for the past month.

"Look at you," he mutters, looking me over from head to toe. "Just look at you. You're stunning."

I'm wearing a denim skirt from the nineties and the standard ranch polo. My hair is pulled up in a bun, and I had just enough time to slap on mascara and lip gloss before coming downstairs. I'm anything but stunning.

I should say *thank you, welcome, it's so nice to see you,* but all that comes out is, "What on earth are you doing here?"

Stanley shrugs. "I thought you could use a friend."

And just like that, my eyes well up.

"Oh, Katie…" He hugs me, even as I remain as stiff and unyielding as a corpse.

"I'm working," I mumble. "Don't make me emotional."

"I'll be on my best behavior, I promise." He pulls back and looks around. "So this is it, huh?"

I follow his gaze. Around us guests are milling about, taking in the sights, following wranglers to their cabins. The mountains are perfect, beautiful in the early evening sun, and the sky and clouds look like something out of a pastoral scene. Shane is nowhere in sight, but Hailey and Lisa are still on the porch gawking at us.

"This is it."

Stanley turns back to me. "It's working for you."

"Stop."

"No, really," he insists. "It is. I thought you were insane when you told me you were coming to spend the summer in some shack in the forest, but it seems to be helping. You've got some color again. You're not just skin and bones."

I roll my eyes. "Thanks." Though I had been noticing my clothes getting a little snug. Stanley had referred to my six months at home before leaving for Thailand as "much needed palliative care," and had watched me like a hawk. As my next door neighbor and closest friend, he'd been the one to help me get my head on straight and find the courage to get back to traveling. Which hadn't worked out so well. After just three days in beautiful, wonderful Thailand, I knew I couldn't stay. All I wanted to do was hide out in my beach-side shack with the curtains drawn and a bottle of wine. When I'd called Stanley to tell him I was returning early to work at the ranch, he'd tried desperately to talk me out of it.

"Well," I say, smoothing my skirt. "Let me show you to your cabin."

When Stanley doesn't budge, I shoot him a suspicious look. And when he finally meets my eyes it's with that guilty little-boy face he knows I can't get mad at.

"Stanley," I say icily. "What have you done?"

There's a tap on my shoulder.

"Hi, Kate."

My jaw drops as I slowly turn around. Over Kevin Drew's suit-clad shoulder I see Hailey and Lisa leaning on the balcony, very close to drooling. My financial advisor and sometime fuck buddy is a handsome, sleek man who looks as though he would be equally at ease in the financial district as on the pages of a fashion magazine. He's smart, rich, and good company — all qualities I have enjoyed — and when he smiles, it's impossible not to smile back.

"Hi, Kevin. This is a surprise."

"I'm surprised too," he says. "And I don't mean your outfit. I didn't know I was coming out here until yesterday."

"Anton had to work." Stanley shrugs, referring to his surgeon husband. "And I wanted the double-occupancy rate."

"Of course."

"You look great," Kevin says. "Turn around."

I smirk. "Absolutely not."

He smiles. "Okay, then just walk ahead of us."

We all laugh. "Which cabin are you guys in?"

Stanley consults the brochure in his hand. "Cabin ten," he says.

I almost choke. "Ten?"

"Yeah, why? Is that one haunted?"

I shake my head. "No. No. Not at all. Let me show you the way."

Hailey, Matt, and Lisa grilled me incessantly about Kevin Drew until I was forced to describe him as an ex-boyfriend to make myself sound more principled than I really am. Was. Anyhow, now they're at O'Malley's, kicking off another week of drinking and dancing. I stayed behind to hang out with Stanley, who declined the offer to go out, even if it meant seeing the Summer Skank he'd heard so much about.

Now he and I soak in the hot tub with an assortment of tiny bottles of alcohol he pilfered from the airplane. Kevin claimed the fresh air was exhausting and begged off early, giving Stanley and me time to catch up.

"I still can't believe you're here," I say for the tenth time.

"So you keep saying."

"Why didn't you tell me?"

Stanley shrugs and sips his wine. "I was on a waiting list," he answers finally. "I didn't want to tell you I would be here if I wouldn't be."

"It's good to see you." It is, but even though Stanley is my favorite person in the world, his timing couldn't be worse. Work is crazy busy, I'm finally getting used to being country Kate, and I have no idea where Shane and I stand. There are a lot of things I need to wrap my brain around, but Stanley is a demanding mistress, and after traveling across the country to surprise me, will no doubt expect my full attention.

"So?" he says after a moment.

"So what?"

"Where's my picture?"

I laugh and finish my vodka, setting the bottle on the deck behind me. "There's no picture."

"Then where's the real deal? Here." He thrusts another bottle at me but I demur.

"No, thanks. I'm done."

"Katharine Burke, done at one?"

"Doesn't sound right, does it?"

"Something has gone horribly awry!"

"I'm older and wiser," I say seriously. "Which means I don't get drunk every night."

"Do you still dance on tabletops?"

"Nope."

He gasps. "Who are you and what have you done with my best friend?"

I snicker. "I left her behind," I confess. "On a beach somewhere. She couldn't hack it in the mountains."

"Don't you find it boring out here? Too...serene?"

It's my turn to shrug. "Sometimes."

"And sometimes..."

"And sometimes it's nice."

"All right, we've gotten off topic. Which one was he? The blond with the baggage? Because that man makes Kevin look like a donkey."

"No, not him. Did you see the redhead on the porch when you came up?"

"I did."

"That's Hailey. Those two have something going on, but can't figure out what."

"That's interesting. I thought the guy with the ponytail was ogling her. Is my sixth sense failing me?"

Stanley is excellent at sussing out relationships.

"No, your sixth sense is working. There's something there too. It's complicated."

"I love it, but stop trying to distract me. Which one is Shane?"

I sigh and wipe a damp hair off my neck, regretting that I ever divulged his name to Stanley. The guy is like a dog with a juicy bone. "Promise not to do anything to embarrass me?"

"No."

"He's the guy with the dark hair and cargo pants. He wasn't wearing cowboy boots—"

"Wait. The lumberjack?"

I burst out laughing. "Yes."

"Is he still ignoring you?"

I hesitate for a nanosecond, but Stanley catches it.

"Are you fucking him?" he exclaims.

"Stanley!" I hiss. "Lower your voice! This is a family establishment."

"Oh my God. How is he? Rough? Powerful? Enduring?"

"He's...great."

Stanley peers at me closely. "Do you *like* him?"

I open my mouth, but the denial won't come out. "I like him," I admit. "But I don't like-like him. He's just...It's casual. He made that clear."

"He's nuts. No way will he ever have his fill of you."

"Oh, Stanley. Now I remember why I like you."

It's almost one thirty when I head up to my room. If I'm being honest, I'm more than a little disappointed that Shane's not waiting in the hallway. I noticed a light on in his trailer on my way up the stairs, but I haven't seen him since the guests arrived. I switch on the ceiling fan and curl up on the bed. Though I expect to lay awake for hours, I fall instantly asleep.

The next two days are a blur of work and Stanley. While I clean cabins between breakfast and lunch, he and Kevin join the other guests on horseback rides, something Stanley describes as "both dreadful and thrilling." In lieu of my afternoon naps, we hike, lounge at the pool, or sit in their cabin catching up.

Kevin is a big hit with pretty much every female guest and staff member, but still doesn't seem comfortable with this rustic environment. Stanley finds it all hilarious and is having a great time.

The two of us are alone in the cabin on Tuesday afternoon—Kevin is going back to the pool to give the women something to drool over—and as we watch his tanned body walk away, Stanley sighs. "What a waste."

I look at him. "What are you talking about? Is everything okay with you and Anton?"

"Not me, you fool. I brought him out here for you."

"What?"

"Anton's not working. He laughed his ass off when I suggested he come with me to a dude ranch. He thought it was a gay sex resort."

"I have no idea what you're talking about."

"I thought you and the lumberjack were still fighting, so I brought Kevin along to relieve your sexual frustration."

I stare at Stanley in horror. "You did not."

"What?"

"He's not a call girl! You can't fly him out to have sex with people!"

"Please. You know he'd be more than willing."

"Does he know that's why he's here?"

"No. He still believes Anton's working. And the double-occupancy thing. Plus I told him you were having a hard time. He came because he cares about you."

Kevin is almost as good with his hands, tongue, and cock as he is at managing my money, and if I had nothing better to compare it to, I'd declare him pretty damn great in bed. But knowing the things Shane is capable of, my time with Kevin is just a hazy memory.

"That is mortifying," I say.

"I was trying to help."

"Thank you."

Stanley laughs. "Did you take tomorrow night off?"

"I did." He and Kevin are going stir crazy stuck at the ranch, so we made reservations at a nice restaurant in town.

"Good. I need some traffic, you know? Rude people, congestion, high prices. All this…peace is giving me a headache."

"Which town do you think you're going to? Dawson has about two thousand people."

"Goddammit."

"I have to go start setting up for dinner," I tell him as I stand. "Some of us have jobs."

Stanley flicks a hand. "Bring me some ale, wench!"

I laugh. "That's not how it works here."

He winks. "We'll see."

No one complains about being called "wench" during dinner service, so I assume Stanley behaves himself for the meal. I'm on dish duty tonight, which means I'm the one who stays behind to mop up the kitchen floor when everyone else has gone. I push the last load of dishes into the sanitizer and turn back to collect the mop, coming to a halt when I see Shane enter through the back door, a stack of dirty dinner plates in hand.

"Hey," I say awkwardly.

He scans my rubber apron and yellow gloves. "Hey."

He brushes past me with the dishes, and I follow, mop bucket in tow. He drops the dishes in the sink and starts to rinse them. I linger behind him.

"I can do that."

"It's no trouble."

"Okay."

When he doesn't look at me I start mopping. I normally hate mopping, but this feels excruciating. The last time we spoke was after the most intense sexual experience of my life, and now it feels like we're back at day one, strangers.

"How do your friends like it out here?"

I look at Shane, who looks away quickly, sticking a plate in the rack.

"Um, they like it. Though they've described things as being a little too 'serene.'"

"Is that what you think?"

"What?"

"Do you miss the city?" He over-enunciates, as though I'm hard of hearing. "Is this place too simple for you?"

I frown. "No. It's not too simple. I love it here." I have a sneaking suspicion he's wondering if I think he's simple too, but when he acts like this it's difficult to tell him otherwise.

"So how is it you know them?"

"Um, Stanley is my best friend and agent, and Kevin is just someone I've known for a few years. We run in the same circles."

Shane nods, jaw tight.

"What have you been up to?" I ask. "I haven't seen much of you."

"Working." The sanitizer finishes, and he wrenches the door open, shoving out the clean dishes and pushing the next load in before slamming the door and hitting the power button.

"Okay, well—"

"That guy's your ex-boyfriend?"

"Kevin? No, not really."

"That's what everyone's saying."

"That's kind of what I told them, to get them to stop asking questions."

"So you were never together?"

"We never dated."

"But you fucked him."

"Shane!"

"What? I'd just like to know what I'm dealing with."

"I beg your pardon?"

He shrugs, wiping water off the counter. "He's your type, that's all. You already know my type."

I feel the blood drain from my cheeks. Is he throwing Cassidy Reyes in my face?

"Why would you say that?" I demand. "What did I do to deserve that?"

He slams down the wet cloth. "You haven't done a damn thing."

"I had no idea they were coming, Shane."

"Of course not."

"Why would I lie about this?"

"So it didn't look like you were killing time until your *GQ* boyfriend showed up to take over?"

"Do not insult me." I feel my chin quiver, but am determined not to cry.

"Don't insult you? You're the one who thanked me for my 'services' on Sunday!"

"I thanked you for helping me clean. I already told you that!"

"Sure, Kate."

"I've been busy with work, Shane. And when I'm not working I'm trying to be polite and hang out with the people who flew three thousand miles to surprise me. I'm not ignoring you."

"So where have you been these past couple days? You know where my trailer is."

"I just told you!"

"All right. Well, thanks for the fun. Have a great summer."

"I don't know why you're acting like this. You're the one who said you wanted a one-time thing, something casual."

A cruel smile twists Shane's face. "You're right, Kate. I did. Thanks for the bonus rounds."

And then he leaves.

I don't see Shane the next day, but Hailey tells me Brandon's given up cornering her—his new pastime since their early morning kiss—so I take it Shane's on the warpath again.

By the time Stanley and Kevin are ready for our evening out, I'm antsy. Because we're going "out on the town" (Stanley's words), I'm wearing my one nice item of clothing: a pretty emerald green dress with a cinched waist that ends just above the knee, and a pair of gold heels. Lisa has styled my hair so it hangs in curls over my shoulders—declaring it "so much better than normal" and earning a snort of laughter from Hailey, who has been watching enviously.

"You're sure I can't come?" she says again. She's been trying to put off Matt's advances, but the guy is cute and charming and with Brandon's mercurial behavior, she hasn't been entirely successful.

"Sorry. You're in charge while I'm away."

"I know this is your first night off in forever, but it still feels incredibly unfair."

I smile. "You'll be okay."

"Have fun with your handsome men."

"Will do."

I wave goodbye and head down the stairs. It's just after five, and I want to be out of the way before guests start showing up for dinner.

I hold on to the railing and step carefully, watching my ankles sway. High heels have been my normal footwear for most of my adult life, but I feel like I've forgotten how to walk in them. Or it may just be the splintering wood steps and gravel road that make it difficult.

I reach the bottom of the stairs and wave at Stanley and Kevin, who wait in front of the ranch vans. A chill runs up my spine, and I make the unwise decision to glance toward the Airstream—and the man leaning against it, arms folded across his chest, watching me. Our eyes lock, and Shane doesn't look away.

I don't know what he wants from me, but I know what I want from him: an apology. But he's stubborn and stupid, and I know it's not forthcoming, so instead I settle for distance. And revenge.

I turn on my brightest smile and aim it at Kevin Drew.

Chapter Sixteen

"Tell us everything," Lisa demands the next morning. I'm limping in my cowboy boots as I hurry around the kitchen preparing toast and coffee for guest breakfasts.

"I already did," I insist. "We went shopping—"

She and Hailey swoon.

"…followed by dinner at Alberto's, then dancing at Wild Rose." Hence the aching feet. Both Stanley and Kevin can dance, and dance we did. Then, despite the fact that it was nearly two o'clock when we returned to the ranch, they drunkenly insisted that I come to their cabin to teach them how to line dance in preparation for tonight's festivities. As the designated driver, I'd found the lesson to be slightly less hilarious, though I am curious to see how they make out this evening.

"God," Lisa sighs. "Two handsome men fighting for your affection…How do you handle it?"

"Neither of them were fighting for anything," I point out. "Stanley's married—to a man—and Kevin had to beat off women with a stick all night. Women much prettier—and wearing much less clothing—than me."

She scoffs. "Let me have my fantasy."

"I thought you did have your fantasy. What's wrong with Pete?"

She shrugs. "Nothing's wrong, exactly. It's just...He doesn't really try."

Hailey returns with dirty plates and listens in. "Who doesn't try?"

Lisa looks around to make sure the coast is clear. The only other person in the kitchen is Alec, who's used to our talk.

"Pete," she whispers. "I think I made a mistake becoming his girlfriend so fast, you know? So now he doesn't have to try to make me like him. He just assumes I do."

Matt enters with a tray of glasses. "Sorry to break up the gabfest, but can we get some help out there, please?"

Lisa snatches up a tray and disappears. Hailey and I exchange a look.

"Did an eighteen-year-old girl just give us some pretty sound advice?" she asks.

I'm equally horrified. "She may have."

There's a knock on the in door, and we look up to see Stanley waving from the dining room. "Check out my new duds," he tells Hailey when she ushers him in. "I'm a cowboy!" He's modeling last night's purchases: tight jeans, plaid shirt, boots, and white hat.

Hailey whistles. "You look phenomenal."

Stanley tips his hat. "Thank you, milady."

I swat at him. "Get out of here, you idiot. No one says milady. It's not sixteen ten."

"Duly noted."

Stanley shuffles out, and Hailey looks at me. "Don't tell me that man's not trying," she says.

I don't see Shane until after dinner. We're finishing up in the kitchen, and he's been recruited to help move tables to prepare for the dance. I exit via the laundry room so I don't have to pass him to get outside.

Upstairs Hailey and I bemoan that we have to go to the dance in the first place, then grumble that we have nothing to wear. "Wear the dress from last night," she urges. "You washed it, right? It's good as new."

"I don't want to wear it," I complain. "If I wear it I'll have to wear the shoes, and my feet hurt. Why don't you wear it?"

Hailey hesitates, and I realize she wants to.

"Go for it," I urge. "As you say, it's clean, and it will look amazing with your hair. Put it on. Shoes too." We're the same size, and after a little rustling behind my closet door, the dress looks awesome on her fit figure. "Matt and Brandon are going to duel over you, milady."

She snorts and twirls in front of the mirror. "Stanley and Kevin said you gave them dance lessons," she says, pinning up her hair.

I laugh. "Yeah. They were drunk, though. We'll see how much they remember."

"Shane's coming."

I'd been sorting through a pile of clothes for something to wear, and I freeze at the words. I'd assumed Shane would be at the dance, so that's not what has me suddenly immobile — it's something in her voice. I turn to meet Hailey's gaze in the mirror.

"What's going on with you two?" she asks.

I look at my hands, wrapped around a wrinkled yellow sundress, and make a show of smoothing it out.

"Kate."

"I don't know," I mumble.

"What's been going on? Brandon's been mentioning Shane's mood swings, and I've started to realize that they correspond with yours: When he's happy, you're happy. When he's not, you're not."

"I'm not nearly as bad as him!"

"No, you're not mean, but there's something there, isn't there?"

I nod, guilty. "Please don't say anything," I plead. "We promised to keep it casual…to keep it a secret."

"Why would he want to keep you a secret? You're a million miles out of his league."

"That's not true." I think of his words the other night in the kitchen. Shane feels that way too — he thinks *I* feel that way. Though after his insulting behavior, he might be right.

"Are you two fighting?"

"He's mad that Kevin's here," I admit. "He heard we used to have a thing and now…He thinks I knew they were coming, even though

I had no idea. He wouldn't listen to anything I said, either. He just decided: judge, jury, executioner. It was awful."

"I asked Brandon what was up with his hot-and-cold behavior, and he said that at the beginning of the summer Shane told them to stay away from the staff, that he was tired of his workers getting in trouble for following their dicks."

"That sounds like Shane."

"But he's not taking his own advice."

"And he's taking it out on everybody else."

"So ironically, he may have had a point."

I can't help but laugh.

The dance is in full swing when we get downstairs. The dining room is packed, but it takes less than half a second to spot Stanley's white hat bobbing in the middle of the dance floor. I smile as I watch him twirl an elderly female guest around the room, though my smile quickly fades when I see the familiar shape of Shane's broad back—and the fingers stroking up and down it. They turn, and I recognize the profile of the cougar from cabin four.

"Alert, alert," Hailey intones. "Incoming."

I turn to see Brandon weaving his way through the throng to reach us. "Cover me," she hisses. "I'm going in." Then she disappears into the dancing crowd, ducked low so Brandon can't follow her red hair. The green dress, on the other hand, stands out like a beacon in the sea of denim.

"Well," Brandon says, stopping at my side. "That could've gone better."

I shrug. "Sorry."

The band kicks off a slow number, and he takes my hand. "Let's dance."

I try to protest, but his grip is unyielding, and soon I'm wrapped in his arms, shuffling awkwardly from side to side. Brandon knows how to dance, but given Shane's proximity and general temperament, I can't help but feel like he's putting himself in harm's way. He's a complete gentleman, however, keeping one hand firmly above my waist, the other holding mine.

After a moment he says something, but I can't hear it over the music.

"What?"

"Where'd she get that dress?" he repeats, mouth near my ear. I follow his gaze over my shoulder, where Hailey dances with a guest.

"What's going on, Brandon? You kiss her, you ignore her…Which is it?"

"The first one, definitely." A pause. "Unless it's the second one."

"She's not going to wait for you to make up your mind, you know."

"She's not exactly waiting, is she?" He scowls as we watch Matt cut in, pulling Hailey close as they dance. She smiles and hides her face in his shirt. She looks happy, not like my conflicted, tormented friend of recent weeks.

"Maybe you're too late."

The song ends and Brandon releases me. "Maybe."

I turn to leave the floor and find something to drink, but crash right into Stanley, who was standing behind us, waiting his turn. He bows. "Milady."

"Where do you think you are, exactly?"

He takes my hands and dances to the upbeat number. "I think I love it here," he shouts over the music. "I'm considering moving!"

"You really look the part!"

"I know!"

He lifts my hand over my head and twirls me. My skirt spins, and the world whooshes past as I turn, coming to an abrupt halt as I bang into Shane's shoulder. He turns to look at me, dark eyes too close, too knowing.

"Sorry," I mumble to him and the cougar he's still dancing with. Stanley tugs me back, and I glare at him. "You did that on purpose!"

"What's with the freeze out?" he asks, watching Shane over my shoulder. "The man's burning up and icy cold. What's going on?"

"Nothing's going on," I admit. "Not anymore."

"What?"

"I don't want to talk about it."

"Well, you look fabulous. Every man in the room is looking at you in this wonderful yellow cotton dress with just one small stain on the hem."

"Thank you. That means a lot."

He kisses my cheek. "Any time."

The band switches to a popular country song, and Kevin appears behind Stanley. "May I?" he asks.

Stanley winks at me. "You absolutely may."

I kick him in the shin as he two-steps away, and Kevin takes my hand, expertly executing the steps he learned last night. "You're a pro," I laugh.

"Right? The music just moves me. Even in jeans so tight they threaten the lives of my future children."

Aw. I'd forgotten that in addition to being smart, handsome, and super rich, Kevin Drew is funny.

"Stanley said you worked here when you were a teenager?"

"Yeah, for three summers." We're dancing closer now so we can hear each other over the music. "I loved it."

He looks out the window at the mountains and the dark sky overhead, filled with a thousand twinkling stars. "I can see why. It looks good on you."

"A little fresh air works wonders."

He scoffs. "Kate, you're getting more than fresh air."

I laugh in surprise. "Kevin!"

He winks. "Nothing gets past me. Tell me about him. He's not what I would've picked for you."

"There's no longer anything to tell."

"Liar."

"It's true."

"Come on. No matter how much I wined and dined you, you never looked at me like you look at him."

"You didn't want me to look at you like that."

He shrugs and avoids my eyes. "You never know."

Over Kevin's shoulder I catch a flash of white. Stanley is jumping up and down, waving to get my attention. "Let's get some fresh air," I suggest.

Kevin spots Stanley and takes my hand, tugging me down the hall after him. We follow Stanley outside into a group of guests who had the same idea.

"Is there somewhere we can go?" Stanley asks, looking around.

I lead them to the steps outside the kitchen and close the gate behind us, then notice Stanley has a ridiculous-looking satellite phone in his hand.

"What on earth are you doing with a satellite phone?" I demand. "This is supposed to be a vacation!"

"I have to go back early," Stanley admits. "Duty calls. Quite literally."

I try not to whine. "What? When?"

"Tomorrow."

"So soon? You've barely stayed for half your visit."

Kevin stands and clears his throat. "If we're leaving early, there's something I have to do."

Stanley snorts. "More like someone."

I look between them. "Who?"

Kevin avoids my eyes so Stanley answers. "Lana."

"The wrangler?"

"That's the one."

Kevin backs toward the gate and pushes it open. "Excuse me." He disappears into the dark, the door swinging shut.

"Maybe Kevin can find something to love about ranch life after all," I muse.

"I don't think love is what he has in mind."

I turn back to my friend. "You really have to go?"

"I'm sorry, Kate. I want to stay, really, but this place got a last-minute cancellation, and I shoved a lot of things aside to come. If I thought you needed me I'd stay in a heartbeat, but…You seem okay. Better."

I think back to my last fight with Shane. How ironic it is that things were fine before Stanley came to save me, and now they're a mess. But I'm not going to guilt trip him. He's been beating himself up long enough.

"You don't have to worry about me," I tell him.

Stanley hugs me. "I didn't used to."

"I'm okay. Really."

"Call me if you need anything. Like a new wardrobe. Anything."

I've got first shift the next morning and despite getting to bed at a relatively early hour, I'm still yawning when the wranglers show up for breakfast.

"Morning," I say, pouring coffee. I take a second look at Lana—a strong, pretty wrangler who grew up on ranches—and wonder how her evening went with Kevin Drew. If her flushed cheeks and relaxed demeanor are any indication, she found quite a lot to like.

"Hey, Kate," Brandon says, entering through the front doors, followed by Connor and Chase, the other ranch hand. Connor snatches a bagel and hurries out the door—he's the one driving Stanley and Kevin into town to catch their early flight.

"Hey." I take breakfast orders, trying not to watch the clock. The wranglers and ranch hands are normally gone by six thirty, and when six thirty comes and goes with no sign of Shane, a sense of dread builds in my stomach.

Lisa, Pete, and Hailey show up at seven. Something feels off—there's tension between Lisa and Pete, and even Hailey is avoiding my eyes. I try to question her, but hungry guests pour in and she hurries away with a coffee pot and order pad. Alec's got today off, so it's just Mark working, and I help chop fruit and mix French toast batter, this time without spilling the vanilla.

Suddenly a delicious, sugary aroma reaches my nose and I sniff, looking around. "What is that?" I ask.

Mark looks at me. "What's what?"

"That heaven-sent smell."

He laughs and holds up a donut, so freshly made I can see the heat wafting off of it. "You mean this?"

My mouth waters, and I forget my earlier anxiety. "Since when do we make donuts?"

"Alec said I could try something new, so last night I whipped up some dough and this morning we're making them to order."

"Oh God. Am I allowed to place an order?"

"I ordered for you. This one's yours."

I bite into the cinnamon sugar-covered ring of paradise and close my eyes. "I'm dying. This is so good."

"I'm glad you like it."

"They're going to forget all about Alec. This place will be your kingdom."

Mark laughs. "That was my plan. Donut domination."

I finish the donut and lick my fingers. "Thank you. I needed that."

"Any time."

I spot a flash of movement over his shoulder and see Shane just inside the back door. He sets down a stack of plates from last night's dinner and freezes when our eyes lock. I expect his usual anger, but instead find something else: He looks tortured. Guilty. But before I can ask what's wrong, he's gone.

"The donuts are a big hit, Mark," Lisa says, coming in with tray of dirty glasses.

"Thanks, Lisa."

Hailey enters with a new order, and I drag her to the side. "What's going on?" I demand. "You're acting weird, and I just saw Shane and he looks awful. Did something happen? Is everyone all right?"

"Kate..."

"Spit it out."

"Later, all right?"

"Hailey!"

"Everyone is okay. It's not that...It's just...Later, okay?"

"Lover's spat?" Matt asks, leaning against the counter and looking on with interest. "Don't let me interrupt."

Hailey uses the opportunity to escape.

Matt frowns. "What am I missing?"

I shake my head, frustrated. "Beats the hell out of me."

Hailey avoids me all morning. It's not until we're climbing the bunkhouse stairs after lunch that she gives me a look and follows me down the hall to my room.

"Ready to talk?" I ask, closing the door behind us.

She sits on my bed, holding something in her hand. "Please know," she begins, "that in no way do I want to be the one to show you this."

My earlier anxiety returns in full force. "What is it?"

"And," she continues, when I sit next to her, "the only reason I'm doing this at all is because if I don't, you'll hear from someone else."

"This is torture. You know that, right?"

She sighs. "I know." Then she hands me a cell phone.

"What's this?"

I don't recognize the phone, but Hailey says it isn't hers as she fiddles with the buttons on the screen, eventually finding the video she's looking for and pressing play. The screen is relatively large but it's dim, and even with the audio it takes me a moment to realize it's footage from O'Malley's.

"Am I on here?" I ask. "When was this taken?"

"Last night. You're not on it."

I've been the featured star of the past videos I've seen, so I'm not sure what the problem might be. The footage is bouncy and largely unfocused, but at the fifty-second mark I see what Hailey didn't want me to see. Shane.

And Cassidy.

Together.

He sits with his back to a table, empty glasses and beer bottles littering the scene. Connor and Chase look on, laughing, as Cassidy straddles Shane in his seat, her horrifyingly short skirt riding up high enough to show the underside of her ass. She begins to grind against him, hips gyrating in time with the slow music, and his eyes are locked on her face. I recognize that look. Desire. Determination. Control.

I inhale painfully as I watch his hands trail up the outsides of her thighs, catching under the hem of that short skirt and offering us a peek of her red thong before moving up higher, over her tiny waist, fingers stroking the sides of her massive breasts.

He cups her face, she lowers her head, and the video is just clear enough to show her tongue slipping into his willing mouth as the crowd cheers.

Fingers numb, I hand the phone back to Hailey.

"Kate," she whispers. "I'm so sorry."

It's stupid, but my eyes fill with tears. "I'm such an idiot," I moan.

"You're not an idiot."

"I shouldn't even care. After the stuff he said to me...Even from the beginning, he—he didn't want anyone to know, and I just... Who else knows?"

A pause. "Pretty much everyone," Hailey says. "But no one knows about the two of you, so they just seem entertained by the news that Shane—the one who forbids his workers from having any fun at all—went out and did...that...last night."

"But he was at the dance."

"He left halfway through. I saw him go."

"To her." Tears spill down my cheeks, and I swipe them away angrily.

"He's an asshole."

"I know."

"He doesn't deserve you."

"I know."

"You can do so much better."

"Don't tell anyone about this, okay? About me?"

"Of course not." Then Hailey sets down the phone, wraps her arms around my shoulders, and lets me cry.

Chapter Seventeen

Friday night is the guests' last evening, and the dining room is full of rambunctious tourists unwilling to admit it's the end of their vacation. We're run off our feet, which is a blessing, because it prevents me from dwelling on the footage that's been running on a loop through my mind all day.

It shouldn't hurt this much, I think. *I barely know the guy.* We had sex a handful of times, and he's moved on. I knew this would happen. Hell, I even warned myself about it. This thing was bound to end. I guess I just thought it would be over when I left, not when he did. When he went to *her.*

I drop dirty dishes onto the counter with enough force that Pete—on dish duty tonight—jumps. "What did I do now?" he asks, resigned. I look at his smooth, guileless face and can't help but smile.

"Nothing," I say. "Sorry."

"It's something," he says. "Lisa's barely speaking to me. You and Hailey are always running off together."

"You didn't do anything," I assure him. "Really." That's actually exactly the problem, but I'm hardly in a position to dole out relationship advice, so I return to the dining room and keep a smile plastered on my face.

"Coming to O'Malley's, Kate?" Lisa asks when dinner service finally ends.

I shake my head. I may never return. "No," I say. "I'm going to bed early."

She pouts. "Hailey won't go either. Nobody's going."

Pete pipes up. "I'll go."

Lisa spares him a glance. "Um, never mind."

Pete, Matt, and I watch her leave. "Tell me she's not mad," Pete insists.

"Dude, she's mad," Matt says.

I try not to smile.

"What did I do?"

Matt slings an arm around his shoulder and leads him out of the kitchen. "Women," he begins, "are complicated, beautiful creatures…"

"What are you still doing here?" asks a voice behind me.

I turn to see Mark tying on an apron.

"Just finishing up," I reply. "What brings you back?"

He hefts a container of flour onto the counter. "Donuts."

"Mmm. Donuts."

"I could use an assistant."

"Like a sous chef?"

"More like an assistant. You in?"

I glance out the window. I can see Connor, Brandon, and Chase piling into a pickup, heading home for the night. That means Shane will be alone, and if I don't take up Mark on his offer, so will I.

"I'm in."

The next morning I'm on first shift again, only this time when I enter the dining room with a pot of coffee, I see Shane sitting with the other ranch hands, his back to me.

Hailey and I debated my best course of action and settled on honoring the original agreement Shane and I made: casual, no-strings attached. If he knows how hurt I am, things will be weird and awkward, so I'll act like everything's fine. Like we've both moved on. Easy.

I pour coffee for the wranglers and take orders, returning with a fresh pot for the ranch hands.

"Morning," I say brightly.

"Hey, Kate," Brandon answers.

I hear Chase and Connor mumble tired greetings, but nothing from Shane. I'm tempted to look at him, but a sudden ache in my chest suggests that's not a wise idea.

I pull out the order pad. "What's everyone having?"

Brandon, Chase, and Connor order copious amounts of food—and donuts—and finally it's just Shane left. I turn toward him, but can't seem to lift my gaze from the order pad, pen poised. I don't want to look at him. I know he'll see something more than I want him to see. But he's not speaking and things are getting weird, so finally I raise my eyes to meet his.

His dark eyes burn. His face is impassive, but the eyes say it all. Everything I want to hear but can't possibly bear to. I look away. "Any time now," I say, prompting a laugh from the ranch hands.

"Just coffee," he answers.

I exhale and hurry back to the kitchen, pouring a glass of water and drinking it quickly. *It will get better*, I remind myself. *You'll just ask Hailey to take first shift. Or Lisa. Or anyone else.* There's no way I'm going to be able to handle the rest of the summer in close proximity to Shane if I don't get over this.

"Order up," Mark calls, and I pick up the hot plates. "I've got your order here," he adds, gesturing to a plate stacked high with steaming donuts.

"Are those the ones your sous chef made?" I ask, straight-faced. "I heard she's really talented."

He shrugs. "She's all right."

I'm laughing as I back through the door and distribute the plates to the wranglers. I can see Shane watching me, but I deliberately keep my eyes averted, a smile on my face. The guests will be gone after lunch, then the kitchen/cabin girls (Matt and Pete aren't entirely okay with the name, but have been out-voted) and I are heading into town for the rest of the day, giving me some much-needed distance.

A short time later the dining room is packed with hungry guests, and Mark is cooking like a fiend. "Kate," he calls when I return with plates. "Can you take out the trash? Sorry to ask, but I'm swamped."

"Of course," I say, setting down the dishes. "No problem."

I drag the metal can to the back door and tie off the bag before tipping it sideways onto the deck and hopping down to the ground to pull it out. The bag is so large and heavy that this is the only way any of us have ever managed to budge it.

I don't hear Shane approach, but I certainly feel it as his chest presses against my back and his arm reaches over mine to take the bag. "Let me help," he says. I feel his breath on my neck, and goose bumps spring up along my spine.

I don't move as he pulls the bag free and sets it on the ground. Then he doesn't move either, standing so close behind me that I can feel the warmth of his body on my back.

"Move," I say softly.

"I wanted to talk—"

I push back with my ass so he's forced to move, then climb up the steps to the kitchen. "There's nothing to talk about."

"Kate."

I can't look at him, so I stare at his hand, clenched around the neck of the bag.

"Thanks for your help," I say.

"It's so nice to get away," Hailey remarks as we pull into town later that afternoon.

"You can say that again," Pete agrees.

Matt shrugs. "I don't know. I like it there."

We all groan.

"You're so disgustingly positive," Hailey accuses.

To my tremendous surprise, Matt leans over and kisses her square on the mouth. "You like it," he answers, then climbs out.

Hailey's eyes meet mine in the rearview mirror. I raise my eyebrows in question, but she merely blushes and shrugs before exiting the van. I guess she's made her choice.

"What's first?" I ask when we're all on the sidewalk.

"Shopping," Lisa says instantly.

I smile. I know exactly how she feels. Though I grew up in a wealthy family, working at the ranch was the first time I ever earned my own money, and I couldn't wait to spend it. I felt incredibly rich and powerful, though when I got home at the end of that first summer, I had fifty-five dollars in my bank account and nothing to show for it.

"Lead the way," I say.

Three hours later everybody's hot and tired. We're each carrying bags. Pete hasn't bought anything, but he's laden with Lisa's purchases. Apparently Hailey clued Matt in on Pete's girl troubles, and Matt has quietly been giving him advice on how to get back into Lisa's good graces—namely, work for it.

We drop the bags back at the van and debate where to go for dinner. After a brief discussion—helped along by our rumbling stomachs—we settle on a nearby Mexican restaurant and order far more than five people could possibly eat.

"So this is your fourth summer here, Kate?" Matt asks, once a mountain of guacamole has helped take the edge off our hunger.

"That's right," I say through a mouthful. "Hard to believe."

"First for everybody else?"

The group nods their agreement.

"Why?" I ask. "You thinking of coming back?"

He shrugs. "I don't know. It's fun—and different—but I don't know if I'd come back. How about you guys?"

Lisa says she's seriously considering it. Upon hearing her answer Pete quickly says the same thing, but Hailey hesitates.

"Hard to say," she says. "Nothing's as simple as it seems."

An older woman comes by with a basket of roses, and Matt buys one for Hailey. After a stern look from his older, wiser friend (Matt, not me), Pete buys one for Lisa, who beams. "Thank you," she says, hugging him.

Pete looks relieved, and I glance away in time to see Matt and Hailey exchange a look that's far more meaningful than I would have expected. Suddenly there's nowhere else for me to turn, so I leave for the restroom, eager to get away from the lovefest. It's hardly my first time being the lone single in a group of couples, but all the other times were on trips abroad when everyone was a stranger to me and there was no one I wished would buy me flowers.

There's no one now, I remind myself. *Have some pride.* He fucked Cassidy Reyes. There's no coming back from that.

After dinner we practically roll back to the van. I'm stuffed and a little nauseous. "Want to walk this off?" Matt suggests. "Just look around?"

Everyone agrees we're not ready for the winding, bumpy drive back to the ranch just yet, and we stroll the pretty streets of downtown Dawson. Most of the shops sell country-western gear—some for tourists, some for real cowboys—and we laugh when we find a mannequin clad in the same outfit Stanley wore to the dance.

"Hey, I want to stop in here," Matt says when we pass a bookstore. "Let's check out Kate's book."

Hailey looks at me. "You have a book?"

I hesitate. "I—Yeah, I do," I answer. "It's nothing."

"It's great," Matt says, holding the door as we all enter. When I pass by he whispers, "Sorry, was I not supposed to say anything?"

I shake my head. "No, it wasn't a secret." There's just no smooth way to work "So, I wrote a book!" into conversation.

Matt leads the way to the travel section, scans the Bs and—to my surprise and everyone else's excitement—extracts the lone copy of *The Sunshine Schools* by Katharine Burke. Hailey and Lisa *ooh* and *ahh* over my name and picture on the cover of "a real book," as Lisa describes it, and I blush, a little bit embarrassed, a little bit proud. Despite my vows to be older and wiser this summer, my poor decisions have given me little else to be proud of.

"I'm buying it," Hailey announces. "And then I'm going to read it. Just think—a real, live writer in our midst, and we didn't even know it."

"You knew it," I point out.

"Well, I knew about the articles, not the book. This is different. This has your picture on it."

"You look so pretty, Kate," Lisa gushes. "So glamorous." A pause. "I mean, not that you aren't pretty now. You're just…different."

Everyone laughs at her discomfort. "Got it," I say, patting her on the shoulder. "Compliment sort of taken."

I follow Hailey to the checkout while everyone else continues to browse.

"Why didn't you tell me you had a book?" she asks, scanning the accolades on the back. "A number one bestselling book?"

"It's a very awkward thing to bring up." I purse my lips and try to sound boastful-casual. "Oh, speaking of bestselling things…"

She laughs and places the book on the counter. "I suppose."

The cashier scans the book, then turns it over in her hands. "Is this good?" she asks.

Hailey looks at me. I'm not about to toot my own horn. "I don't know," she replies. "I haven't read it yet. But I've heard good things."

"I just sold a copy last week," the cashier tells us, putting the book in a bag. "We hardly ever sell travel books. Must be popular."

"It's awesome," Matt says, overhearing. "The author is a friend of mine."

I shoot him a warning look, and he doesn't embarrass me further.

"Thank you," I say, and we all head back to the van.

The next morning is Changeover Sunday. One week since the last time Shane and I had sex. Since the day he made me feel things I didn't think were possible. With the memory of Shane's visit lingering, I ask Hailey if she'll work with me. We normally clean cabins solo, but I feel like I need moral support.

And sure enough, Shane stops by the second cabin. We're making the beds in the guest bedroom when there's a sharp knock on the door, followed by his voice. "Kate?"

Hailey and I exchange a look. "She's in here," Hailey calls innocently.

"Who is that? Hailey?"

Shane stops in the bedroom doorway. I keep my back to him and focus on making my hospital corners particularly tight.

"Did you need something?" I say, not turning around.

Shane sighs. "Mary asked me to tell you we're going to have two extra staying in here this week. Last-minute addition. She wants you to make up the pull-out couch."

I stand and spread the quilt on the bed. "Okay. Thank you."

"You going to turn around?"

"What for?"

There's a pause, then he curses under his breath and leaves.

When the slamming door stops ringing in my ears I turn to Hailey. "How was that?"

She nods. "Very strong."

"It was stupid."

"No, it was great."

"He'll know I care if I can't even make eye contact."

She nods and avoids my gaze.

"What?" I press. "What?"

"Well…maybe it's best you don't look at him."

"Why? Does he look different?"

"No. He looks the same. But the way he looks at you…That's what's different. Like he's not trying to hide it."

"It's too late."

"I know."

"Can you go get the extra sheets?"

"Yep."

"And if you see Shane moving this way can you come racing back to protect my honor?"

"Absolutely."

But Shane doesn't come back, and I don't "see" him again until later that afternoon when the guest vans arrive. As we do each week, the staff stands on the front porch and smiles and waves. Brandon's barely able to conceal his hatred for Matt as he and Hailey stand just a little too close, and Shane doesn't hide the fact that he's staring at me while he helps the guests out of the van.

Hank and Mary are up front, which is unusual, greeting the guests and chatting amiably about what they can expect from their visit. When the bags are loaded and most of the guests have dispersed, I send everyone into the dining room to prepare for dinner service.

"Kate," Shane calls.

I freeze mid-step. The door to the lodge is so close, all I have to do is reach out my hand, pull it open, and dash inside. My arm is extended and freedom is mine when I hear Hank say, "Kate. Shane's calling you."

I plaster on a pleasantly surprised expression and turn. "Oh, sorry. I didn't hear." *Dammit.* I can't very well run away while Hank and Mary are here. I owe them at least the pretense of professionalism.

"Can I talk to you for a second?" Shane asks. His voice is raised to cover the distance from the vans to the lodge.

I shoot a look at Hank and Mary—they're barely listening.

"Can it wait?" I ask tersely, remaining on the porch. Behind me I can hear the sounds of chairs being pulled out as the guests take their seats.

Shane crosses his arms. "It won't take long."

"Go for it, Kate," Mary says absently. "They're just sitting down now. You have a few minutes."

I force a smile. "Okay. Great."

"In here," Shane says, entering the barn.

Oh hell no. I know for a fact that the ranch hands are still out delivering luggage, and I am not going anywhere alone with Shane. I stalk across the road and stop resolutely at the entrance to the barn. I risk a look over my shoulder just in time to see Hank and Mary disappear into the lodge, foiling my plan not to face Shane one-on-one.

"Come in here," he orders. It takes a minute for my eyes adjust to the dim lighting, and I spot him a few steps away, shuffling his feet.

"No."

"Kate."

"Shane."

"What are you afraid of?"

"Nothing," I say deliberately. "I think you've done your worst."

He takes a deep breath. He's still studying his feet. Finally he looks up at me, so handsome and wounded that it somehow manages to hurt even more.

"I'm sorry," he says.

"Don't."

"I'm so sorry about everything. Everything I said. Everything I did."

"You don't have to—"

"I do," he says forcefully, taking a step forward. For a second I think he's going to touch me, then he stops himself, fisting his hands at his sides. "For what I said to you in the kitchen and for the stuff at the bar—"

I feel my eyes well up, and I start to back away. "Don't do this now," I say tightly. "I have to go back in there and face everybody, and I can't—"

"Kate."

"No." I turn back to the lodge.

"I didn't fuck her."

The words stop me in my tracks, but I don't turn around.

"I know you saw the video. I know it was bad. But that's all that happened. I left right after. Nothing else…There was nothing else to see."

I'm trying so desperately not to cry. I don't know why Shane thinks this revelation will help—but it does. A very tiny bit. But not enough to turn around. I take another step toward the lodge, and this time he comes after me, gripping my arm and forcing me to look at him.

"Everyone can see," I say.

"Let them."

"No."

"Talk to me later then."

"There's nothing to say."

"You don't have to say anything. Just listen."

"Shane—"

"Please, Kate?"

This sudden change in demeanor is so extreme and so confusing that I really don't know how to feel. But the look in his eyes, the feel of his skin on mine…I curse myself, but it's enough to make me agree.

Chapter Eighteen

I'm stalling. After dinner service I insist it's time to de-lime the drinking glasses, claiming they look splotchy from the well water. And they do look a little splotchy...But not life-or-death splotchy like I'm making it out to be.

By the time the glasses are gleaming, everyone is hot and cranky, and I shoo them away so I can mop up. I'm alone for approximately thirty seconds before Shane appears in the back doorway.

"You done stalling?" he asks.

I keep my head down and focus on mopping very thoroughly. "No."

Wordlessly he takes the mop from my hands, scours the floor with rather impressive skill, and rolls the bucket back to the corner. "Let's go," he says.

I shoot him a suspicious look. "Go where?"

"To my trailer. Where do you think?"

"Let's talk here."

"In the kitchen?"

"Yes."

He sighs and runs a hand over his face. "Is that really what you want? Anyone can come by. Listen in."

I stare at his tormented face. I want him to be tormented. I want him to feel exactly how I feel (in addition to guilty)—like he lost something he didn't know he was going to miss quite so much.

"Please come to my trailer," he says quietly. "I won't touch you."

I nod and remove my apron, tossing it in the laundry pile with the others. I trail after him out the door, closing it behind us. The night is dark and warm, and the stars are out in full force. But all too soon we're standing awkwardly in Shane's living room, squaring off from opposite ends of the coffee table.

He just stares at me, those dark eyes seeing too much. When I can't take the silence anymore, I look away and cross my arms. "You wanted to talk," I say, pleased that my voice doesn't shake. "Talk."

"Do you want a drink?"

"No."

Shane sighs. "I'm sorry."

I study a piece of laminate flooring that has a bump in it. I'm surprised this squeaked past Shane's "detail-oriented" regime.

"Would you look at me?"

I want to stick out my chin and refuse, but worry that would make me look weak and childish. Eventually I raise my eyes.

"Kate, I'm sorry about what I said in the kitchen. It's none of my business who you've…dated. I know you didn't know your friends were coming. I shouldn't have said any of that stuff."

I blink and look away. This is the apology I wanted on Tuesday, pre-Cassidy Reyes. Now, who knows what I want. Will any apology cover the damage?

"But that's not the worst part. You saw the worst part on that damn video, and I'm sorry you did. I'm sorry you saw it, and I'm sorry I did it. I'm really, really sorry. I meant what I said earlier: I didn't fu—nothing else happened after the stuff on the tape. I went over there looking to blow off steam, drank too much, and one thing led to another. Next thing I know I'm sitting there realizing I don't want to be doing what I'm doing. I left before it went too far."

"Too far?"

Shane clears his throat. "Further, then."

I force myself to shake my head. "You said from the beginning that you wanted things to be casual. I can't blame you for anything. Like you said, I have my type, and apparently you have yours."

"Shit." Shane runs a hand through his hair. "I didn't mean that either, Kate. Maybe a month ago, before you showed up, I would've thought that was my type, but now…That's not what I want."

I blink away tears, but not before one slips out. I don't bother wiping it away. He's not falling for this unaffected act anyway. "Then why, Shane? Why run off to her when you knew I was more than willing?"

He starts to answer, but I interrupt. "That day in the cabin you asked if I wanted to be done, and *I said no*. Did you just want to hear me say I wanted more so you could be the first one out?"

"No. Jesus, no." Like before, Shane steps toward me but stops himself.

"Then why? Why her?"

He stares at his feet. He looks humbled and tortured, and it's not nearly as satisfying as I'd imagined. "Because I was jealous," he admits in a very low voice.

"What?"

He struggles to meet my eyes. "I was jealous."

"Of my gay agent and an old friend?"

"You left the dance with him!"

"What?"

"First you leave with them in that green dress—looking like some sort of…*fantasy*—and then you come back in the middle of the night and go to their cabin. Then you dance with him, and he takes your hand and leads you outside to do who knows what…"

It's taking me a minute to follow along, and finally I realize he's talking about when Kevin and I left the dance to talk to Stanley.

"Nothing happened!"

"I know that now." Shane sinks onto the couch and rests his elbows on his knees, studying the floor. "The next morning I heard how he and Lana had…Well, anyway, I knew you didn't—"

He looks up at me. "Kate, I was jealous. I've never been crazy about anyone this way. I don't act like this, I swear. You have me on edge. Everything about you catches my eye. I can't focus when you're near. And I guess I can't handle the thought of anyone else touching you."

"You didn't have to watch a video of someone else dry-humping me in a bar."

He squeezes his eyes shut. "I know."

"Someone you hate."

"I know."

"What do you want me to say, Shane? That every time you're angry it's okay to insult me and run to Cassidy Reyes so long as you apologize after?"

"No." He looks miserable.

"Then what?"

"I want you to say you'll take me back." It looks like it's killing him to utter such humbling words. And for a second I'm stunned.

"What?"

"I want to do this, Kate. For real. I know you're leaving, but until you go, I want to do this. No secrets. Not casual. Just...us."

I slump onto the far side of the couch, completely flabbergasted. There's no other word for it. I can't decide if I'm more shocked by the fact that he's actually saying these things, or that I'm seriously considering them. A week ago I would have jumped at the chance to be "real," but now that I know how "real" things can get, I don't know if I'm up for it.

"It'll never happen again," Shane says, facing me. "I swear it."

"How do you know?"

"Because I've never felt this bad in my life, and I don't want to feel this way again. You're too good for me, Kate. Everyone knows it. But what the fuck? Let's pretend we're equals for the next couple of months."

"We are equals."

"Then take me back."

"How can I trust you?" I wipe a tear off my cheek.

"I'll do whatever you want. As long as it takes. Just try again."

"If you touch her I'll kill you."

"Agreed."

"If you even talk to her."

"Whatever you want."

"I'm not going to fuck you because you apologized." *Even though I really want to.*

Shane clears his throat, like the words are a physical blow. "I understand."

"Well, all right then."

We sit stiffly on opposite ends of the couch, like a couple in the Victorian era.

He glances at me. "What now?"

"I guess I'll go back to my room."

"Okay."

I stand and smooth my skirt. "Good night."

Shane stands too, then goes to the door and pushes it open. I have to brush along his body to get outside, but I suppose that was the point.

"Good night, Kate."

I call up my self-control and refuse to throw myself at him, despite what my hormones are urging. I return to the lodge with my back straight, wounded pride on the mend.

Chapter Nineteen

I sleep through my alarm the next morning and stumble into the kitchen at seven thirty.

"Well, look who decided to show up," Hailey croons.

I glower at her and pour myself a cup of coffee.

"Late night?"

"Not really."

"So what happened?"

It's on the tip of my tongue to say nothing happened, but then I consider Shane's proclamation that he doesn't want things to be a secret, and I try to tell Hailey we're together. As in, *together*-together. But I can't. It feels weird.

"We talked," I say.

"About?"

"About—"

"Sleeping beauty hath arrived!" Matt announces, coming in with an empty coffee pot. "Thank you for joining us."

"Glad to be here." I shoot Hailey a look. "We'll talk later."

"You bet we will."

Midway through the service I'm making toast for a guest when I hear someone clear his throat. I already know who it is, but still my heart beats a little faster when I see Shane framed in the back doorway, thermos in hand.

"Morning," he says, watching me carefully.

"Morning."

"I came for some coffee."

"Sure."

He unscrews the thermos cap, and I pick up the fresh pot and fill him up.

"Thanks."

"You're welcome."

He glances over my shoulder, and I follow his gaze. No one's looking. The only person in the kitchen is Alec, and he's busy cooking.

"I guess I'll see you."

"Yeah. Okay." God. I sound like I'm thirteen. So does Shane.

"Right."

He hesitates, makes a move to leave, then turns back. "Come here, then."

I'm only a foot away, but I shuffle closer, as ordered. Eyes open, he bends down and presses his warm lips to mine. We linger for a moment, then pull back.

Shane clears his throat. "Later."

"Later." I watch him go.

When I turn around Hailey is right behind me, arms crossed. "*That's* what happened?" she asks, her tone a weird mix of surprised and smug.

I shift awkwardly. "Sort of."

"Well…"

"Do you think I'm pathetic?"

The corner of her mouth quirks up in a smile. "Honey, I think you're alive."

I return her smile and scurry off to work, but spend the rest of the morning unsuccessfully trying to dodge additional questions. I finally relent when she corners me in cabin seven and demands details in exchange for carrying back the load of dirty towels I've amassed. It's a fair trade, so I recap the previous night's making-up story and she leaves, satisfied.

After lunch I visit the pool to swim before my nap. When I came to the ranch I promised myself I'd swim regularly, but so far I've made it out just a handful of times. Fortunately the pool is free, and I'm just finishing my tenth lap when I feel the water shift as someone dives in.

I'm at the deep end, so I tread water and watch as a large, tan figure swims along the bottom of the pool, stopping in front of me. Shane floats up slowly, fingers trailing over my legs before releasing me when he surfaces.

"Hey." He smiles.

We're so close I can see the sun reflected in his eyes. The smile is contagious, and I can't stop one from spreading across my face. "Hey."

"Busy morning?"

"As always. You?"

"Same."

He runs a hand through his wet hair, water sluicing down the sides of his face. His foot bumps mine under water and our eyes meet. "Want to race?" he asks.

"I beg your pardon?"

"You heard me. Let's race."

"Where?"

"To the other end of the pool."

"What the hell for?"

"Are you afraid?"

I scoff. "Please."

"Then let's go. You ready?"

I can't believe this is happening. Who is this man? But I prepare myself to race. We each grip the side of the pool and brace our feet against the wall.

"On three," Shane says. "One, two, three."

We push off and race to the far end. My front crawl is decent, but Shane's is predictably stronger. He beats me by five lengths and waits in the shallow end until I pull up, breathing hard.

"Good try," he says.

"Shut up. You cheated."

"You want a head start?"

"Yes. Ten seconds."

He laughs. "That's how long it takes to complete the race!"

"Deal or not?"

He shakes my hand, calloused palm tickling mine. "Deal. I'll count when you leave. Whenever you're ready, Flipper."

I take a deep breath and push off, swimming hard. I can't hear anything over the sound of the splashing water, but I can see the end getting closer. And then a rough hand wraps around my ankle, yanking me to an abrupt halt. I flail for a second, then flounder as I see Shane swim past me.

"You did not just do that!" I shout, swimming to the far end.

"Do what?"

"Shane Maddox, who are you? Foreman, handyman, swim cheater?"

He smiles—a slow, sexy smile that reaches right between my legs. "I'm whatever you want me to be, Kate Burke."

"I want you to be you."

"Then yeah, I'm a swim cheater."

He swims closer, pinning me to the wall, an arm on either side of my head. I hook my hands over my shoulders and grip the ledge so I don't sink under, then close my eyes as moves in to kiss me. It's weird, the heat that rises inside me despite the cool water I'm immersed in. And it's distracting the way these simple, shy kisses touch somewhere inside that's not used to being found.

I wait for Shane to deepen the kiss, to push his fingers into my hair and hold me still for his tongue, but it doesn't come. He kisses me sweetly and thoroughly, but it's the kind of kiss that's not going to lead anywhere. Maybe it's because he's still apologizing or because he doesn't know how I'll react, or maybe it's just because we're in a public pool and anyone could come by, but he pulls away first and swims backward, watching me.

"I have to go track down a wayward calf," he says.

"Does that mean what I think it means?"

"If you think it means I'm going to go look for a lost baby cow, then yes."

I swim to the middle of the pool and tread water, watching as he climbs the stairs and picks up a towel, drying his hair as water runs down his gorgeous chest and drips onto the deck.

"Well…happy hunting."

He smiles at me. "Thanks. See you later."

I watch him go, perplexed. And maybe a little charmed.

The next four days are more of the same: chaste, sweet encounters that Shane initiates and ends. He finds me in the laundry room or between cabins, and each meeting involves silly banter and harmless kisses that stoke a fire that's growing hotter each day. And as much as I wouldn't mind more, some part of me holds back. Maybe it's the older, wiser part finally taking the reins, but I think it's more like my inner self-preservationist is coming forward, reminding me that the last time I said I wanted more, I got nothing at all.

Finally it's Saturday. The guests are gone, and we have a whole afternoon and evening to ourselves. Shane and the ranch hands left an hour ago to take the guests to town, and we've just finished cleaning up the kitchen. Everyone else drifts off to nap or swim, and I beeline it to the office to pound out an email to Stanley, updating him on the new developments at the ranch. We played phone tag all week but never quite managed to catch each other, so this will have to do.

I click open a new message, type in Stanley's address, and watch the cursor blink in the Subject line. *Relationship status*, I type. Then my mind goes blank. What exactly is my relationship status? Are Shane and I in a relationship, albeit one with a firm two-month deadline (as printed on my return plane ticket)? Or are we just openly, monogamously fooling around with the understanding that it's not forever?

I don't know how long I stare at the blank message, but I'm vaguely aware of Gina saying, "Back there." A second later I look up to see Shane standing in the doorway. It's a small office, and it feels almost claustrophobic with him in it. But claustrophobic in a good way, like the walls can't bring us close enough together for my raging hormones.

"Hey," I say. "I thought you were in town."

"I'm back."

"That was fast."

He shrugs. "What are you up to?"

I sigh and close the message window, no closer to finding answers. "Nothing."

"All right. Let's go. Put on some sneakers."

"Why? Are we racing again?"

Shane smiles—that sexy, beautiful smile that makes my heart pound. "No. We're hiking. Get dressed. I'll meet you out front."

After changing into shorts and a T-shirt—and the requisite sneakers—I find Shane in front of the barn. He's swapped work boots for hiking boots but is otherwise dressed exactly the same, with the addition of a canvas rucksack slung over his shoulder. "What's in there?" I ask as we walk down the road. There's a decent hiking trail on the other side of the river, and we head in that direction, the bright July sun beating down.

"Water. Supplies. The usual."

"I didn't take you for a hiker."

"I don't go out often. You?"

"Once in a while."

We cross the small bridge that spans the river that marked the beginning of our "relationship." I stare at the shallow water and remember how my heart raced when Shane touched me, when he whispered the things he wanted to do to me. I remember how much I wanted him to do those things, how much I still want them.

I find him watching me and blush, wondering if he can read my mind. If he can he doesn't say so, just takes my hand as we reach the mouth of the trail and enter the forest. The trees loom large and dark around us, providing welcome relief from the heat. At some point Shane lets go of my hand—okay, it's almost immediately, when it becomes obvious he's a much better hiker than me—and we trek along in companionable silence.

Sweat trickles down my temple, and I wipe it away. But soon there's a line snaking down my spine, and another between my breasts. I'm too stubborn to tell Shane to slow down, so I plod along after him, making the occasional noise to show I'm listening when he points out a bird or plant of interest.

"What'd you do before you came here?" I ask finally, so I don't have to study another fern.

"I told you. We brought the guests to town."

"I mean before you came to the ranch. For the first time."

"Oh. I was in school."

We reach a small ledge and look out at the neighboring mountains: lush, green rolling hills surrounded by clear blue sky. Shane hands me a bottle of water, and I drink gratefully, listening as he tells me he got a degree in physical therapy at LSU.

"Louisiana State?"

"Uh-huh."

"Is that where you're from?" I hadn't noticed an accent.

He shakes his head. "I'm from California. We lived on the coast, but my grandfather had a ranch inland. Every summer my brother and I had to work out there."

"That must have been fun."

"We hated it. We wanted to be with our friends, skateboarding, chasing girls, swimming in the ocean. Instead we were trucked off to the desert to slave away for three months."

I laugh. "I thought you liked this work."

He smiles. "I do now."

"LSU, huh? I guess that explains how you helped my shoulder."

"Told you it wasn't a ploy."

"So why didn't you become a physical therapist?"

"Do you really want to talk about this?"

"Not if you don't."

Shane sighs. "My grandfather died the day before I graduated. I had a job lined up and was thinking about grad school, but I went back to help with the ranch, to keep it running until they could find someone else to take over. What I didn't know was that the ranch had been struggling for a long time, and I couldn't fix it. I tried for two years, but eventually we had to sell."

"You wanted to stay?"

"Ironic, right? The place I hated the most became the one thing I thought I'd die if I lost. But I lost it. And I didn't die."

"And now you'd like to own this place."

He shrugs. "One day. I figure Hank and Mary will be ready to retire in ten years. Maybe we can work something out. I should have enough saved by then."

"I like your goal."

"You do?"

"Sure. I love this place. It's important that somebody who cares about it keeps it running."

Shane finishes his water and puts the empty bottle back in his bag. "Let's keep going. You ready?"

"We're not done yet?"

He laughs. "A little farther."

Turns out Shane's idea of "a little farther" is two grueling hours away. By the time he says "We're here," I've decided I'm willing to beg him to put that degree to good use. Just as I'm about to fall to my knees, I see what he wanted me to see: nestled into the cliff face is a sparkling waterfall that spills into a small, dark pool.

I've seen waterfalls before—bigger, prettier, more tropical waterfalls—but this one takes my breath away. This time I'm with someone who wants to show me, not because he's my tour guide and it's his job, but because he wants me to see something he thinks I'll like. Something he likes.

"It's beautiful," I say.

He shrugs. "I like it. I know it's not *Ban Gioc*, but..."

I look at him oddly. "What?"

"That waterfall in Vietnam you wrote about."

I cock my head. "Did you—"

"I read your book, Kate."

"You're the other buyer?"

"What?"

"Hailey bought a copy this week, and the cashier told us someone had recently purchased the other one. That was you?"

Shane looks away. "Yeah."

"How did you even know about the book?"

"I overheard Matt trying to join your fan club."

I laugh. "That's an overstatement."

He looks at me suddenly, his eyes dark and serious. "I hope so."

"What do you mean?"

Shane sets the pack on the ground and comes closer, stopping close enough to touch, but not bridging the gap. "That guy likes you."

"He likes Hailey."

"And the sous chef likes you too."

"I'm a really nice person."

"And Kevin Drew likes you."

"Do you like me?"

"You know I do."

"Then stop talking about them and kiss me already."

Shane smiles and lowers his head, his lips finding mine and brushing back and forth gently. I press my tongue against the seam of his lips but they remain resolutely closed — just more simple, chaste kisses.

I pull away, frustrated. "What's going on?" I demand.

"What do you mean?"

"With this seventh-grade kissing!"

My favorite eyebrow arches, this time in offense. "I beg your pardon?"

"Do you want me or not?"

"I want you."

"Then why doesn't it feel like it? We're back together, but we're not? I want you, Shane. You don't have to treat me like I'll break if you touch me."

"You got mad in the cabin."

"What?"

"After, when I was putting my shoes on. You were pissed about how I treated you. I thought you didn't like it."

"I was pissed because you left me there after the most intense — " I break off to regain my composure, so I don't put all my cards on the table. "I was pissed because you were trying to run away, not because of what you — of what happened."

"So you liked it?"

"I came, didn't I? I'm sure you felt it."

"I thought you felt like I was using you. I mean, you 'dated' that Kevin Drew guy, and I'm sure he's all fancy and rich, taking you to nice places...I thought that's what you wanted. Respectful."

"Shane, look at me."

Eventually he returns his gaze to mine.

"I like everything about you."

He looks doubtful.

"No one has ever made me come the way you do. You're right—I'm used to guys like Kevin Drew. But I don't miss them. I miss you. I miss the way you touched me. I love it when you say you're going to fuck me—I don't think it's disrespectful. But this sweet, preteen style of kissing…"

"Preteen?" Shane exclaims.

"It's not going to cut it. If you're not going to man up—"

"Man up?" He takes a threatening step forward.

"And do what I know you're capable of doing—"

"You don't know what I'm capable of, Katharine Burke." Now he's trying not to smile.

I back away from his advancing form. "I don't know. Should I write this down for you?"

He undoes his belt buckle with deliberate menace, sliding the leather through the loops. "No," he says. "I think I've got it."

"I've already warned you about belts."

He laughs and drops it, then lunges forward, hooking a leg under mine and toppling me to the ground. He uses an arm to cushion my fall and covers my body with his, his delicious weight pressing me into the spongy earth. One knee grinds between my legs and rubs against me roughly, eliciting a groan.

"Is this what you want?"

"You're on the right track."

Suddenly Shane rolls off and I sit up, confused. "Wha—?"

I watch as he crouches in front of the rucksack, undoing the clasps and pulling out a wool blanket, which he spreads over the ground. He looks at me from under a critical eyebrow. "Why are you still dressed?" he asks.

"You brought a blanket?"

Still low to the ground, he comes back over and pulls my T-shirt over my head. He pushes a hand down the front of my shorts, cupping my damp pussy through my panties. "Take off your clothes," he growls, "and get in the water."

I look at the waterfall. It's beautiful, but it can wait. "I'd rather—"

He cuts me off with a kiss. "Now."

Shane steps out of his boots and whips off his shirt, standing to remove his pants. "I wanted to fuck you in the pool so bad I thought I'd die," he says, eyes never leaving mine.

I take off my bra. "Was there really a wayward calf?"

"Yeah, but Connor could have found it."

"So why didn't you?"

"Fuck you? Because anyone could have come by."

I stand and wiggle out of my shorts. "Is that the only reason?"

"No, Kate. I wanted to fuck you—hard—and I didn't think you wanted me to. So I wanted to wait until I'd cooled off and could do things slow and polite. But every time I got near you, slow and polite went out the window."

"But today you feel…polite?"

He takes my hand and wrenches me forward, then pulls off my flimsy panties with a tearing noise. I stare in shock at the scrap of fabric hanging from his fingers. No one—and I mean no one—has ever literally ripped off my clothes before.

"I'm feeling very polite," he says, shucking his boxer briefs before tossing me over his shoulder and striding toward the water.

I shriek and punch at his bare ass. "Careful," he warns. "Anything you do to me I'm going to do to you ten times over." I stop hitting, and he laughs. "Good to know."

He has one hand slung behind my knees to hold me in place, and I squeal as the other delves between my thighs, testing my wetness. "Not there yet," he says matter-of-factly, though my clit would beg to disagree. "Maybe this will help."

Shane dumps me into the water and jumps in after. It's surprisingly deep—and cold—and I shoot back to the surface, hair in my eyes, sputtering.

"Not helpful!" I squawk, shivering. "That was the opposite of helpful."

He moves toward me, just his head and shoulders breaking the surface. "I don't know," he says, reaching forward to pick me up, lifting me out of the water so my breasts are visible. Thanks to the cold, my nipples are tight and aching, and he sucks one into his mouth, his hot tongue making me moan.

My head drops back. "Oh God."

"He can't help you now." Shane turns his attention to my other nipple, biting down harder than expected and making me jerk in his arms. "Remember," he warns, not removing his mouth. "Only say no if you mean it."

"You make me forget," I whisper.

Shane looks up and pulls me forward to straddle his waist, raising his lips to mine. "Me too."

Finally — *finally* — he kisses me. A real, passionate kiss with his hand in my hair and his tongue taking control. The kind of kiss that leaves no doubt he wants this as much as I do.

His free hand slides down my back, tickling my spine. Then he cups my ass, the tips of his calloused fingers sliding between my slick cheeks, stopping at the one place no one has ever been.

I pull back and look into his eyes. "No," I whisper.

The hand moves lower, finding my waiting core and pushing one finger inside. He swallows my groan and finger-fucks me like this for a long time, eventually adding a second finger. I'm bobbing up and down on his hand, his cock pressing into my stomach, growing harder and harder with each passing moment.

"I want to come with you," I plead.

"You will," he answers. "Later. But I want you begging for it."

"I don't beg."

He smiles. "You will."

He lets me go, and the pool is too deep for me to stand, so I tread water as he advances on me, stopping only when my back meets the cold, wet rock face. The waterfall splashes down beside us, drowning out the forest noise. Shane puts two fingers in his mouth then lowers his hand beneath the water, back to my pussy.

"Spread your legs," he orders softly.

"I'll drown."

He hooks a hand under my arm and holds me up. "Do it."

I do, gasping when those same two fingers push into me, curling forward to stroke the spot on my inner wall that makes everything else cease to matter. "Shane."

His thumb finds my clit and presses down hard, circling roughly. "Come."

I come. My eyes squeeze shut as though I can't handle seeing him as well as feeling him. My legs try to clamp together, but he's blocking them with his body, forcing me to remain open while he presses harder and deeper and makes the orgasm go on forever.

I don't know when we left the water or how much time has passed when Shane finally removes his hand, toying with my nipples as he waits for me to come back to earth. "I don't know how much more of that I can take," I breathe.

He kisses me. "You said you wanted to do it my way."

Shane's way soon has him leaning back on his arms as I take him in my mouth, doing my best to repay the favor. At one point I look up to see him watching me and remember how he watched me the first time in his trailer, when I thought we'd never do this again.

"I'm going to come in your mouth," he warns.

"Do it," I say around a mouthful of cock.

"Jesus." His hand covers the top of my head, holding me still as he spurts long streams of come into my throat. I swallow, laving him while he groans, and when he's spent I pull away and flop back on the blanket to give us both some time to recover.

After a while Shane pushes himself up to his knees and looks down at me, studying every inch, naked and bare for his gaze. "Open your legs."

I bite my lip but follow the order.

"Wider."

He strokes a finger through my wet lips and circles my clit. Then that same hand trails up my stomach to my breast, his other hand mirroring the action. My breathing quickens as he plays with each breast, pinching each distended nipple, harder and harder until I gasp.

"Shane," I warn.

"I can see your pussy getting wetter," he says softly.

I clamp my legs shut, horrified at my body's betrayal, but instantly feel Shane's hands on my knees, gently tugging them apart. "I said open your legs," he reminds me. "Don't close them again."

I moan. "You're not the boss of me."

"Why don't you like this?" he asks, twisting my nipples again, making me whimper.

"It hurts."

"Does it? This is nothing."

"What would you know?"

He laughs. "I think you're used to finesse, Kate, and you're not used to fucking."

One hand massages my breasts while the other delves between my legs, flicking my clit, pulling back the hood and stroking the small bud. My hips buck upward, and I can't stop the cry that spills from my throat.

"But finesse is okay too," he whispers. The finger that torments my clit slips down lower, past my throbbing entrance to the darker, tighter hole beneath. "So is this."

My eyes flutter open. "Shane, no."

"I won't do anything you don't want me to."

"I don't want you to fuck my ass."

"How about just a finger?"

I force myself to breathe, slowly and evenly. No one has ever touched me there before. They haven't been allowed. Even in my drunkest, wildest moments, I've never agreed. And now, older, wiser Kate is actually considering it.

Shane swirls that deviant finger in my copious juices and holds it up so I can see it shining in the sunlight. Then he dips his hand far back between my legs and presses in slightly. The tight muscles refuse to budge.

"Let me in," he whispers.

"I'm afraid."

"Of what?"

I try to find the words but they won't come. His finger rests on that forbidden place and now his other hand is tormenting my clit.

"I don't know," I say weakly.

"I'm going to lick your pussy the whole time," Shane promises, lying on his stomach between my spread legs. "Then," he continues, "when you can't take it anymore, I'm going to come up there and fuck you long and hard. Do you understand?"

All I can do is nod.

"You can still say no."

I shake my head.

"Good."

His face disappears between my legs, tongue swirling, and that slick finger presses harder and harder on my untried opening until it breaks through and pushes inside. My legs fall open, my heels dig into the ground, and I thrust up into Shane's dangerous, practiced mouth. He parts his lips and sucks me in, tongue pushing high into my depths, teeth grazing my clit. His finger plunders in deeper and deeper until it can't go any farther, then he pulls out, fucking my ass gently but firmly.

I clamp a hand over my mouth to smother my cries. My eyes fly open to watch the speckled light in the trees, a kaleidoscope of blue and yellow and green. Shane holds me down, having his way, then circles my clit with his mouth and sucks hard.

"I'm going to come," I cry.

"I know."

"Hurry."

"Say it."

Even in my pre-orgasmic haze, I know what he wants. "Please."

"Please what?"

"Please fuck me!"

In an instant Shane is on top of me, elbows on either side of my head. His cock rams inside, making me scream and bite his shoulder. His fingers find mine, and he holds on as his hips pound forward, again and again. I know I don't have long, but I want us to come together.

I open my eyes and find his already open, inches away from mine. I refuse to look away, and that's what does it. Shane cries out and comes, grinding into me. I spasm tightly around him, legs locking around his hips to hold him in place as his pubic bone rasps my clit and forces out every possible ounce of pleasure, taking and taking and taking until there's nothing left to give.

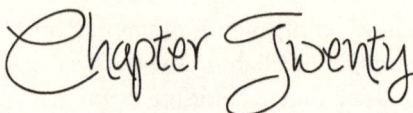

Chapter Twenty

July passes in a blur of work, sun, and Shane, not necessarily in that order. We don't hold hands or kiss in the dining room — well, except for that one time that had the wranglers groaning — but we're not a secret, and I'm surprised by how comfortable I am with the idea that this man, who by all means is not my type, is mine. And he certainly seems to consider me his, if his penchant for control is any indication.

As a woman who has run her own life somewhat successfully for thirty years, it's taken some time to get used to sharing control with someone else. Not that Shane's great at sharing, but he's trying. And I can't lie — most of the time his "detail-oriented" control freak ways end up with me in the throes of a phenomenal orgasm. So I'm not complaining.

"I'm jealous," Stanley moans when I tell him as much.

"What do you have to be jealous of? You have a gorgeous surgeon husband who lets you wear your new cowboy boots in the house."

"I know. I'm just jealous I'm not there to spy on you two. I've never seen Kate Burke in love before."

I laugh. "I'm not in love. I'm in lust. It's different."

"I saw the way that man looked at you. That was more than lust."

"That was a month ago, and it was mostly fueled by rage and jealousy. You're confused."

"Suit yourself."

"Stanley. Don't put ideas in my head."

"Why not? What's the harm in falling in love?"

"There's nothing wrong with falling in love—with the right person. But it's already August, and I'm leaving in a month."

"Why?"

"Why what?"

"Why are you leaving?"

"I have a plane ticket."

"That's a terrible reason."

"Is not."

"And where will you be going?"

"Back to Boston! To live next door to my best friend and constant nag, Stanley Goldblatt!"

"There's nothing for you here."

"Now you're just being mean."

"I'm serious, Kate. What's the harm in staying?"

"Well, first of all, the ranch closes for the winter, and I'd have nowhere to live. I'd have nothing to do—"

"You're self-employed, not to mention loaded. You don't need to work. And you know how off-putting it is to see rich blondes complain about boredom."

"That's mean."

"It's true."

"Stanley—"

"Just think about it."

I lower my voice. "Think about falling in love with Shane? It's not something you can train yourself to do!"

"I don't think you need to 'train' yourself on this, Katie. You dated that handsome hotelier—thanks again for the lifetime room discount—"

"I regret that."

"…for two years, but you never once talked about him the way you do this guy."

"I'm hanging up now."

"Stop punishing yourself for what happened—"

"Nobody's being punished. I have to go."

"You aren't stupid and reckless anymore. You can trust your judgment. Fall in love."

"I am in love, Stanley. With you. Or at least I was until this conversation. Now I have to go. Bye."

"Bye, sweetie."

I hang up.

I'm not lying to Stanley. I really do have to go. For the third time in as many days I watch Hank and Mary wave goodbye to a new group of power suits in a shiny rental car. I dash out of the phone booth and walk/run around the lodge to intercept my seasonal parents once the guests have gone.

"Hey!" I gasp, breathing hard.

They turn to me in surprise. "Hey, Kate," Mary says, tucking a wayward strand of hair behind my ear. "Where are you off to?"

"Nothing. Nowhere. I mean, who was that?" I gesture at the retreating cloud of dust disappearing under the arch.

"Oh, just some…people."

"I couldn't help notice that you guys have had several 'people' drop by for tours this summer. Is it a new promotional thing you're doing?"

They look at each other. Mary scuffs the ground with her boot. "Um, no…"

"Then what's going on?" I'd like to consider myself a fairly calm and rational person, but that goes out the window when I'm suddenly struck with a horrifying thought. "Are you two all right?" I demand. "They're not doctors, are they?"

Hank lets loose with a big belly laugh. "No, Kate, they're not doctors. They're…well, why don't you come inside and we'll talk about it?"

I refuse their offer of iced tea but follow them down the lane to their house, taking a seat in the cluttered country kitchen. Hank begins to talk, and all I can do is stare at them across the scarred wooden table.

"You're selling?" I echo, lips numb.

"It's time," Mary says. "We're getting old, and running this place just isn't as much fun as it used to be."

"You're the one who gave us the idea," Hank adds.

I stare at him in horrified confusion. "Me? How—?"

"Your writing," he clarifies. "All those beautiful places you've been. Over the years we've been keeping a list of the places we'd like to visit, but we can never find the time. If we sell the ranch we'll have the best of both worlds: money and time."

My heart is pounding so hard I can feel it through my chest. All I can think about is Shane. Shane wants to buy this place. Shane doesn't have the money.

"B-But what about the winter?" I stammer. "Can't you travel all winter? Isn't that the American dream? Warm summers here, warm winters there?"

Mary frowns. "That's not the only American dream, Kate. What about the one where you get to retire and stop working?"

"Are those people going to buy it?"

"I don't know," Mary answers. "Maybe. They seem interested."

"And will they keep things the same? What will they—"

Hank runs a weary hand over his thinning hair. "That's the tough part," he admits. "We've been trying to find someone who wants to keep the ranch intact, but that's a lot to take on."

"Shane wants to buy it," I say impulsively. "He'd keep it just like it is. And he loves it here."

Mary pats my arm. "I know you care about him, dear, but we've spoken to Shane in the past, and he's not even close to having enough money. He'd be in debt for the rest of his life. It's too much to take on. It wouldn't be fair to anybody."

"Tell me, will you?" I plead. "If you find a buyer. Just…tell me?"

"Of course." Mary nods. "No problem."

"Well," Hanks says, pulling a huge photo album off the counter and thumping it onto the table. "Now that the cat's out of the bag, I guess you can help us plan our trip."

I can only stare in shock when he flips open the first page of the photo album to reveal copies of my old travel articles, recommending people travel to Bali or Hong Kong or Rio. There are hundreds of them—page after page, some flagged with sticky notes.

"Isn't this exciting?" Mary asks. "I can't wait. And it's all thanks to you."

It's a Saturday and the guests are gone, so Shane and I are going to town for our first official date. He's begged me to wear "that damn fantasy dress," meaning the green one, which I am. Now I'm upstairs with Lisa, who helps me curl my hair and paint my nails.

"God," I say, staring at my shiny red toes. "I can't remember the last time I had a pedicure."

"Was your life super glamorous?" she asks enviously.

I smile. "Sometimes."

"Did you meet any celebrities?"

"A couple."

"Have you ever been in a private jet?"

"Yes."

She flops back onto the bed in mock devastation. "I'm so jealous."

"It was pretty cool."

"You must miss it. Are you excited to go back to your real life?"

I open my mouth, then close it when I realize I don't have an answer. Or maybe I do. "I like it here," I say finally. "I'm not ready for it to be over yet."

"Because you have a boyfriend?"

"That's part of it. How about you? Are you excited to go back?"

"Yep. Did I tell you I changed schools?"

"You did? I thought you wanted to go to UVA."

"I thought I did too. But now I don't. Janie's going there, and I'm going to do something different. I got in some other places, and Texas State still had a spot for me."

"That's great."

"I'm excited. It's about time I tried something new."

"You're eighteen. You have lots of time for new things."

Lisa shrugs. "Why wait?"

I can't argue with her reasoning, so I just hold up a hank of hair to give her curling iron access to the pieces underneath. I remember the days when "trying something new" meant a new cocktail or new lipstick. I gradually upgraded to new restaurants, new hotels, and new countries, and now, evidently, a new life. Not the one I imagined myself living, but I'm not complaining.

With nails gleaming and my hair bouncy and shiny, I twirl in a circle for Lisa's approval (granted) and make my way downstairs. Shane has parked one of the lodge trucks next to the bunkhouse, and he leans against it, watching my descent. The last time I did this he was standing next to the Airstream, and I was smiling at Kevin Drew. Now I turn that smile on Shane, who looks me up and down, face impassive.

He shrugs. "You'll do."

"That's sweet."

He opens the door and helps me in, swatting my ass on the way. "I know."

I'm starving by the time we get to town. Shane made reservations at a fancy Italian place on Main Street, and heads turn as we make our way to the corner table.

"Did you see that?" I whisper when we're seated. "Those woman were gawking at you."

"I didn't notice." He shrugs. "I was too busy staring down all the men ogling you in that damn dress."

"You like this dress."

"Damn right I do." He gives me that devastating grin, and I smile back. This is only the second time I've seen Shane in a suit, and he looks great. Black jacket, black pants, open neck white shirt—and no work boots. He's a sight.

The server arrives with our menus and water, and I order a bottle of wine, testing and approving it once it's poured. When the server leaves I see Shane watching me, amused. "What?"

"That," he says, mimicking flicking his wrist and swirling imaginary wine in an imaginary glass. "You're so fancy."

"Please. That's how it's done."

"You would know."

I shrug. "Just drink it."

"Do you like this place?"

"The restaurant? Yes, it's nice."

"Nice enough?"

"For what?"

"For you."

"Shane."

"What? Answer the question."

"Yes, it's nice enough. I'd be happy anywhere with you." I shoot him a look. "You're not trying to pick a fight, are you? Because the truck keys are in my purse. You're the one who'll be walking back."

He smiles. "I was just thinking about the places you've been. They're so much better than anything you'll find here."

I sigh inwardly. "You can't be a travel writer if you're constantly wishing you were somewhere else," I tell him. "You have to live in the moment, be where you are, and enjoy it. Otherwise it's wasted. And I happen to love where I am right now. Satisfied?"

His dark eyes glow. "Yeah."

I return my gaze to the menu, but I'm barely registering the words. All afternoon I've been trying to figure out how to tell Shane the ranch is for sale, but his preoccupation with our imagined "class difference" makes discussing finances an unpleasant proposition.

The server returns and we order, then stare at each other when he leaves.

"So," I say.

Shane arches that brow. "So?"

"I was talking to Stanley today, and he told me the old woman living above us died."

"You two live together?"

"No, we're neighbors, but the penthouse is above us, so technically we share an upstairs neighbor."

"How'd she die?"

"Food poisoning."

"You think Stanley did it?"

I laugh. "I wouldn't put him past him. He's been wanting to buy that place and turn his apartment into a two-story mega-palace for years."

"Will he?"

"He wants me to invest with him. Maybe divide the penthouse into two, then convert both our apartments into two-story units."

"Why does he need you?"

I shrug, uncomfortable. "Because it's expensive."

"Isn't he rich?"

I shrug again. "Sort of."

Shane clues in. "But not as rich as you."

"It would just be easier with two people, that's all."

Shane leans back in his seat. "Are you a millionaire?"

I stare at him in surprise. "I—"

"I'm not asking how much. Just...are you?"

Finally I nod, watching his face grow tense. "The book helped."

"And you grew up rich? In New York?"

"Yes."

"Must be nice."

"It's not something I can change, Shane."

"I'm not blaming you. It's just...different. You're like one of the guests instead of the workers."

I roll my eyes. "If one of the guests cleaned everybody else's bathroom."

That drags a smile out of him. "Yeah."

"You really think I'm different? Stuck up? I thought we were past that."

His foot finds my leg under the table and strokes my calf reassuringly. "We're past it. I was just wondering."

After dinner we stroll around downtown. I window shop, but Shane pretends to faint at the mere idea of actual shopping, so I don't go into any stores. I don't think I'd want to buy anything with him around, anyway. He nearly bit off my head when I offered to split the dinner bill. Financial discussions are temporarily off the table.

"Hey," he says when we're driving home.

"Hey yourself." It's closing in on eleven o'clock, and because Shane is driving, I was forced to drink most of the wine by myself. My eyes have been closed for the past ten minutes.

"Want to do something?"

I crack open an eye. "Like what?" I half expect him to reach over and hike up my skirt, but instead he pulls the truck over, stopping near a small bridge that spans a wide part of the river below.

"Get out."

Shane climbs out of the truck and I do the same, taking his offered hand and following him onto the bridge in the darkness. There's a full moon tonight, and I watch its reflection shimmer on the rushing water twenty feet below.

"Very pretty," I say, because I don't know what he wants me to see. Or say. Or do.

"Let's jump."

"What?"

"Let's jump in the river."

"I like you, but not enough to form a suicide pact."

"You're hilarious. Everyone jumps here. It's tradition. The water's deep, and there's a path to climb back up through the rocks. Let's take off our clothes and jump."

I'm not about to tell Shane this, but I've said those words more than twice—fine, four times—before. But those days are behind me, wobbling around drunkenly on high heels, making stupid decisions, being foolish. I know better now.

"Let's not," I say.

"Why?"

"Because. It's crazy. Let's just go back to the ranch." I try to return to the truck, but Shane's got an iron grip on my hand.

"It'll be fun."

"I'm not that person anymore," I protest.

"What person? A fun one?"

"A reckless person. A let's-take-off-our-clothes-in-public person."

"I like reckless Kate. I like striptease, Janie-battling, bat-saving Kate."

"Those Kates were not supposed to follow me to this ranch."

"Let them out." He kisses the tip of my nose and removes his suit jacket. "Come on. I've never jumped before. Jump with me."

"I'll wait up here."

"I'll hold your hand."

"I'm not worried about drowning!" Actually, with most of a bottle of wine in my system, perhaps I should be.

"Please?" He turns those dark eyes on me, only for once they're pleading, not demanding.

"Don't look at me like that."

"Katharine Burke, would you please take off your clothes and jump off a bridge with me? You'd be my first."

I snort with laughter. "This sort of thing is supposed to be in my past."

"Why?"

"Because," I say, faltering. "It just is."

Shane shucks the rest of his clothes until he's left in only his black boxer briefs. "Don't make me jump alone," he says.

I sigh and unzip my dress. "You're a terrible influence."

One minute later we're standing on the edge of the bridge, fingers entwined, staring down at the dark water below. "You're sure it's safe?" I ask again.

"I'm sure."

"And you're not too scared?"

Shane shoots me a look. "One. Two. Three."

We jump. I scream the whole way down. Shane will deny that he screamed too, but I know what I heard.

We hit the water and plunge deep, our hands coming apart. I hold my breath and wait until my momentum slows, never touching the bottom, then swim back up. I break the surface and look around for Shane. Nothing.

"Shane?" I whisper.

Suddenly he surfaces behind me, shaking his head like a dog, water droplets flying. "Awesome!" he exclaims, beaming. I see the moonlight glint off his teeth. "That was amazing!"

I can't help but smile back. "Do you feel better now?"

"Hell yes," he says, pulling me close and kissing me thoroughly. "I feel fucking *reckless*."

Chapter Twenty-One

As it turns out, I'm a huge coward who can't tell her boyfriend his beloved ranch is going to be sold to callous strangers. Every time the subject of money comes up he gets so...testy. And I don't want to fight anymore. I like getting along with Shane. It turns out that under that strong, silent exterior lies a halfway-decent personality and even a teeny-tiny sense of humor.

A few days later I visit his trailer after lunch service has finished and knock on the door. No answer. He gave me a key a little while ago, so I let myself in and sit down with one of the gossip magazines Lisa picked up on her last trip to town. Four divorces and one affair later, I look at the clock. We agreed to hang out this afternoon, and Shane is late, which is very unlike him. Just as I start to wonder where he might be, the man of the hour strolls in.

"Hey," he says, kissing me on top of the head and pulling a bottle of water out of the small refrigerator.

I set the magazine aside. "Hey. Where have you been?"

"On the phone."

"Come again?" It's next to impossible to picture Shane doing something as mundane as speaking on the phone.

He gives me a meaningful look and downs half the bottle.

"Are you parched?" I ask. "Did you get in touch with your inner chatterbox?"

"Actually," he says, finishing the water, "someone got in touch with me."

"Who would want to talk to you?"

Shane drops down next to me on the couch. The arm he slings around my neck is a little tighter than is strictly necessary, making me laugh. "Stanley," he answers.

I try to straighten, but he keeps my head pinned to his chest. "Stanley?"

"Yep. Your good friend Stanley Goldblatt."

"What did he want?"

"He wanted to know when he could expect you back in Boston."

"What did you say?"

"I figured September. Right?"

The thought makes me sad, but I keep my voice neutral. "Right."

"And then he asked me how I felt about you."

Now I put real effort into wrestling out of his choke hold, eventually succeeding. I pull back and stare at Shane, horrified. "He didn't."

"He did." His expression is carefully blank, dark eyes fathomless.

"And...you said..."

"I said..."

"That you're in awe of me?"

"Uh-huh."

"That you admire my work ethic?"

"Yep."

"And envy my wicked sense of humor?"

"No."

"My fabulous legs?"

"Meh."

"You lie!"

Shane smiles at me. He's being deliberately infuriating.

Well, we can both be frustrating. I yawn dramatically. "I think I'll go take my afternoon nap now. Alone."

"Why alone? I'm right here. I'll make sure you don't fall out of bed."

"I'll risk it."

"Kate."

"What?"

"What happened in Jamaica?"

For a second it's hard to breathe. When I speak, my voice is barely audible. "What?"

"Stanley told me to ask you what happened in Jamaica."

My mouth is dry. "Why would he tell you that?"

Shane hesitates, obviously unprepared for my shaken reaction. "I may have asked him what it was you keep saying you want to leave in the past. Why you're trying so hard to be…different."

"What did he say?"

"To ask you about Jamaica."

"I hate him."

"Tell me about it."

"It was just…a rough time, that's all. It was months ago."

"What happened?"

"Shane…"

He gets up from the couch and goes the trailer door, leaning against it and effectively blocking the exit. "Tell me."

It was my second of four weeks in the beautiful Caribbean country. I'd spent my first week in Kingston and was on day three of my week in a new resort development on the north side of the island. It was beautiful. Sun, sand, new friends, new restaurants, new clubs.

I'd been to Jamaica before, and I'd always enjoyed myself. It's hard to complain about an all-expenses-paid trip to a beautiful island, but I was already getting bored. And not just with Jamaica. It was starting to feel like all my days were running together: wake up late, swim, eat, shop, drink, dance, sleep in. Carve out a few hours to write. It didn't matter where I was; the pattern was always the same.

That day I'd joined up with a group of Dutch tourists, and we'd spent the day snorkeling and complaining about the lack of a party atmosphere at the resort bar. Some locals we met on the beach told us about a club a mile down the road that not a lot of tourists went to—a place we should visit it if we wanted a "real" island experience.

My Dutch friends were up for the adventure, and I was desperate for something to break me out of my monotony. After a late dinner at the resort, washed down with several glasses of wine, we flagged a cab and rode the short distance down the two-lane road, surrounded on either side by palm trees and sand.

Because this area was just starting to be developed, there weren't a ton of tourists, but we were far from the only ones. We were warmly welcomed and soon fell into the regular routine of shots and dancing and more shots. But it just wasn't doing it for me. As nice as everybody was, all I wanted to do was go back to my hotel room, fall asleep, and wake up somewhere else—somewhere new, somewhere with a purpose. I knew that was unlikely to happen, but the idea of climbing into bed held serious appeal, so around two o'clock in the morning I left by myself, weaving through the small parking lot and pausing on the side of the road to find a cab.

It was dark and warm, and there was no traffic. No cabs. I waited a few minutes, then reasoned that it was just a mile to the hotel—no reason I couldn't walk back. The combined effects of alcohol and high heels made progress slow, but I was determined, picking my way along the edge of the road by the moonlight. It wasn't ideal, but it wasn't bad either, until suddenly it was. Until suddenly it was awful.

People find it hard to believe that in ten years of traveling alone I don't have any real horror stories to tell, and compared to some I've heard, this one isn't all that bad. But for a single woman alone on the side of the road in the middle of the night, surrounded by three strange men reeking of alcohol and contempt, it was as bad as it got.

"Give us your purse," one ordered. Another came up behind me and shoved me when my shocked limbs didn't move fast enough. I almost never carried a purse when I traveled, but I'd felt safe in my group of friends and wanted to keep my notepad in case I needed to jot down story ideas.

I stumbled. One heel caught in a crack and snapped in two, and I crashed to my knees on the pavement. My mind told me to get up, to run backward or forward—I had to be halfway between the resort and the club—but I couldn't seem to move. I was too drunk. I'd had so much to drink that I hadn't even realized how drunk I was until it was too late. I recognized that this was becoming a habit with me—waking up more mornings than not with a patchy memory of the night before—but this was one night I wouldn't forget.

I felt a boot hit my back and searing pain shot up my side. Someone else kicked my thighs and shins, and my purse was yanked off my arm so hard that the strap broke. I tried to scream for help but managed only a moan. The person who grabbed my purse dumped the contents on the ground and roared in outrage when he found just a few American dollars and a handful of local currency. "Where's the money, bitch?" he shouted.

"No money," I mumbled. This got me a whack in the face with my empty purse. My lip split, and I tasted blood. Kicks rained down all over me, and I covered my head with my arms and finally managed a scream when a foot connected with my forearm, snapping the bone.

"Then you can give us something else," a sour voice hissed in my ear. I was wearing a short designer dress, and I felt fingers at the hem, yanking hard at the fabric.

"No," I gasped, lowering one hand to hold the dress in place and exposing my nose, which was a mistake. Someone punched me in the face, and I felt blood pour over my cheek and into my mouth. I covered my head again and felt more hands on my dress, trying to pull my legs apart, pinning me down.

I'll never forget the softly accented voice of my savior, the sharp but calm "What's going on here?" that sent my attackers scattering. I can still feel the smooth skin of his fingers on my shoulder. He asked my name, asked if I could stand. The closest hospital was an hour away, and he took me in his cab, refusing payment and helping me limp inside, my broken arm shrieking in agony.

I had no identification — the contents of my purse were strewn on the side of a dark road sixty miles away. The doctors and nurses were kind and efficient, and the police were too, though we all knew it was unlikely anyone would ever be charged for the crime. When a young nurse asked if there was anyone she could call to come stay with me, I had to admit to her and to myself that there was no one. I barely knew my Dutch friends, I couldn't explain to my mother why I'd been staggering down the road drunk in the middle of the night, and the only real friend I had was Stanley, who was away on his honeymoon with his new husband, Anton.

I spent the night in the hospital, then returned to the resort, locking myself in my room and jumping whenever anyone passed by in the hall outside. I tried desperately to convince myself I would be fine in a few days, the bruises would fade, the cast would come off, everything would be okay. But it wasn't okay. I was alone. I was friendless. And there was nothing I could do about it.

On the third day I caved and tried to call Stanley, but his phone was turned off. On the fourth day I tried again, cursing myself for not writing down the name of his Parisian hotel. I tried on days five, six, and seven too, though I knew the result would be the same. I cried myself to sleep, rich and blond and sorry for myself, and on the eighth day, I called the airline and booked a flight home.

When I finish the story I look up at Shane. He's staring at me with a mix of shock and horror. Carefully he lifts my right arm, the one that was broken, and inspects the smooth skin.

"It's okay," I whisper. "It was months ago."

"I'm sorry that happened to you," he says.

"I don't want anyone to know."

"Why, Kate? Why keep it a secret?"

I shake my head and force myself not to cry. "Because I was stupid. I was drunk. Not just then, but all the time. I made terrible decisions, and I'm lucky that's the worst thing that happened to me. I learned a lesson from it. It's fine."

"It's not fine!"

"I'm not glad it happened, Shane, but it did, and all I can do is move past it."

He's struggling to control his temper. "Did they catch the guys?"

"No."

His calloused fingers trace the contours of my face, finding the small scar on my hairline that once held eleven tiny stitches, the hollows under my eyes that were stained black and blue for weeks. "You think this happened because you were reckless?"

"I think I needed to grow up, and this was the catalyst."

"So now you're older and wiser?"

I sniffle. "I'm just older."

Shane kisses me very carefully. "You should get some rest."

"Lay down with me."

"I've still got some stuff to do in the barn."

"Please?" I know he has time to lay down with me. We freaking scheduled this visit. He opens his mouth to say no, but I try again. "Please?"

He sighs and nods. "Yeah. Of course."

We move to the small bedroom, and I climb in bed first, slipping out of my jeans and socks so I'm wearing just the ranch polo and panties. Shane lies beside me, fully dressed, his body stiff as a board.

"Don't be weird," I say, putting a hand on his chest.

"I'm not."

I lean over and kiss him on the mouth. His lips are soft and warm, but he doesn't kiss me back. "Do you want me to go?"

He looks startled. "Of course not."

"Then kiss me."

"Kate."

"I'm not broken, Shane. This is why I didn't want to tell anyone my sad little story. It's in the past. Let it go. I have."

"You haven't if you're still punishing yourself for it."

"How am I punishing myself? By not jumping off bridges every day?"

He stares at me, struggling with something, but then his eyes flatten and I know he's not going to tell me what he wants to say. I lean over and kiss him again, levering myself on top of his broad chest, soon straddling him. Eventually he kisses me back, and I slip my tongue into his mouth, enjoying the novelty of being the one to instigate things.

I smooth my hands over his shoulders, down his arms, stroking his fingers. I touch his chest, rubbing my thumb over his nipples until I feel them tighten through the thin cotton of his T-shirt. At length I feel his cock start to stir, and I gently rub myself over him, feeling him harden and grow.

"I want you," I whisper.

"Kate…"

"What?"

"I would never hurt you."

"I know."

"All that stuff…the rough stuff, if you don't like it—"

"I love it. I love everything you do. I'd tell you if I didn't."

"You would?"

"Of course. Just like you'd tell me you love everything I do, even if you didn't, right? Because I can do no wrong?"

I feel him smile against my cheek. "You're one hundred percent right."

"Knew it."

We reverse positions so Shane's on top, and he laces his fingers through mine and kisses me leisurely, thoroughly. I wrap my legs around his waist and grind my pussy against his now-straining erection. He frees one hand to gently stroke my breasts, tweaking my nipples—but not painfully so—before sliding his hand down my belly to cup the heat between my legs.

I groan and writhe, and he dips beneath the thin fabric of my panties to push one finger inside me, stroking deep, spreading my moisture everywhere, readying me for his cock. I slide a hand between us and unbuckle his belt, pushing down the zipper and slipping my hand inside to find him, making him groan.

"Kate," he breathes into my neck. "Dammit."

He rises over me to take off his T-shirt, then pushes his pants and underwear down, kicking them off. He swiftly divests me of my top and bra, then covers me again, his hot, hard weight a delicious reminder of his strength, his power.

I jerk his cock harder, knowing he likes it this way, enjoying the emotions that rage in his dark eyes. He spreads my legs and takes away my hand, holding it aside as he leans back on his heels. "Are you on the pill?" he asks.

"I have the shot."

"I want to come inside you." He raises his eyes to mine. "Is that okay?"

I swallow. No one has ever come inside me before. Even in my committed relationships—however brief—I required condoms. But now the thought of Shane being inside me with no barriers, of him leaving a trace of himself behind, makes my heart pound. "Yes." I nod. "I want to feel you."

"Watch."

I look down as he positions himself and slowly pushes inside. My tender muscles quiver, straining to accommodate his thick cock. His thumb circles my clit as he forges ahead, and I sigh and force myself to relax until he's in to the hilt.

"You're so tight," he groans into my ear.

"You're so big."

"Right again."

I laugh, but it's immediately cut off when he pulls out and slides back in. Shane begins to thrust—deep, languorous strokes that touch every part of me. Soon I'm slippery and moaning, and he's pushing in harder, faster, his tongue mimicking his cock, fucking my mouth. I groan and suck him in, wanting him everywhere, feeling everything.

He hooks his elbows under my knees and pulls up my legs, opening me farther, grinding us together. My clit can't take the pressure and I lose my breath, gasping as the tremors build, so swift and unforgiving that all I can do is arch my back and let them drag me under. My inner walls clasp Shane tightly, milking him, pulling him deeper, demanding everything.

He thrusts impossibly hard, answering the request, shouting his release as he comes inside me. I feel a sudden wet heat between my legs and clutch him tightly, unable or unwilling to let go. When he shudders one last time, we're both breathing hard. I can feel his heart beating against my chest, the echoing thud of mine, his sweat-damp hair on my temple.

Eventually he eases out, and as my body struggles to release him, I realize he was wrong that day on the hike when he told me I wasn't used to fucking. The truth is, I wasn't used to making love.

Chapter Twenty-Two

Things reach a comfortable, happy status quo around the ranch. Summer is winding down, and there are just two weeks left in the season. Once the last guests leave we'll take a few days to prepare the cabins for winter, then everyone will go their separate ways before the cold comes. I'll head east, Shane will head west, and everything will be fine. Fine and dandy.

I'm in the process of purposely not thinking about this when Hailey raps loudly on the open door and walks in. "What's going on?" she demands.

I'm making the beds in cabin eight and look around for the answer. "Should I know what you're talking about?"

"Shane's on a rampage. What did you do?" That last line is a joke, but I can tell from the look in her eyes that the first part is not.

We hurry out of the cabin and around to the front of the lodge just in time to see Shane storming from the barn into his trailer. He slams the door so hard behind him that it bounces back open.

I have no idea what's happened to make Shane upset. I'm not so conceited as to think it's me, but I'm not willing to approach the trailer right now either. A second later the choice is made for us when Shane stomps back out to slam the door again, stopping when he sees us. We freeze like deer waiting to be run over—*Move, fools!*—and instead of retreating inside, he stalks over to us.

"What do we do?" Hailey hisses.

"Act invisible."

Shane's shoulders are tight, his cheeks are flushed, and I can almost see steam rising from his neck as he approaches.

I'd like to make a joke to ease the tension, but my mind is blank. "What's wrong?" I say instead.

He takes a deep breath, clearly trying to calm himself but not succeeding. "Connor just met the ranch's new owners."

My entire body goes numb. Yes, I knew the ranch was for sale, but my shock at this news is genuine. "What?" Hailey and I ask in unison.

"Yeah. Some yuppies from fucking Maryland who want to turn it into an eco spa. An eco spa!" He nearly shouts the words. "Goddamn rich idiots who think they know how to run a business because their GPS told them how to find it."

My heart is pounding. Guilt will do that. "When is this happening?"

"As soon as possible. This is our last season. Everything will be sold, I assume. All the horses, all the land…It's gone."

My face is burning. I knew this was in the works, and I didn't say anything. I could've done something. I could've tried harder. If I'd just told Shane maybe he could've done something. Maybe he had a plan.

I feel terrible, and I feel even worse when I see he's next to tears. I reach out to touch his arm, but he shifts away. "I'm really sorry, Shane."

He forces a smile to take away the sting of his rejection. "It's not your fault. I'll find you later, okay?"

Hailey and I nod, and he returns to the trailer, closing the door with a little less force but just as much finality.

"Oh God," I breathe, resting a hand on the rail so I don't topple over. My knees are weak and my vision is blurry. I am a horrible, horrible person.

"What?" Hailey asks.

"I have to talk to them."

"To who? Kate?"

She calls after me, but despite my shaky legs I'm already running down the road to Hank and Mary's small house. I pound on the door and let myself in. "Hank!" I call. "Mary?"

"Kate, is that you?"

I find them sitting at the kitchen table, surrounded by a mountain of paperwork. "Did you do it?" I ask, hand trembling as I steady myself against the wall. "Did you sell the ranch?"

They look at each other. They look almost as guilty as I feel. "Pretty close," Hank admits. "There are still a few details left to work out."

I skip the accusations, the self-righteous reminder that they were supposed to tell me when they'd found a buyer—they promised!—and get right to the point. "Please don't do it," I beg. A tear slips out the corner of my eye, and I wipe it away. "Don't sell them the ranch."

They look pained. "Kate…" Mary begins.

I see the photo album sitting open on the counter, their dreams of rest and relaxation just a few signatures away. I know their decision has nothing to do with me, nothing to do with Shane. And technically, it's none of my business. But still I hear someone talking, someone completely crazy—the kind of crazy that only makes sense to other crazy people.

"Sell it to me instead," I hear myself plead. "Let me buy the ranch."

"You coward," Stanley says again.

"You don't have to convince me," I mutter. "I know."

"You have to tell him."

"I know!"

"He's probably in his trailer right now, crying his heart out, thinking his precious ranch is gone forever when really it's right where it should be."

"It's not right where it should be, Stanley! It's with me! This is not my dream. It's Shane's dream, and I bought it. I *bought* it!"

"It was for a good cause, like a charity."

"That's a terrible way to phrase it."

"You're right. More like…a placeholder."

I slump onto the milk crate. "A placeholder. That's it exactly. I'll buy it now, and then in ten years when Shane has the money, I'll sell it to him. In the meantime he can run it like he wants to, and nothing has to change."

"There you go."

"Except..."

"You still have to convince him of all that?"

"Uh-huh. Stanley, you have no idea how he gets about money. When we go out to eat, he won't let me pay for anything, and he keeps asking if the places we go are nice enough for my 'tastes'..."

"Did you tell him you've eaten scorpions?"

I laugh. "No."

"Cockroaches?"

"No! That's not going to help. Then he'd become convinced I'm bored with him and could never be happy."

"That man is crazy about you."

"We'll see how crazy he is when he finds out what I've done."

"I mean it, Kate. He's got some control issues—"

"No kidding."

"But he wants to make you happy, and buying this ranch, for him, makes you happy."

"You'd think. Instead I've got a bottle of antacid next to my bed and my hair is turning gray."

Stanley gasps. "Do it now."

"I will."

"Today."

"Today?"

"That's right."

"Don't you dare call him again, Stanley."

He laughs. He's already gotten an earful about his whole "ask about Jamaica" shtick. "I won't."

I sigh. I feel sick. "I'll do it after lunch," I say. "We're supposed to hang out...I'll tell him then. He's going to hate me."

"He'll get over it. You're there for good now."

"That's just it, though, isn't it? I'm not sticking around. I mean, this place closes up for the winter, and in two weeks there'll be nothing left for me to do. I'll have to come back in the spring, but it's probably going to be so I can hire a new foreman."

"I'd do it." Stanley sounds genuinely interested.

I can't help but laugh. "You might be hired."

We hang up, and I walk over to the dining room for lunch, though I'm not remotely hungry. It's Sunday and several staffers are sitting around, cobbling together sandwiches from the supplies Mark and Alec set out. I join Hailey, Lisa, and Matt and chew halfheartedly on a piece of bread, trying to focus on the conversation.

My appetite disappears completely when Shane and Brandon walk in, and if Hailey's sudden aversion to her sandwich is any indication, she's lost interest in eating too. She and Matt are still together, and Matt appears completely oblivious—or just not interested in—the friction between Hailey and Brandon, though if anything the tension has grown.

Shane nods at me but tips his head toward Brandon to indicate he has to sit with his friend, and because Brandon can't sit with Hailey…It's junior high all over again. We even gossip about them sometimes late at night when we can't fall asleep.

I'm so distracted I don't hear Gina the first time she calls me. Hailey kicks me under the table to get my attention, and I jerk toward the hallway where Gina is waving.

"Kate," she repeats. "Phone call for you. I think it's Kevin Drew again. He says it's urgent." She disappears back down the hall, and though the dining room activity never slowed, I'd swear all the sound and oxygen in the room vanished with those words. My gaze flickers to Shane, who's staring at me across the room, brows drawn in hurt and confusion.

I shake my head, though what message I'm trying to convey—*Don't be mad? I'll explain later? It's probably a wrong number?*—I don't know. To make sure things really look bad, I scurry out of the room with my head down and rush into the back office to slump into the seat and pick up the extension. I know why Kevin's calling me, but his timing could not be worse.

"Hey," I say. "Now's not a great time."

"It won't take long." He's in business mode, his smooth voice crisp and efficient. "I have a few things I need to fax over for you to sign, but I wanted to make sure you were near the fax machine so they don't end up in the wrong hands."

A shadow falls over the desk, and I look up to see Shane looming in the doorway.

"Okay," I say into the receiver. My voice is hasty, guilty. "Send them."

I hang up and stare at the phone for a long moment. I haven't quite planned my I-bought-the-ranch speech, and I don't know how to begin.

Shane takes a step inside and shuts the door. I don't know why I didn't close it, or maybe I do: he would have followed anyway. Nothing can keep Shane away when he wants something, and likewise, nothing can bring him back once he's gone. And I know I'll lose him when he learns what I've done. The final two weeks we could have spent together will be lost, strained and awful like before.

He doesn't come any closer, just stands by the door, arms folded across his chest, face blank. His dark eyes tell another story, however, flashing with hurt and anger. I'm sure my intensely guilty behavior hasn't helped matters.

"Why is he calling you?" he asks when I make no move to speak or get up. Outside I can hear the fax beep, signaling a transmission.

I run a hand through my hair. "He's my financial advisor," I mumble finally. So much for new and improved Kate. I'm acting like a guilty teenager, and there seems to be nothing I can do about it.

When Shane speaks, his words are slow and measured, like he's trying very hard to keep his temper in check. "Why does your financial advisor need to speak with you? Urgently?"

"Just to go over some…financial matters."

"Did you buy that place with Stanley?"

"No."

"Then what?" He sighs heavily when I don't answer. "Would you want to know if I was getting secret phone calls from Cassidy Reyes?"

I raise my eyes to his. I can feel the tears swimming, threatening to spill over. I nod weakly.

He frowns. "What's going on?"

I open my mouth but can't force out the words.

"Your financial advisor is calling you…at a ranch…about financial matters…now?"

I nod again. Then I wince when I see the realization dawn on his beautiful features, the way shock and disbelief and horror and anger and hurt swirl together.

"You bought this place?" he utters.

"Yes." The tears slip down my cheeks. I shouldn't feel guilty about making a business decision—one that's good for us—but I do.

"Did you know they were going to sell?"

I want to tell him the whole story, that I didn't have any intention of buying the ranch, that it was a surprise to me too, that the eco spa people were going to change everything, but the words lodge in my throat.

Shane slams a fist down onto the desk, making the phone jump, scaring me half to death.

"Yes!" I shriek, startled. Guilty, frightened, angry.

"And you didn't tell me?" His voice is rising in volume, little by little. His cheeks are flushed, hands fisted.

"I wanted to."

"But you wanted to buy this place yourself."

"They told me you couldn't afford it. Those people—the ones from Maryland—they were going to buy it and sell everything. You said so yourself. So I did the only thing I could think of."

"Did it ever occur to you to tell me?"

"All the time. Every—"

Shane laughs roughly. "All the time, Kate, really? All the time?"

"It's impossible to talk to you about this stuff!"

"About you buying my dream?"

"It's a placeholder," I say hurriedly. "You can buy it from me when you have the money."

I couldn't have shocked him more if I'd punched him in the stomach. "I'm sorry," he says tightly, "did you think you were doing me a *favor?*"

His face is like a car wreck, and I can't look away. I'm as unlikely to describe this as a *favor* as I would a *charity*, but I suppose that doesn't change the truth.

"I did the only thing I could. I didn't plan it."

"You own the ranch. You."

"What's wrong with that? I love this place, Shane."

"Yeah. I love it too, Kate."

"So what's the problem? Nothing changes. You're in charge. And in a few years…"

"You know why Brandon didn't get involved with your friend? Because I told him not to. Because I told my guys that screwing around with the staff only leads to trouble."

"This isn't—"

"You're in charge, Kate. Not me. This is your place now."

"You're being ridiculous."

"On the contrary. I'm finally coming to my senses."

"We can—"

"Thanks for a few good lays and one hell of a blowjob. You've got a great mouth."

The blood drains from my face. "Don't you dare insult me. This has nothing to do with sex. Nothing—"

"No, you're right, Kate. It has nothing to do with sex. You're in charge now, and I can't fuck my boss."

I swipe a hand under my eyes, but there are too many tears to make much difference. "You don't have to be like this."

"There are two weeks left in the season. You sign my paycheck, and I'll do my job. That's it, got it?"

I take a deep breath and set my jaw. "If that's what you want."

"That's all I want."

I look him in the eye, hoping I appear more confident and less heartbroken than I feel. "Then that's what you'll get."

Chapter Twenty-Three

Sundays are normally awful — spending a solid six hours cleaning cabins is never fun — but today is looking spectacularly bad. They probably couldn't make out the words, but I'm certain absolutely everyone has heard our fight.

Shane storms out of the office and back into the dining room, telling everyone to "Meet the new boss," and all eyes turn to me. No one seems to have taken the news of the ranch's sale quite as personally as Shane, but they still appear surprised to learn I'm the one who bought it.

There's nothing for me to do but stand here awkwardly, silently confirming that what Shane said is true. When I can't take it anymore, I announce that I'm going to get back to work and hurry off to hide in one of the cabins, where I promptly bawl my eyes out. Eventually I regain some measure of self-control, mop up my tears, and get on with my work.

Three hours later I'm standing on the porch with Matt, Hailey, Lisa, and Pete — who we still call the handyman though he's been working with us full-time since the beginning — smiling and waving at the arriving guests. Shane's there, holding open doors and helping people out, but I keep my gaze averted. I can't decide if I want to cry some more or rage against his stupidity, his infuriating ego, and the unfairness of the situation.

When I got out of the shower half an hour ago, Hailey was waiting for me. She understands why I didn't tell anyone about buying the ranch and agrees that Shane is being unfair. "All ranch hands are jerks," she declared, and I concurred.

The week passes in a confusing blur. As though to compensate for Shane's coldness — he doesn't even come in for breakfast — everyone else is really nice: Alec makes me special French toast; Mark saves me donuts; Lisa compliments my hair. Even Brandon is kind, helping me unclog the pipes in one of the cabins, a task I'd normally have to tackle myself.

I'm cleaning cabin nine on Friday when I hear a loud shriek. I rush outside to see Lisa racing out of a cabin, swatting frantically at her head.

"Lisa!" I shout, catching her attention. "What's going on? Another wasp's nest?"

Matt had had an unfortunate encounter with a wasp's nest while sweeping spider webs from under the eaves one changeover day. For a while we were all extra paranoid, but the ranch hands went around with smoke spray and cleaned everything out, and we hadn't had any more trouble.

"Bat!" Lisa heaves, skidding to a halt in front of me. "There's a bat in cabin eight! It hit me in the head! It's still in my hair!"

I inspect Lisa's hair, but there's nothing in there but her hands. "Your hair is fine," I say. "No bat."

"I'll have to cut it all off!"

"You definitely won't. Fill out a requisition slip and ask Brandon to come look at it." I keep my voice deliberately calm so as not to further incense her.

We head into my "safe" cabin and I hand Lisa a form, watching her fill it out with shaky hands. "Now go deliver it," I say. "He's probably in the barn. If not, give it to Connor or Chase. Just hurry and get back to your cabins."

"I can't go back in there!"

I sigh. "Fine. I'll switch with you. I'll take Eight, you do Ten."

Her voice trembles. "Okay."

It's all I can do not to roll my eyes. Lisa has come a long way since her first days as Janie's minion, but watching her stand in the doorway, expecting to be dive-bombed at any second, is a little much.

"Lisa. Bats don't attack people. You'll be fine."

She takes a deep breath and races outside. I watch her until she disappears around toward the front of the ranch, then brace myself for cabin eight. I prop open the door as I enter, remembering Shane's advice that the bat will most likely fly out on its own.

Lisa returns to tell me she gave the requisition slip to Connor, and I gather her stuff from cabin eight and send her on her way. I finish cabin nine, clean up eleven, then walk back to eight, hoping the bat found its way out. The door is still propped open, so I leave it that way, assuming Connor hasn't stopped in yet.

Cabin eight had a group of six men here on an annual boys-only getaway, and I have a fleeting moment of doubt about the whole bat situation when I see the state of things inside. It'd be enough to send me screaming too. I grumble about Lisa but get to work, gathering up the dirty towels — that's every single one — and lugging them down to the laundry room.

When I return with clean towels, I can hear Connor in the bedroom searching for the bat. "I don't know where it is," I call as I enter the bathroom to restock the towels. "Lisa said it was flying around. I left the door open, so it might have flown out." I place the bathmat on the edge of the tub and turn to leave, uttering a yelp of surprise when I see Shane in the doorway.

He is not pleased to see me.

"This is Lisa's request," he says, holding up the requisition slip.

"She gave it to Connor."

"He gave it to me. What are you doing in here?"

"Lisa was too afraid to come back. Why didn't you ask Brandon or Chase to come?"

"I guess they have better things to do."

I push past Shane, though he doesn't make it easy, and yank the crumpled sheets off the pull-out couch. "Don't bother staying," I say. "I'll look for it myself. It's probably gone, anyway."

Shane's silent for a long moment, and finally I look up at him. "It's in there," he says, jerking a chin at the master bedroom.

"Oh. Thanks."

"It could be the same one, getting to be a nuisance."

"I doubt it."

"If it keeps coming back…"

"I said I'd take care of it. No one asked you to kill anything."

"Aye-aye, boss."

I inhale angrily, but refuse to give in to his pettiness. "That's all, Shane."

"Is it?"

"That's what you wanted."

"I guess it is."

"Then why are you still here?"

"Why didn't you tell me the ranch was for sale?"

I roll up the couch and slap the cushions back on top, keeping myself busy so I don't have to look at him. Shane and I and a cabin are not a good combination. "When Hank and Mary told me it was for sale, I said you wanted it. They said they'd already talked to you, and you didn't have the money yet. You'd be in debt forever. It was too much to ask."

"So you bought it."

"No. I already told you this. I asked them to tell me when they had a buyer and for some reason they didn't, so when I heard about the eco spa, I found them and practically begged them not to sell. But they want to retire, Shane, and it's not fair to ask them to stick around for ten years until you can afford it."

He looks predictably pissed at my reference to money, but I cut him off.

"Deal with it, Shane. You don't have the money, and I do, so I bought the ranch. I'm not going to turn it into an eco spa, and I know I can't run it by myself, so you can stay on doing exactly what you have been, but I'm going to be here, and I'm not going to put up with your hissy fits. There are other foremen out there, and if I have to, I'll find a new one."

"I beg your pardon?"

"You heard me. I'm rich, deal with it."

He makes a sound that's equal parts exasperation and anger. "Deal with it?"

"Yeah. I'm leaving in ten days, so you'll have the winter to think about it. If you're here when I get back, I'll assume you're in. And if you're not, I'll start looking for someone who is." My chin wants desperately to quiver, and I keep my hands busy fluffing pillows so he can't see them tremble.

His dark eyes bore into mine, and I refuse to look away. I can see from the tense set of his shoulders that he's still angry, but it's his ego at work. If he doesn't know how to get past this, there's nothing I can do about it. Like it or not, we're adults, and I'm doing my very best to act like one. He needs to do the same.

I see a muscle tick in his jaw and think he's about to speak, though I don't know if I want to hear what he has to say. If he quits, I'm fucked. If he doesn't, I'm screwed. Because there's no way I can fire Shane: he's good at his job, and people respect him. But every day will be a little bit of torture, seeing him and knowing I can't have him anymore. I've given this a lot of thought over the past week, and if I'm going to be the boss, I'll have to make tough choices. This is the one I've settled on. I'll let Shane decide. On my terms. Sort of.

"Kate? Are you a vampire now?" Hailey appears in the doorway, cleaning basket tucked under her arm. "You're taking awfully — Oh." She cuts off abruptly when she sees Shane and me facing off. "Sorry, I'll—"

"No." I stop her. "That's fine. Are you done with your cabins?"

"Yeah. Do you need help?"

I stare at Shane pointedly while I answer. "Yes. But only if you're willing."

Hailey gives me a weird look. "I'm willing."

"Great. Thanks."

We're interrupted by a faint fluttering noise. I turn toward the master bedroom just in time to see a small black shape zip through the room and zoom out the open cabin door.

The look Shane gives me is full of meaning, though what he's trying to convey I can't — or simply won't — guess. And then, as always, he leaves.

Chapter Twenty-Four

"**K**ate, this is tragic. A heartbreaking tragedy."

"It's not. It's fine."

I'm back on the milk crate, listening as Stanley almost sobs in my ear about the unfairness of unrequited—and unacknowledged—love.

"Nothing's fine!" he shouts. "You know how many men I've seen you with? Dozens. A hundred maybe."

I wince. "Stanley!"

"But you didn't love any of them. I wondered if you even knew how."

"I'm going to hang up."

"And do you know how many parties we've been to? How many bottles of expensive wine we've shared? How many hours we spent photographing all the shoes in your closet?"

That was one of the "tasks" Stanley insisted we accomplish during my recent recovery period. He enjoyed it. I did not.

"What are you getting at, Stanley?"

"Kate, you've been to the best places with the best food and wine and clothes and music, and, arguably, some of the best people—namely me. And, oh, fine, Anton. But I've never seen you as at home as you are out there, in the middle of some godforsaken forest, on the top of a mountain, with a bunch of hillbillies."

"Thanks?"

"You belong there. You're in love with that place and that man. Don't let him chase you away."

"No one is chasing anyone. The season is done. Two more days of cleanup and we're out of here. Half the staff has already gone."

"I've said it before, and I'll say it again——"

"Do not tell me I have nowhere better to be!"

"You don't!"

"You're hurting my feelings."

"Kate, my dear, they were already broken. I'm just pointing it out. You can fix this."

"How? Sell the ranch to someone else and ask Shane to date me now that I'm not his boss?"

"You've got a lot of arguments, Katharine Burke, but you know the one thing you haven't argued with?"

I sigh. "I suppose you're going to tell me."

"You haven't denied that you love him."

"Stanley——"

"Think about it." And then, like a jerk, he hangs up.

Matt leaves that afternoon. No notice, just one minute he's here, helping clean cabins and nail boards over windows, and the next he's got his pack slung over his shoulder and is coming to say goodbye.

"What?" I ask lamely as he hugs me.

"A friend of mine is having a party in Phoenix in two days. I thought I'd go."

"Just like that?"

"Season's over."

"But..."

"Peace out, Kate. You're going to be an awesome owner."

We're standing in the kitchen where I've been helping Alec and Mark do inventory.

"Well…Bye."

"Bye." He waves to the chefs, they wave back, and he walks out the door without a backward glance. Through the window I watch him amble down the road, disappearing from view.

"I'll need a minute," I tell Alec, then hustle over to cabin two where Hailey is working.

"Hey," she says when I enter.

"Hey. Did you know Matt left?"

"Yeah. He just said goodbye."

"Did you know?"

"Like in advance? Nope."

I study her closely. She seems fine. Not sad in the least. "How come you don't seem upset?"

She shrugs. "I don't know. He'll be fine. I'll be fine. It was just a summer thing. Summer's over."

I slump on the bed. "Hell. It's over."

Hailey sits next to me. "We've still got two days left. Let's not be sad."

I eyeball her. "I have two days left. You're not going anywhere."

"True." Just last week Hailey was hired as the kitchen/dining room manager at a resort thirty minutes down the road. Located near a small ski hill, they stay open year-round and cater to winter-sports enthusiasts. They take people snowshoeing, cross-country skiing, and ice climbing. Pretty much anything you can do in the snow.

"What about Brandon?" I ask.

"What about him?"

"Does he know you're staying?"

"No, and don't tell him!"

Brandon and I rarely speak at any length, so the odds of me letting this slip are slim to none. Fine, they're none. Anyway, according to Connor, Shane invited him and Brandon to Texas to help out on his friend's ranch. After that, things are up in the air.

As for me, I've got a plane to catch. We'll finish up work tomorrow, and the day after I'll take Pete and Lisa to town for their early-afternoon flights, then kill time while waiting for my own that evening.

Hank and Mary packed up their house as soon as the ink was dry and took their newfound money and freedom to Bali. At this point all that's left are the ranch hands, the remaining kitchen/cabin staff, Alec and Mark, and two or three wranglers.

"Coming to O'Malley's tomorrow for our going-away drinkfest?" Hailey asks.

"Yeah, why not?"

"Let's dance those boys right out of our heads."

"Dance?"

She laughs. "With a little help from Jose Cuervo."

Jose Cuervo is a kind man. The only ranch hand at the bar is Connor, who seems to have taken an interest in Cassidy, as gross as that makes him. Mark has made a game out of it, insisting we all take a drink every time Cassidy shimmies her breasts in Connor's face and he responds by tipping his head back and howling. Needless to say, everyone's pretty drunk.

An old-school country song comes on, and everybody lines up to dance, hooking our thumbs in our belt loops and kicking up our heels.

"I'm going to miss you!" Hailey shouts over the music.

I look at her and smile. This is the best I've felt since my fight with Shane. It's the first time I've been able to imagine myself coming back here year after year and not feeling awful and alone. Hailey has already promised to come back to work next summer, and while I don't know how true that is, I certainly appreciate the gesture.

"I'll miss you too!" I shout back. "Come visit me!"

"I'll be working at a resort—you come visit me!"

I toss my head back and laugh just as Cassidy dances her way over. Hailey and I exchange a look, and I just barely resist an eye roll, pretending not to see Summer Skank sidle up to Mark. Hailey doesn't need to speak to ask the question we're both thinking: *Does Cassidy think I'm with Mark again? Really?*

Even Mark appears to be on the same page, shooting me a questioning look. To mess with Cassidy I try to appear outraged, and he laughs. Then Hailey laughs too. Cassidy's cheeks flush and she looks pissed, but when she tries to approach me, Connor cuts in and sweeps her away.

"Seriously?" Hailey asks, boot-scooting to the right.

"What's left to take? The ranch?"

"Does she know you bought it?"

"Beats me."

"You might need to hire bodyguards next summer. Accidents can happen in the mountains…when there's no one around to hear you scream."

I laugh again, tripping over my own feet but catching myself before I fall. "On that note," I say, "I think I'll head out."

"What? Are you sure?"

"Yeah. I think I saw Randy outside. I'll catch a ride with him." A minute later I stumble out into the parking lot, hunt around for a patchy yellow Volkswagen, climb in, and stagger out again when Randy parks back at the ranch.

"Thanks!" I call, handing over a fistful of bills and waving goodbye.

Randy drives away, and I stand alone on the dirt road. The night is silent and warm and a thousand stars twinkle overhead. Behind me the lodge is dark, the paddock before me is empty. *This is mine*, I think. Followed promptly by, *What the hell was I thinking?* But even as my mind starts to race, I can't help but smile. It's mine.

As I turn toward my room, my boots crunching on gravel is the only sound. With Lisa and Hailey at O'Malley's, the girls' bunk is empty, and I don't bother turning on any lights until I get to my room. I shut the door behind me, switch on the fan, and swap my going-out clothes—jeans and a tank top—for my pajamas: shorts and a different tank top. The window is already open, but I push it as far as it will go, letting the night air wash in and, okay, fine, risking a quick glance at Shane's trailer: it's dark. As far as I know, I'm completely alone on the ranch, which is also a fairly accurate description of how I feel about my new business venture.

It's a little after midnight and I yawn, switch off the light, and crawl into bed. Now that I'm here, however, I can't seem to fall asleep. I listen to the fan spin and remember my first night back, lying in Hank and Mary's house with the fan turning and the window open and feeling like I was home. And now this place *is* my home, at least for one more night. Then I'll leave again, like always.

Stanley once pointed out that I never talk about arriving someplace or being someplace, but always about leaving—like the visit never happened. I suppose that's because when the time came, I'd always been ready to go. Sure, the departures were sometimes sad, but they were necessary. Only now I don't feel that way. Like Stanley—*damn him*—keeps mentioning, for once I don't have anywhere better to be.

Unfortunately I also have no reason to stay. And certainly no place to stay. As of tomorrow afternoon the water and electricity will be shut off, the horses and cattle will be taken elsewhere, and the ranch will be abandoned to the elements until spring.

I try to imagine myself living in Hank and Mary's house, greeting the staff, signing checks, dealing with problems, being the boss. It's a weirdly welcome feeling. I'm just starting to get drowsy when I hear something at the door. I jump as a knock sounds—two quick raps, close together.

"Hello?" I call warily.

The door swings open, but the hallway is dark and I can't see who enters.

"Who is it?"

A pause. "Me."

I sit up abruptly, heart racing. "Shane?"

In quick succession I hear the door click shut, three footsteps cross the floor, and the faint squeak of the mattress as Shane kneels beside me, his hands finding my face in the darkness. I can't see anything, only feel, and the pressure of his mouth on mine is very, very welcome. I part my lips for his insistent tongue, and the heat he always stirs up spreads to every part of me.

He presses me into the mattress, my head landing on the pillow, and follows with his body, kicking off his boots until he's covering me completely, his weight a welcome anchor.

"What's happening?" I mumble against his mouth.

"Last time," he answers, silencing me with his tongue.

It doesn't take long. He swiftly removes my clothes before stripping out of his own, and uses his knee to spread my legs before slipping his hand between my thighs and pushing two fingers high inside. He groans, working his fingers back and forth, stretching me, drawing out the moisture.

I touch him everywhere I can reach, committing each muscle to memory, each indent, each curve of his body. Once he's moving his fingers easily through my slick center, he finds my clit and teases it out from its hiding place, making me moan as he bites my neck and torments me before settling between my thighs, the thick head of his cock finding my entrance and pushing inside.

I stretch for his invasion, accepting, acquiescing, memorizing the feel of him. Belatedly I realize he's not wearing a condom, and my blood rushes to the surface, making my skin flame, every thrust stoking the fires. I feel him everywhere, from my head to my toes, and curl my fingers around his as he holds my hands on either side of my head, tongue mating with mine.

It takes forever, and it's over too fast—the simple friction of Shane's body over mine, within mine—no games, no words, no pretense. He's saying goodbye, the only way he can.

Chapter Twenty-Five

I'm not surprised to find Shane gone when I wake up the next morning. I'd woken up a few times during the night to feel him next to me, fast asleep. Perhaps it was simply because it was the last time, but the sound of his chest rising and falling, all the hurt feelings and anger forgotten—albeit temporarily—had felt right.

I pull myself out of bed and climb into the shower to wake up. It's just after eight, and Lisa is entering the other bathroom at the same time. She looks like hell.

"Rough night?" I ask.

She rolls her eyes, then winces. "Gah."

I laugh.

"What'd you do?" she demands. "Why do you look so good?"

"Good? I'm just getting up."

"I think I'm going to be sick."

She rushes into the bathroom, slams the door, and seconds later I hear her hurling. I'm not sure how O'Malley's has managed to remain open this long when every time an underage employee goes in there they seem to come back over-served.

I clean up and dress, then go downstairs to begin my final inspections. I see Pete lugging his suitcase around to the porch, looking awful. "Late night?" I ask.

"I think I'm going to die," he moans, dropping onto the steps.

"Drink some orange juice. It'll help."

"I'm not hung over, I'm heartbroken!" he cries.

I look at him closely. His shaggy brown hair flops into his face, and I realize the eyes I thought were bloodshot are actually filled with tears.

"You'll be okay."

"I'll never see her again!"

"Maybe you can keep in touch."

He swipes a hand across his eyes. "It won't be the same. I love her, Kate. I love Lisa more than anything."

I smile. "She's a great girl."

"The best."

I pat him on the back and stand. "Try to enjoy the time you have left. You can cry on the plane."

I find Hailey standing just inside the lodge with two cups of coffee. "If this ranch thing doesn't work out," she says, "you could be a counselor, advising young lovers on the ways of the heart."

"I don't have any advice," I say dryly, accepting the coffee.

"Are you all packed?"

"Mostly. You?"

"Yep. I'll go when you go." Unable to stomach the idea of sleeping alongside horny teenagers for a minute more, Hailey rented a small house near the resort where she starts work next week.

"I can't believe you're staying," I say.

"I can't believe you're going."

"I'll be back."

"Yeah, but not for six months."

"The time will fly by. You'll see."

Brandon enters from the kitchen, chewing on a bagel. "Hey," he says.

"Hi." I nod.

"Hey," Hailey says.

We stand there awkwardly. "Almost ready to go?" I ask to fill the silence.

Brandon swallows his mouthful. "Yeah. Nearly done. Water's off in an hour, so make sure you've got what you need. We'll cut the electricity last. What time are you heading out?"

"About an hour."

He turns his attention to Hailey. "What about you?"

"What about me?"

"When are you leaving?"

"I'm going to the airport with Kate." This is not true. "When are you leaving?"

"A couple hours."

"Well…safe trip."

"Thanks." Brandon lingers for a second before crossing the dining room and disappearing down the hall to the offices. We watch him go.

"He's so pretty," Hailey whispers.

"Just be strong a little while longer."

"How do you do it?"

"Do what?"

"Pretend you don't want Shane as much as you do?"

"It's called self-preservation. If I pretend long enough, maybe I'll start to believe it."

"I've been trying all summer, and it's still not working."

"You heard the man. He's leaving in two hours. They all are. Soon they'll be en route to Texas, I'll be headed to Boston, and you'll be, well, nearby."

We turn around as Lisa enters, looking refreshed after her morning hurl. She's wheeling two suitcases behind her.

"You look well," Hailey remarks, "for the girl who threw up everything and anything just an hour ago."

"Thanks." Lisa shrugs. "I feel better."

I think about Pete, lost and forlorn. "How's Pete?"

"Sad."

"And you're not?"

"I'm sad. Just not that sad."

I look between my friends. "You two are like rocks," I accuse. "Emotionless stones!"

Hailey looks affronted. "What are you talking about?"

"Both of your summer flings are coming to an end, and you don't even care!"

Now Lisa looks offended. "I care! But I'm also looking forward to what happens next. I'm going to college, I'm going to pick out stuff for my dorm room, Janie won't be there—I'm kind of excited."

Again Stanley's words come back to haunt me: I don't have anywhere better to be, but I'm still leaving.

"I'm going to finish packing," I say, polishing off the coffee. "We'll leave in an hour."

"Sounds good."

Upstairs I tidy my room and double-check both bathrooms to make sure I haven't forgotten anything. I packed most of my stuff yesterday, so there's not much else to do. I strip the bed, put the quilt in a plastic bag to protect it from moths and small animals, and wheel my suitcase to the door. Before I go, I turn to look at the room one last time, refusing to feel sad. *I'll be back*, I remind myself. In just a few months this will start all over again.

I stare at the bed, feeling Shane moving over me, his hands stroking my hair, tongue twining with mine for the last time. I wish I could picture it, but all I have to remember last night by are the feelings. Memories that will fade with each day, week, month. Memories that will cease to comfort, and, hopefully, cease to hurt.

"It's no use," Pete says again. "They're gone."

We're sitting in the van—Pete, Hailey, Lisa, and me—loaded up and ready to go. The ranch is locked, the electricity has been shut off, and the ranch hands are nowhere to be found. Pete mentioned that he heard them say something about checking the fences one last time, and Shane's truck is gone, which supports the theory. All the same I peek inside the barn—empty—and knock on the trailer door. No answer. I try the knob: locked.

I nod to myself. Okay.

"All right," I say before anyone can get restless. "Let's beat it."

"*Via con Dios!*" Lisa shouts as we drive under the arch. "Thanks for the memories, bitches!"

"What is it you're going to study?" Hailey asks. "Poetry?"

Thirty minutes later we drop her off. She hugs each of us, blinks back tears, and promises to keep in touch. I watch her tiny form shrink in the rearview mirror, waving until she's gone. Soon we're parked at the small Dawson airport where I arranged to have Randy pick up the van later and drive it back to join the other vans at a garage for the winter.

We wheel our suitcases inside and check in. Pete's flight leaves forty-five minutes before Lisa's, but because mine isn't for another six hours, I'm stuck with my bags. We visit the food court to get something to eat and sit at a small table, listening to Lisa chatter on about the jungle theme she's decided on for her dorm room. Pete looks forlorn. He lives in Michigan. He's never going to see this jungle room, and we all know it.

Finally it's time for Pete to go through security. He tries to convince Lisa to come with him and wait at the gate, but she demurs, saying she doesn't want to make a scene. I'm not sure if that's true, but I play along, saying I could use the company. Pete's lower lip trembles as he accepts the inevitable and says goodbye, clutching Lisa in a hug that garners stares. To her credit, she gives him a kiss that will keep him company on the long flight, and eventually he passes through security and disappears from view.

"Wow," she sighs, slumping back in her seat. "That was exhausting."

"You handled it well."

"Onward and upward."

"What?"

"I'm just starting. This summer was my renaissance."

"You're too young for a renaissance."

Lisa laughs. "I'm starting fresh then. No more following people around. I'm looking forward to it."

"You're not afraid of arriving in a strange place all by yourself? You won't know anybody or where anything is."

"No. It didn't bother you, did it? All the places you traveled?"

"No. I suppose not."

"Then it'll be fine."

We sit quietly for a while, lost in our thoughts. Then I look over at Lisa. "Why'd you come back?" I ask. "When you left in the middle of the night, why'd you come back?"

After a moment she turns to me. We've already had this conversation, but I could use the reminder, or maybe the encouragement.

"I'd been following Janie my whole life," she says, "doing the same thing, but getting nowhere. I thought about something *someone* had said to me the day before, about not leaving a place or a person, but leaving a pattern. And it was time to break the pattern."

I flash back to our conversation in the lodge bar, when Lisa asked me why I'd stopped my travel writing. My answer may have been vague, but it was the truth. It was time to end the cycle of coming and going, loving and leaving, drinking and forgetting. I'd written about so many beautiful places, must-see beaches, must-eat restaurants, and told so many people how to enjoy their own lives that I'd forgotten how to enjoy my own. I'd left every beautiful place I'd ever been, and the one place that meant the most to me, Ponderosa Pines, I'd already left three times. And why?

Lisa's flight lights up near the top of the board, and she stands. "I guess I'll be going."

I rise to hug her. "You're going to be all right," I say into her hair.

Her grip tightens. "You too, Kate."

I watch her until she passes through security, waving goodbye one last time, then buy a bottle of water and a gossip magazine and settle in to wait some more. I mentally vote on who wore which dress best and who looks terrible without makeup, polish off my drink, and buy another. I wheel my suitcases around the tiny airport and try on cheap sunglasses, but my enthusiasm for shopping is conspicuously absent. Something's wrong, but it takes me another hour to admit what it is.

My flight's at six, but at four o'clock I'm in the van, racing back up the winding mountain roads a little over the speed limit. Fine, I'm going nearly double, but there's no one out here, and maybe there's still a little bit of the old crazy Kate left in me.

I've decided I can't leave. If all I'm going to do in Boston is sit around and plan for the coming season at the ranch, I can do that from here. Hailey rented a place, so I'm sure I can rent one too. And maybe I'll take up snowshoeing or knitting or some other way to pass the winter indoors, because there's no way anyone makes plowing these roads a priority.

I make the turn onto ranch property—my property—and pass under the arch welcoming me to Ponderosa Pines. I smile at the serene scene before me: a hundred-year-old lodge surrounded by mountains and trees, nature and freedom. The barn has been closed up, the door boarded like all the others, and the pickup is nowhere to be seen. The ranch hands are gone. It's just me and my ranch.

I park and get out, laughing to myself like a crazy person. I don't know the first thing about running a business, fixing a fence, or birthing a foal, but I guess I have plenty of time to learn. The air is soft and warm, and the first signs of fall color are appearing on the trees as I wind between the cabins, passing the empty pool and the back kitchen entrance.

Eventually I return to the front and sit on the porch, surveying my land. I laugh again, long and loud. *How did older, wiser Kate end up here?* I wonder. Maybe some things are meant to be.

"What's so funny?"

I almost fall off the steps. It's Shane, approaching from the trailer. He's dressed in his familiar uniform of cargo pants and black T-shirt, the dark color highlighting his tan, his dark eyes, his dark hair. The man is perfect. And for some reason, he's still here.

"I thought you left," I say.

He stops in front of me, and I push myself to my feet.

"I thought *you* left," he replies.

"I came back."

"Why?"

"I've been told I have nowhere better to be. Where's your truck?"

He bites his lip and looks away. "Guys took it. They went to Texas."

"Without you?"

"That's right."

"Why?"

"I told them to."

"You chose to stay at an abandoned ranch without any transportation?"

Shane looks thoughtful for a moment, then nods, looking up at me from under those devastatingly sexy eyebrows. "I'm reckless now, Kate. And I think you're to blame."

"Did you think I would come back?"

"I hoped so."

I look away and blink rapidly so I won't cry.

He touches my arm. "You were right to buy the ranch. I'm sorry about how I reacted."

"I understand."

"I don't have an excuse. I've been told I'm a control freak. I'll try to control it."

I laugh under my breath. "Right."

"You'll do a good job here."

"Will I?"

"Yeah."

"Where will you be?"

"Right here, if you'll have me."

"As my…employee?"

"If that's all you want."

"What do you want?"

He leans down to whisper in my ear. "You."

"Me?"

"I can't believe it either."

My blood quickens. "Why?"

"You know why."

My heart pounds so hard I swear we can both hear it. "Tell me."

"You ask too many questions, Kate." He pushes my hair behind my ear and leans forward to kiss me, but I back away.

"Answer them."

Shane stifles a smile and keeps his hand where it is, cupping my neck, rough thumb stroking my jaw. "All right, I hope you're listening."

"Of course I am. I'm three inches away."

"I'm only going to say this once."

"Just once?"

"Just once."

"Because, you know, the last time you said something was only going to happen once, it ended up happening again…and again… and again…"

His lips are getting closer, tempting me, and I tip my face away, though I'm still held in his grip. I can feel the heat from his chest on mine, and get goose bumps up and down my spine.

Shane's eyes lock on mine. "I love you, Kate."

I take a deep breath. It's corny, but I swear my heart swells. That's the first time anyone has ever said those words to me and meant them in this way.

"You do?"

"I do. And I think I have for a very long time."

"You have?"

"Uh-huh."

He brushes his lips over mine, once, twice, three times.

"That's really great news," I breathe.

Shane pulls his head back, hand still holding me in place. "Are you going to leave me hanging?" he asks.

Now I smile, preparing to utter words I have never said before, not in this way. "I love you, Shane."

He smiles back. "You do?"

"Uh-huh."

"Say it again."

"I thought we were only saying things once."

"I love you, Kate."

"I love you, Shane. I'll say it for as long as you want."

This time when he leans in to kiss me, I don't move away. I wrap my arms around his neck and pull him closer, holding on, staying put. It's taken me thirty years to figure out where I belong, and now that I know, I'm not going anywhere.

Acknowledgments

The road to publishing is paved with much rejection, so let me thank the wonderful team of women at Omnific who were the first to say yes.

Lisa O'Hara: For reading my query and requesting pages. Then reading them and requesting more. Then reading those too. Then passing them along. Thank you!

Elizabeth Harper: For being the first person to send me an email with "Manuscript Acceptance" in the subject line. Best. Day. Ever. (Except for that time I stood next to Colin Firth in HMV...)

Jessica Royer Ocken: Editor extraordinaire! Thank you for reading and re-reading and reading some more. And thank you for being patient and funny and helping the things I wanted to say come across as more than a bunch of hopeful stammering. Anyone who knows when and how to use a four-dot ellipsis is a star in my book.

About the Author

Julianna Keyes is a Canadian writer who has lived on both coasts and several places in between. She's been skydiving, bungee jumping, and whitewater rafting, but nothing thrills—or terrifies—her as much as the blank page. She has volunteered in Zambia, taught English in China, and dreams of seeing pink dolphins in the Amazon. This is her first book.

←···→Erotic Romance←···→

The Keyhole Series: Becoming sage (book one) by Kasi Alexander
The Keyhole Series: Saving sunni (book two) by Kasi & Reggie Alexander
The Winemaker's Dinner: Appetizers & Entrée by Dr. Ivan Rusilko &
Everly Drummond
The Winemaker's Dinner: Dessert by Dr. Ivan Rusilko

←···→Paranormal Romance←···→

The Light Series: Seers of Light, Whisper of Light, and Circle of Light
by Jennifer DeLucy
The Hanaford Park Series: Eve of Samhain & Pleasures Untold by Lisa Sanchez
Immortal Awakening by KC Randall
Crushed Seraphim and *Bittersweet Seraphim* by Debra Anastasia
The Guardian's Wild Child by Feather Stone
Grave Refrain by Sarah M. Glover
Divinity by Patricia Leever
Blood Vine and *Blood Entangled* by Amber Belldene
Divine Temptation by Nicki Elson
Love in the Time of the Dead by Tera Shanley

←···→Historical Romance←···→

Cat O' Nine Tails by Patricia Leever
Burning Embers by Hannah Fielding
Good Ground by Tracy Winegar

←···→Romantic Suspense←···→

Whirlwind by Robin DeJarnett
The CONduct Series: With Good Behavior & Bad Behavior & On Best Behavior
by Jennifer Lane
Indivisible by Jessica McQuinn
Between the Lies by Alison Oburia

←···→Anthologies←···→

A Valentine Anthology including short stories by Alice Clayton,
Jennifer DeLucy, Nicki Elson, Jessica McQuinn, Victoria Michaels,
and Alison Oburia

←—⁓→Singles and Novellas←—⁓→

It's Only Kinky the First Time by Kasi Alexander
Learning the Ropes by Kasi & Reggie Alexander
The Winemaker's Dinner: RSVP by Dr. Ivan Rusilko
The Winemaker's Dinner: No Reservations by Everly Drummond
Big Guns by Jessica McQuinn
Concessions by Robin DeJarnett
Starstruck by Lisa Sanchez
New Flame by BJ Thornton
Shackled by Debra Anastasia
Swim Recruit by Jennifer Lane
Sway by Nicki Elson
Full Speed Ahead by Susan Kaye Quinn
The Second Sunrise by Hannah Downing
The Summer Prince by Carol Oates
Whatever it Takes by Sarah M. Glover
Clarity by Patricia Leever
A Christmas Wish by Autumn Markus
Late Night with Andres by Debra Anastasia

coming soon from
OMNIFIC PUBLISHING

Disclosure of the Heart by Mary Whitney

Flirting with Chaos by Kenya Wright

Keeping the Peace (a Small Town novel) by Linda Cunningham

The Weight of Words by Georgina Guthrie

Theatricks by Eleanor Gwyn Jones

The Sacrificial Lamb by Laura Pintus

The Art of Appreciation by Autumn Markus

Return to Poughkeepsie by Debra Anastasia